TOUCHES OF EDEN

A CLEAN, SMALL-TOWN, FIREFIGHTER ROMANCE

TINA NEWCOMB

Touches of Eden

ISBN: 978-1-947786-24-0

Cover Design by Dar Albert of Wicked Smart Designs

CONTENTS

CHAPTER 1

Jillian Saunders jumped when the phone on her desk rang. Since most people called her cell number or texted, she'd forgotten how annoying the sound was. She grabbed the receiver before it could ring again. "Hello."

"I need a personal training session today."

The voice on the other end of the line wasn't much more welcoming than the shrilling ring. She and the demanding woman were friends through mutual acquaintances. When their group from high school met for the occasional girls' night out or to celebrate a birthday, she and Misty Garrett were there along with four other women.

Jillian switched screens on her computer, looked over her completely booked schedule, and sighed to herself. This conversation wouldn't end well. At least not for her.

"Can you come in at five?"

"I can come in now."

Jillian was tempted to laugh, but to do so would only anger Misty. "I have classes and clients until five. If you can come in then for a consultation—"

"I don't want a consultation! I want a complete workout."

"It's smart to start with a consultation so I can see what level—"

"Are you forgetting that your employers are my in-laws?"

"No, Misty." Jillian put an index finger to her left temple. "I'll forget the consultation, but I can't just drop my other clients and classes. Five o'clock is the best I can do today. I'll be off work by then, so I can help you personally." *Not that you care whether I get paid for my time.* As soon as the thought flashed through her mind, she pushed it aside.

Misty was asking for help, which wasn't her style. Demanding an appointment *right this minute* was. Motherhood had smoothed many of Misty's rough edges, but obviously not the I-want-it-now ones. Jillian was surprised Misty had waited almost a year after giving birth to ask for help with getting back into shape.

"I have a baby, Jillian."

"I understand you have to work around your schedule and Sophia's, but I can't just drop my other clients to fit you in. If you can't come at five, I have a couple of openings next week."

"Next week!"

"You're always welcome to come in and work out on your own before that."

Jillian closed her eyes while Misty continued to argue.

"Misty, there is nothing else I can do today. Come in at five, and I'll show you a few exercises you can do until we set up a permanent schedule. I'll send home a few diet plan options as well."

"You're welcome," she mumbled after Misty hung up without a goodbye.

Misty, with her outrageous self-confidence, natural gorgeousness, and venomous tongue, intimidated Jillian to her toes. She always looked like she'd stepped off the pages of a fashion magazine, airbrushed perfection in real life. Beautiful enough to capture any man's attention, Misty could turn around and cut him in two with a single comment.

Jillian replaced the receiver and pushed up from the chair she'd been planted in for the last two hours. Reaching high over her head, she bent, vertebra by vertebra, until her hands rested flat on the floor. The stretch relieved the stiffness in her back and shoulders. Her hamstrings begged for more than thirty seconds, but that was all the time she could spare. Straightening, she did a minute of deep breathing to clear her mind of Misty's domineering demands and juggernaut approach. Then she plastered on a smile before leaving her office to deal with another uncooperative client.

She walked through the free-weight area of the gym. Get Fit was packed with New Year's resolution-makers trying to rid themselves of the ten unwanted pounds they gained over the holidays.

She turned her attention to the main floor and nearly missed a step.

Fireman Brandt Smith was running on one of the treadmills. His brawny arm muscles glistened with sweat while they pumped to the rhythm of his feet. A few locks of his honey-colored hair bounced every time his foot hit the running deck. She stood, mesmerized by the beauty of his shoulders, the power in his leg muscles. She imagined him on a beach, the waves slowly sliding over the sand, his feet leaving tracks as he ran toward a brilliant sunset.

She also noticed the puckering evidence of a burn scar on his shoulder and neck peeking from under his sleeveless T-shirt. She took a step to the left and could see the mark ran from shoulder to elbow on the inside of his right arm. She'd never heard—

"Like what you see?"

Brandt glanced her way.

Embarrassed that she'd been caught staring, she turned toward her next client while sucking air into deprived lungs. She didn't realize she'd been holding her breath until Marty Graw—yes, his real name—spoke. Loudly. He usually looked like he'd just sucked on a lemon, but today his sour expression was replaced with a self-satisfied smirk.

"Appreciating," she said, quietly enough that Brandt couldn't hear. "Just think, Marty. You could have a body like that."

Marty's belly, which hung over the waistband of his sweatpants, jiggled when he snorted. If Brandt didn't know they were talking about him before, he knew when Marty pointed at him. "Only in my wife's wildest dreams would I ever look like that."

Doc Newell told Marty the week after Thanksgiving that he was a dozen chicken wings and a banana cream pie away from a heart attack. For Christmas, his wife gave him the gym's Get Fit and Healthy package, and Doc Newell imparted strict orders for him to follow Jillian's plan.

Marty was in his mid forties, had never worked out a day in his life, and didn't want to start now. Gentle with Marty in the beginning, Jillian was tired of him taking advantage of her easy nature. They'd been working together three days a week since the first of the year. If progress was going to be made, it was time for her to step up his program.

"Not in your wife's dreams. Pure reality. Have you warmed up?"

He glared at her from the corner of his eye in response.

"We've talked about this. You have to warm up before we start. Spend a couple of minutes on an elliptical to get your heart rate up."

"I hate the elliptical."

"Maybe you'll remember that on Tuesday and warm up

on one of the bikes before our pleasure-filled hour together. I'll be back in two minutes."

She replenished a stack of towels and polished the drinking fountain, giving her procrastinator time to build up his anger. He worked a little harder that way. When she turned to get Marty started, her gaze collided with Brandt's in one of the wall mirrors.

He smiled.

This wasn't the first time she'd noticed his disarming smile or the irresistible dimple in his left cheek. This was, however, the first time that smile had ever been directed at her. Or was it? She glanced around, expecting to see a gorgeous woman somewhere behind her. When she looked back at him, his smile grew.

She turned away for the second time, then mentally smacked herself. *Why did you do that? The least you could have done is smile back. He'll think you're a….* She couldn't think of anything stupid enough to call herself. She also couldn't bring herself to glance his way again. To smile now would be as idiotic as not smiling in the first place.

Marty spent forty-five minutes sweating and sputtering rude remarks. As a fast-food franchise owner, he enjoyed what he sold way more than he should. Jillian gave him a simple, healthy diet to follow their first week together, but knew darn well he wasn't adhering to her suggestions. She coaxed and encouraged while Marty huffed, groaned, and hurled more insults. His strength and endurance were slowly increasing, which inspired her. Him? Not so much. She wondered if he even noticed the changes resulting from their three weeks of work.

Even though her attention was focused on her client, she noticed Brandt moving closer to them as his own workout continued.

"You made it through another hour of torture. Good work,

Marty." She held up a finger. "No rewarding yourself with junk food. Eat an apple or an orange instead."

He scowled.

"One more rep, then walk two laps around the track to cool down."

"I used to like you," Marty wheezed.

"Sadly that's one of the drawbacks of my job." She fluttered her eyelashes dramatically. "By June you'll be sending me flowers."

"Don't count on it." He finished his rep, climbed off the rowing machine, and trudged toward the indoor track.

"I like Gerbera daisies," she called after him. "They're cheerful, and will definitely remind me of your smile. See you Tuesday."

"You have a thankless job."

She whipped around, recognizing the voice. Brandt stood behind her. Heat washed up her neck and across her cheeks. "No. Well.... Maybe in the beginning." She turned toward her office, but stopped. *Brandt just opened the door for you. Talk to him.* She sucked in some courage and twisted back. "I thought the fire station had enviable exercise equipment."

"We do, but a Boy Scout troop invaded our weight room this afternoon to work on their fire safety badges."

"I worked with a troop last week on their personal fitness badges." *A tiny something we have in common. Sorta.*

He was close enough that she could reach out and touch the cute cleft in his chin. This morning it was covered in whiskers. Of course, she didn't reach out, but she could have.

"You were great with Marty." He took a step closer and her heart thumped against her ribs, stealing her breath away. "Do you have many clients that cranky?"

Her thoughts veered to Misty. "A couple."

They stared at each other for a heart-stopping moment. She'd waited for him to notice her for two years. Amazingly the day was here, and she couldn't think of anything to say that might keep him talking. She wished she were witty enough to make him laugh or courageous enough to ask him out. Alas, she wasn't that person.

After a year of therapy, she tried not to hold herself responsible for what happened in college. Deep down, she still believed she could have prevented things from escalating.

"I have a class to teach." She thumbed over her shoulder. "Have a nice day."

~

"You too."

Brandt watched Jillian enter a glassed-off room and greet several people before he headed for the showers. He knew of Jillian, knew her friends, but they'd never really talked before and he wondered why. Other than her job as a personal trainer, he didn't know much about her. Her unfaltering good cheer during the hour she worked with Marty proved she possessed infinite patience. The fast-food king wasn't the most pleasant person to be around on the best of days.

He might not have noticed her before, but he made up for it today. Her toned body as she worked side by side with Marty, her beautiful brown eyes sparkling despite her client's constant grumbling. Though Marty might not have noticed, her smile and encouraging words had pushed him to work harder.

Despite all that, what really caught his attention was the blush that touched her cheeks the couple of times their gazes met. When was the last time he'd seen a female blush?

He showered, towel-dried his hair, and dressed in his jeans and a sweater. On his way out of the gym, he glanced through the glass windows. Jillian was still in the classroom teaching what looked like beginner yoga. After she demonstrated the pose, she walked around the room lifting a client's sagging elbow, touching another's back.

Maybe it was time to look into yoga. He'd never taken a class. The thought surprised him in a good way.

Outside, the air was so cold his breath emerged as white clouds. He looked up in time to see Misty Garrett slide out of her car. She spotted him, stopped, and frowned. Not unusual.

His first night in Eden Falls, after accepting the opening with the fire department, he'd gone to Rowdy's Bar and Grill at the invitation of his new crew. They hadn't been there fifteen minutes when Misty sauntered over to their table and propositioned him in front of the men. She'd been single then, and a beauty, with a cascade of black hair and electric blue eyes. He'd met women like Misty before. Her brazenness didn't appeal to him.

Manners, branded into him as a boy, wouldn't allow him to embarrass her in front of four other men. He tried to laugh off her proposition as a joke, but Misty wasn't one to back down. She turned an uncomfortable situation into tacky.

He finally lifted her off his lap and told her he wasn't interested. Misty threw out several insults about him batting for the other team. "Firemen are all brawn and no brains," and "If you'd gotten four more questions right, maybe you could have been a cop." She finished off with, "You guys have the only job where you wake up when it's time to go home," before storming out of Rowdy's.

"One day her house will be on fire and she'll have to eat those words," one of the crewmembers muttered.

Another had clapped Brandt's shoulder. "Congratulations. You just survived your first Misty encounter."

A couple of days later, he'd further insulted Misty when he asked her friend, Alex, out. She'd despised him ever since.

Misty's frown fell away as she started toward him. In fact, for the first time since he'd known her, she actually looked embarrassed. She held up a hand to stop him. "I owe you an apology."

He raised both brows in surprise. "Are you talking to me?"

Misty looked skyward when the first snowflakes of the predicted storm started to fall. She held out her gloved hand and caught one in her palm. "I was pretty awful to you when you first moved to town. I shouldn't have...come on so strong. And I shouldn't have insulted you when you turned me down." She lifted her shoulders, and the bottom half of her face disappeared behind her raised collar.

Misty was apologizing? Brandt wasn't sure how to respond, but did close his mouth when he realized it was hanging open.

"I just want to say I'm sorry."

"Apology accepted."

She looked down. "Apologizing is like step three of the twelve-step program we *mean girls*"—she made quotation marks with her fingers—"have to go through before we can earn our tiaras."

Brandt nodded. He wasn't quite sure what had just happened, but was relieved he wouldn't have to sidestep Misty anymore.

She glanced up at him, the lower half of her face still hidden. "Why did you ask Alex out?"

Because she is the complete opposite of Kacie. "She was kind."

Misty's gaze floated past him as if she had to process his answer. "She is kind and considerate...and icky sweet." Her eyes met his and she lowered her shoulders, flashing a genuine and very un-Misty-like smile. "And I'm pretty lucky to have her as a friend."

"Me too." He and Alex had only gone out a few times, but it was enough to know they weren't a match. She was easy to be around, though, and had become his safety net in a new town. She'd introduced him around, helped him find his bearings.

She was married now and, like Misty, he felt pretty lucky to count Mayor Alexis McCreed as one of his friends.

Misty's mouth disappeared behind her raised collar again. "See you around, Brandt" came out muffled.

"Yeah, Misty. I'll see you around."

~

The memory of Brandt's smile made her hour with Misty a little more pleasant. Though Misty was trying to change her mean-girl persona, the old Misty crept out while Jillian worked her muscles.

"Are you trying to kill me?"

Jillian raised her brows. "I suggested a consult. You're the one who insisted on a full workout."

Misty's blue eyes blazed. "Yeah, a workout, not a torture session."

"This won't kill you, Misty."

"You're working me like you're holding a grudge." Misty narrowed her eyes. "Is that it? I said something awful years ago, and you're getting back at me?"

Jillian laughed, but not hard enough to annoy Misty further. "No. You apologized, and I accepted. The past is the past."

"That's what you say, but—"

"Misty, I don't hold grudges. You're working muscles that aren't used to exercise. In a month, you'll consider this a cakewalk. Keep your arms straight."

"Have you ever done this? Do you have any idea how bad

it hurts?"

"Yes. I do this exercise several times a week."

Misty set the weight down and rubbed her stomach muscles. "You're odd, and I'm not saying that to be mean, but anyone who enjoys exercise is just...odd. You know who you should date?"

This should be good. "Who?"

"Brandt Smith. He was leaving when I came in. I bet he loves to exercise. You two fitness junkies could work out together."

Jillian's cheeks heated for the second time that afternoon. *Nice idea, except he barely knows I exist.* Today was the first time they'd said more than hi to each other.

"You're blushing," Misty said, eyeing her like a hawk watching its prey. "You like him."

Jillian shook her head. She wouldn't reveal her feelings—not to Misty. She did forgive her for any infractions from the past, but that didn't mean she trusted her with long-guarded emotions. "You did really well today. Walk a lap around the track to cool off, then come into my office. We'll set up a workout schedule, and I'll get you those diet plans we talked about."

Jillian walked through the door of her basement apartment and headed straight for the kitchen—four feet away. She dropped her keys in a small bowl on the counter and plugged her cell phone into the charger nearby.

Henry appeared.

"Hey, handsome. Did you miss me?"

"Meeeowww."

She slid her hand under Henry's belly and tucked him against her chest. His deep purr vibrated along her collarbone.

Henry was a rescue, a birthday present from her brother. They got along fine as roommates, as long as she remembered her place. "How was your day?"

He blinked deep gray eyes and meowed mournfully.

"Really? It was that terrible, huh? You'd rather be out in the cold and snow than in this warm apartment? Tomorrow I'll trade places with you."

Jillian wandered from the kitchen to the living room and back again. The confines of her cozy little she-cave were a tight, slightly claustrophobic fit tonight. Her nerves were still jumpy after talking to Brandt. And working with Misty hadn't helped.

She'd been against renting a basement apartment, because sunshine streaming through open windows didn't happen underground. But when she graduated college and decided to move into Eden Falls from her parents' farm, apartments were scarce and money was tight.

The outside door opened directly into her living area. The kitchen—a few cabinets hung on a wall, a single sink, a small refrigerator, and a two-burner stove—was to the right. To the left of the door was a short hall that led to her bedroom and bathroom. Seven hundred square feet turned out to be large enough for her and Henry.

Mrs. O'Malley had converted her basement into an apartment and started renting it out when her husband passed away ten years earlier. She didn't need the money, so the rent was low. With her children living in faraway states, Jillian suspected she just wanted someone she trusted close by. Jillian ran occasional errands for her, shoveled the walks in winter, and mowed the lawn during the summer.

In exchange Mrs. O'Malley let her paint the dark wood-paneled walls as long as she supplied the paint and the labor. A beautiful cream had warmed the space instantly. Then Jillian's mom made colorful drapes for the small basement windows and a coordinated slipcover for the sofa Jillian scored at a garage sale. She splurged on two comfy armchairs that filled the tiny space. The down comforter on her bed was well worth the cost, since the temperature in the basement was run by the thermostat upstairs, and Mrs. O'Malley kept things on the cool side of cozy. She added a few throw pillows, some bright prints for the walls, and was now quite content with her space.

She circled back to the living room and dropped into one of the chairs. "Do you want to hear about my day? It was quite thrilling."

Henry pushed out of her arms and jumped to the back of the chair. "Meeowww."

"Guess who came in today?" She waved her hand. "Oh, I'll just tell you, because you'll never guess. Brandt Smith!"

Henry lay down near her head, his purr rumbling close to her ear.

She turned to look over her shoulder. "I know. I was excited too. He worked out at Get Fit because a Boy Scout troop was using the exercise room at the fire station. We talked. Well, he talked, but still...."

Henry closed his eyes.

"You don't have to be so unenthusiastic about it. Especially since you know how long I've liked him." She sighed. "I know nothing will come of it, but it was a small bit of thrill in my not-so-very-exciting life. You could pretend to be happy for me."

When she got no response, she pushed up from the chair. "You're just acting like that because you want your dinner."

Of course, the word "dinner" got an immediate reaction. Henry jumped off the back of the chair, landing elegantly, and sauntered into the kitchen. He meowed his agreement when she chose his favorite cat food from the cupboard and opened the can.

"Oh, guess who else came in today? Misty. She said she gained fifty pounds over the holiday, when in reality it was only about eight. She wants to get toned for summer."

Jillian spooned the food into her cat's bowl and set it on the floor. "Misty was a little demanding, but only half as bad as she used to be. Of course, she expects results without putting in much work, but that's not unusual. Most people want instant results. We both know that isn't how it works.

She leaned a hip against the counter and crossed her arms. "I think these sessions might be good for me and Misty. Maybe we can get to know each other better."

Jillian released her ponytail band and ran fingers through her hair, separating a few tangles. "She actually suggested Brandt and I might make a good match."

She touched the tip of Henry's tail with her toe.

He scooted around his bowl, out of her reach.

"I guess I'll shower before I eat. I still have the Sunday dinner leftovers Mom sent home."

Henry was too busy scarfing his delicacy to pay her any mind.

"Maybe you should take a breath. You act like you haven't eaten in days."

Still nothing.

Jillian glanced around her quiet apartment. She was having a full-fledged, though one-sided, conversation with a cat. "At least I'm not talking to myself. Right, Henry?"

At the sound of his name, Henry looked up and blinked. "Meeeowww."

~

Three days later, Jillian heard a commotion. She jumped up from her desk and headed for a group of people collected around the men's locker room door.

"An ambulance is on the way, Marty."

At the sound of Dawson Garrett's voice and the mention of the client she just finished with, Jillian pushed through the crowd. "What happened?"

Marty lay on the floor, head elevated on a couple of towels. When he spotted her, he pointed a chubby finger. "This is your fault. I'm having a heart attack because you're a sadist."

She knelt beside them. *You're having a heart attack because you eat too much fast food.*

"Now, Marty, there's no use blaming Jillian," her employer said, patting her shoulder.

Suddenly Brandt was beside her, and she was afraid *she* was having the heart attack.

As the only paramedic in town, Brandt usually arrived just ahead of the ambulance. He set his medical kit next to Marty. "What have we got?"

"Marty says he's having a heart attack. Glenda saw him come out of the locker room holding his chest," Dawson said.

"Then he just laid down on the floor," Glenda added.

"This is her fault!" Marty pointed at Jillian.

"I...." She had no words, but felt her cheeks flame when Brandt glanced at her.

Brandt tugged a stethoscope from his kit and listened to Marty's chest, took his pulse, asked him about the pain. He was in calm control, going through a mental checklist. And Jillian was mesmerized.

While checking Marty, he asked Jillian questions about the workout. He asked Marty about his diet and if there was any history of heart problems in his family. A stretcher was brought in, and Brandt helped load Marty into the back of the ambulance, then climbed in beside him. Right before the door shut, he glanced at her and flashed his beautiful dimple.

She melted into a puddle.

CHAPTER 2

Less than a week after their encounter, Jillian was surprised to see Brandt back in the gym. He and another firefighter were spotting each other in the free-weight area. She took a moment to appreciate the way their muscles bulged and rippled as they worked out. As always, she found the human body and its capabilities fascinatingly marvelous.

When her gaze finally made its way back to Brandt's face, he was grinning. At her. Her heartbeat tripped over itself before jumping to her throat. She'd been caught staring. Again.

She'd crushed on him since he moved to town, her imagination creating many scenarios that of course never played out. In those fantasies, she was self-confident, brave, and friendly in a fun, flirty way. She didn't stand on the cusp of introverted-ness. Instead, she was comfortable, assertive, and could strike up and hold a conversation.

By this time in her life, Jillian knew she would never have the courage to initiate anything, not after what had happened in college. That incident would haunt her forever.

"Hey, Smith, pay attention," the other firefighter said.

The comment brought Jillian back to the present. She flashed a closed-lip smile and even added a little wave—quite proud that she did so without blushing—then retreated to the safety of her office.

She shed her coat and scarf, hung them on the hook by the door, and sat behind the well-worn desk. First on her list of to-dos, revise class schedules for next month. One of their instructors moved unexpectedly, so she'd have to shuffle a few of the classes around. She'd already talked to a kick-boxing instructor in Harrisville who was willing to fill a few openings, and she could lead another yoga or spin class to fill in until Dawson and Glenda hired someone.

Two employees were already here, and two more were scheduled to come in at nine. Since she didn't have a client until ten, she could work uninterrupted for an hour.

In addition to her already-packed calendar, Dawson called her last night to see if she could come in two hours earlier than she was scheduled. He and Glenda were meeting with a realtor this morning to look through the vacant building next door. They wanted to expand, give her an office with windows, and add a climbing wall, a couple of volleyball courts, and an indoor pool. The later would increase their membership exponentially, since Eden Falls town pool was outdoors and only open three months a year.

She bit into the apple she'd brought for a snack.

"Hi."

Ohmygosh. She swiped at the juice on her chin. She knew the voice well, had heard the deep rumble many times, but it was always directed toward someone else. Usually Alex.

"Hello." She cringed inwardly at her breathlessness, hoping Brandt wouldn't notice. Though he was probably used to that sort of reaction from women.

Lifting his arm to the doorframe, the edges of the burn

scar peeked from under his T-shirt again. He must have noticed her looking, because he lowered his arm. "I thought you might like to know Marty's heart attack was indigestion."

"I heard." Marty's wife told Glenda, who'd told her that Marty finally admitted to eating six donuts along with a fast-food breakfast before his workout that morning.

"Just coming in?"

She bobbed her head and swiped at her chin in case she missed a dribble. "Actually I was scheduled to come in later, but the Garretts—do you know Dawson and Glenda?"

He grinned and her heart thudded hard. Twice. "I know the Garretts."

Of course he knows the Garretts, dum-dum. He dated their niece. "Dawson asked me to come in early."

He stepped into her office and leaned back against the wall, crossing his arms over his broad chest as though he intended to stay awhile. His beautiful hazel eyes moved around her small space, lighting on the two framed diplomas on her wall, the short bookcase crammed with health magazines, and the colorful pencil holder on the corner of her desk, before stopping on her.

"What would you be doing if Dawson hadn't called?"

The question took her by surprise. "I…uh…well, I'd probably be cleaning my apartment or doing laundry. Maybe visiting my family." *Cleaning my apartment? Doing laundry? You are one exciting woman, Jillian.*

He ran his fingers through his tousled, ridiculously sexy hair. "Does your family live close by?"

Relieved he'd picked up on that part of her monologue, she nodded. "Saunders' Apple Orchards, just outside of town."

The corners of his eyes crinkled when he grinned, making his dimple wink. "Ahh, that's your parents' place. I didn't connect the last names."

He knows my last name is Saunders? He knows my last name is Saunders! So simple, yet extremely exciting. She wished she could stop the silly blush that heated her cheeks. He knew her last name, which meant he knew a bit more about her than she thought he did.

"I've seen the signs for that orchard. I bet it was a great place to grow up."

The image of a bobblehead doll popped into her mind when she nodded, again. "It...was."

A lone eyebrow rose. "I hear a but."

She lifted a shoulder. "But...my parents believed—still do believe in hard work. Of course it's paid off, but when I was a kid, working every Saturday afternoon wasn't much fun. When all our friends were headed to the movies or to the river, we were mowing, weeding, picking apples, and taking our turn at the fruit stand at the end of the driveway."

"Fruit stand?"

"Besides apples, we have plum, peach, and cherry trees. My parents sell the fruit along with jams, jellies, apple butter, even...soap." *Stop babbling!*

Brandt listened like he was truly interested, his smile still in place. She loved his smile. His white teeth gleamed from a tanned face, which, at this time of year, came from sunny days on a ski slope. Two-day stubble enhanced his strong, angular jaw. He was so handsome she had a hard time dragging her gaze away. Just the sight of him around town sent her heart banging like a snare in a drumline competition.

He shifted his weight.

"Would you like to sit down?" *Stupid! You should have offered when he first knocked.*

"Sure. Thanks." He sat in the only other chair in her small office. "Because you said we, I assume you have brothers or sisters. Maybe some of both?"

She turned a framed picture on her desk. "Two brothers, one sister."

He picked up the photo. His mouth twitched in the cutest way while he studied it. She would remember everything about his visit to her office today. She'd emblazon it in her memory for future use.

"You're the baby." He glanced at her. "Cute pigtails."

She shrugged.

He set the picture back on her desk. "How old were you there?"

"About six." Feeling a little braver, she asked, "Do you have siblings?"

"Four boys, one girl. I'm number two."

Jillian tried to contain the giddiness bubbling through her system like an effervescent IV. She was having a normal as-if-it-happened-every-day conversation with Brandt Smith. Flexing her ankles under her desk, she tried to relax at least one part of her body. "Where does your sister fall?"

"She's the youngest."

"Poor girl."

"Poor girl, my eye," he said on a chuckle. "She was spoiled rotten. Still is."

"Spoiled rotten, as she should be with four older brothers."

His laugh sent her heart knocking again. "Were you spoiled?"

"I might have had a little lighter workload when I was younger, but no, we all had our chores."

"Do your brothers and sister live around here?"

"My oldest brother Joe does. He and his wife built a house at the farm. Sam, a marine biologist, is somewhere in the Gulf of Mexico. My sister Tania and her Air Force husband live in Texas."

He nodded slowly as though he was processing the information. She wondered what was going through his mind, wished she could think of a question to ask. The fear of saying something that might send him on his way overpowered that wish. "Do you go out to your parents' farm often?"

"I try to go a couple of times a week, usually on my day off and Sunday. I'm kind of expected for Sunday dinner."

"Do you have the same day off every week?"

He wants to know about my days off. Her fingertips went numb, followed by her cheeks. She swallowed, hoping her voice wouldn't come out shaky. "The gym is closed on Sundays, and I usually have Wednesdays off unless Dawson and Glenda need me to work for them."

"I have next Wednesday off. Would you be interested in going snowshoeing?"

"Snowshoeing? Next Wednesday?" *Brandt Smith asked me out!*

The thought darted through her mind and then tripped and fell. She was jumping to conclusions. He didn't say it was a date or that going snowshoeing was just with him. He'd probably asked a gang of friends and was kind enough to include her. *Casual invitation to join a group—not a date.*

But, if it is a date...we'll be alone. In the woods.

She opened her mouth to say no, but stopped. If she declined his offer, he might never ask again. Just because one guy in college hurt her didn't mean Brandt would. He was a fireman, the town's only paramedic. He helped people for a living. She'd never heard a negative thing said about him. If you couldn't trust someone with those credentials, whom could you trust?

Torn between yes and no, she shook her head. "I haven't been snowshoeing in a long time."

He flashed his beautiful grin. "Haven't you heard? It's like riding a bike."

What she heard was angels singing. In harmony. There

were definite shouts of joy. *Hallelujah! Hallelujah! She has a date!* "Okay." Bobblehead nod. "I'd like to go."

"Your parents won't be upset if you miss a visit?"

"No. I don't go on a regular basis.... I mean I don't go every day off, just when I don't have anything else"—she flapped a hand—"that doesn't sound right...." *Stop talking!*

He laughed and pushed up from the chair. "I was just making sure. I don't want your parents upset with me."

She stared at him when he braced his hands on her desk. Her breath hitched in her throat. *He's going to kiss—*

"I'll need your number so I can call with details."

"Oh! Of course. Sure." She grabbed a Post-it notepad and scratched out her cell number.

He took the piece of paper from her. "So it's a date."

She did another bobblehead impersonation, knowing full well she was wearing a goofy grin. *It is a date! He said it's a date!* She wanted to jump up and down, clap her hands like a giddy schoolgirl, cover her heart so he wouldn't notice it pounding out of her chest. Instead, she stayed perfectly still.

He straightened. "Have a nice day, Jillian."

"You too."

She waited a full minute to make sure he wasn't coming back, then stood and eased the door shut. Her happiness, too huge to contain, bubbled over into a silly giggle. She hugged herself, then grabbed her cell phone and scrolled through her contacts, accidentally bypassing her friend's work number twice before hitting the Call button.

"Owen Danielson's office. Jolie speaking. May I—"

"Jolie, it's Jillian."

"Hey, Jillie-Bean."

"Are you busy?"

"Nope. Owen took the morning off. One of his boys had—"

"He asked me out." Jillian was too energized to hold the

news in a moment longer. So excited she was feeling light-headed. This just might be the very best day of her life.

"Are you all right? You sound out of breath."

"Did you hear what I said? He asked me out."

"Who asked you out?"

"Brandt Smith. He asked me out. On a date. He even said, 'It's a date', so it's for real!"

~

Brandt walked into the house he bought two months earlier. Boxes still lined the walls in the spare bedrooms and filled the closet, boxes he had ignored until now.

On the way home from the gym, he decided today was a good day to make a plan. He went from room to room of the three bedroom-two bath fixer-upper, listed things he'd like to change, and prioritized the lists while eating lunch. He'd start in the largest spare bedroom, because it needed the least amount of work. The space would become his guest room. He'd sort through the boxes in the closet and prep the walls for a coat of paint. Then he'd pull up the dingy carpeting to reveal hardwood floors, which were begging to be refinished. They'd been a wonderful discovery he made soon after moving in.

He loved that an old house could be made new with a little elbow grease. And he was up to the task. He'd helped his dad restore several old homes while in high school. In the process he'd acquired the handyman skills needed for this renovation.

After lunch, he went to the bedroom's closet. Tucked in the back were three boxes he hadn't opened in two years. He tugged out the first, cut the tape sealing it shut, and folded back the flaps. On top was a framed photo of him and Kacie just after he asked her to marry him. Their happy smiles in place, she held out her left hand so their special moment would be frozen for all time.

The photo was taken two weeks before his accident.

He wasn't sure why he'd kept things reminding him of her, but it was time to clear both his mind and his house of their time together. He was tired of hanging on to old memories. And that's what he was doing by keeping these things. *Time to let go and move on.*

He pulled out another framed photo. This one was taken on a trip to the Oregon Coast. They'd hiked down to a beautiful beach full of driftwood. Again, before his accident.

That was how he categorized his memories with Kacie. Before and after.

He'd always been pretty confident about dating, but Kacie decimated that confidence. He should have seen it coming, should have noticed her pulling away, but he'd been too focused on his own recovery. He was sure her love ran deeper than just skin and looks. He'd been wrong.

His thoughts wandered to Jillian. The second he left her office, he started questioning his decision to ask her out. Did he dare put himself out there again? The only person he'd dated since Kacie was Alex. As mayor of Eden Falls, a business owner, and a mother, she'd seemed safe, steady, and trustworthy. He felt he could build back some of his shaken trust with her. Though he respected her as a friend, and appreciated her sense of humor and sweet nature, there just hadn't been enough flame to build on.

His parents shared a happy, loving relationship. They'd never been afraid to show affection in front of their children. By observing his parents' open devotion for each other, Brandt and his siblings had learned to appreciate the bond they shared, and to look forward to having the same.

He ran the pad of his thumb over the image of him and

Kacie grinning for the camera. They both looked happy. They had been happy.

The third picture he pulled out was of him in a hospital bed, three weeks after the accident. Kacie was leaning awkwardly toward him, her smile tight. He remembered her stepping away when he reached for her waist. "I don't want to hurt you."

This was the day he should have noticed the structure she'd been slowly and discreetly erecting between them. He'd been too caught up in his own shrunken world that consisted of a hospital room and rehab and pain. He had an army of "should haves" that still stood at attention, waiting for a dismissal order.

Today was that day.

One last time, he let himself remember the look of horror on her face when she walked into the emergency room and saw his burns for the first time. He remembered the fear in her eyes when he first tried to stand, to walk. He remembered her excuses for not visiting, believing them at the time, knowing different now.

He also remembered the day he was released from the hospital and she wasn't there. The day he was driving to physical therapy and saw her with a man, embracing, kissing openly on the streets of downtown Tacoma as if he, her fiancé, didn't exist. As if their wedding wasn't weeks away. That day would be a hard one to forget.

When he confronted her, she denied nothing. She said she hadn't broken off their engagement yet because she pitied him. Until that moment, he'd been so proud of his progress.

She also said she couldn't bear seeing the scars covering his right side from neck to knee. She admitted their puckered ugliness disgusted her.

Decimated? Yes. If the woman who planned to marry him didn't want him, who would?

The wedding, put on hold because of the accident, was cancelled. He often wondered what would have happened if he hadn't seen her with another man. Would she have told him, or just gone through with the wedding and crushed him later?

He didn't know where she was now and, for the first time since he saw her with that other man, he realized he didn't care.

His thoughts turned back to Jillian. He wasn't sure what prompted him to ask her out, other than she'd been on his mind a lot since he saw her the week before. He had no intention of doing anything but talking to her when he went to her office door. Getting to know a little about her was interesting enough that a snowshoeing invitation popped out of his mouth before his thoughts caught up.

Now he was second-guessing his decision to ask her out. And snowshoeing as a first date activity— What was he thinking? Most women liked to dress up and go somewhere nice for a first date. He shouldn't have assumed Jillian was any different.

He took all three pictures out of the frames, tore them in half, and set the frames aside to be given away. Next item in the box was a sweater Kacie gave him. Expensive and a great color, yet he knew he'd never wear it again. He set it in the giveaway pile.

~

Jillian almost skipped into her apartment after work. She hung her coat on the rack by the door. "Hello, sweet Henry," she said when he ambled into the kitchen. She picked him up and whirled in a circle. "Did you miss me? I have some more thrilling news. Brandt came into the gym again today and he asked me out. Can you believe it?"

Henry blinked, his complete lack of interest apparent.

"I'm still shaking I'm so excited. And a little nervous."

"Why?" She lifted Henry so they were eye to eye. "Because of what happened in college."

Henry batted her cheek softly.

"I know. I know. It's time to forget about the past." She tucked Henry against her chest. "It's hard, but I'll try. I've never heard a negative thing said about Brandt since he moved here. Everyone likes him. That's promising, don't you think?"

She walked into the living room. "He's taking me snowshoeing next Wednesday. Isn't that the perfect first date? Well, maybe not to you, but I think it's perfect. I haven't been snowshoeing in years."

Lying back on the sofa, she adjusted a pillow and Henry settled on her lap. "I'm not sure if it's just the two of us. I didn't have the courage to ask, but he did say, 'So it's a date,' which means I'm not fantasizing all this. It *is* a date. I really am going on a date with Brandt Smith."

Her cell phone rang. She carried Henry into the kitchen to answer, but stopped short. What if it was Brandt? Maybe he was calling to cancel. She peeked behind the bananas and sighed in relief when she spotted Jolie's wedding picture on the screen.

"Hi." She wondered if her friend could hear the relief in her voice.

"Hey, Jillie-Bean. Stella just called. She and Alex are headed to Rowdy's for an impromptu girls' night out. You in?"

Just what she needed to burn off some of her pent-up energy. "Sounds perfect."

. . .

Rowdy's Bar and Grill was packed for a Thursday night. Country music drifted from well-hidden speakers, but Jillian could barely distinguish who was singing over the noise. She spotted her friends at a table in the back and made her way through the crowd, waving and speaking to those she knew.

Life was interfering with their traditional girls' night out. They used to get together at least once a month, but they hadn't been able to arrange a time since before Christmas. Alex McCreed was busy with her many roles as mayor, owner of the only flower shop in town, wife, and mother. Stella Adams had a classroom full of second-graders zapping her energy during the day and an unreliable boyfriend making dates then cancelling at night. Jolie Klein worked full-time for attorney Owen Danielson while pregnant—due very soon—with her first baby, a girl. Carolyn West, who moved back to town on Memorial Day, managed Patsy's Pastries and was dating Alex's brother, police chief, JT Garrett. Jillian expected them to announce their engagement any day. And Misty was...Misty. She juggled a husband, a one-year-old daughter, and worked as a top stylist at Dahlia's Salon.

Jillian rested her hand on Jolie's belly, which probably irritated the soon-to-be mom, but she was kind enough not to say so. "How are you feeling?"

"Fat. The doctor said my ankles are swollen but I can't even see them."

Jillian pressed a finger to Jolie's ankle. "They aren't bad."

"I have pimples. It's like I've reliving my chubby high school years." She blinked rapidly as if fighting tears. "And my hormones are raging. Poor Nate is going to divorce me before this baby is born."

Jillian put her arms around Jolie. "You have one little pimple on your chin. Your skin will clear when your hormones settle. Soon you'll be holding a beautiful baby in your arms and nothing else will matter."

Misty snorted. "Don't listen to Little Miss Positive, Jolie. Your breasts fill with milk that leaks every time the baby cries, you never have an uninterrupted night of sleep again, and the love life you had before you got pregnant—gone."

Alex reached over and patted Jolie's arm. "Don't listen to Little Miss Negative. You and Nate will enjoy every second of parenthood."

"I didn't say she wouldn't enjoy it." Misty glared around the table. "I just said nothing goes back to normal. Except your skin. After a year. And your ankles. Eventually you'll see them again."

"Everything will be fine," Jillian said, trying to smooth over the worry Misty had put on Jolie's face. "You and Nate will invent a new normal together."

Stella slapped hands on the table. "Jolie's baby is the reason I called an impromptu girls' night out. Let's plan a shower tonight."

Jillian had thought about that very thing a dozen times, but her apartment was too small to hold more than the five of them, and Jolie would want to invite both her own family and Nate's.

"We can have it at my house," Alex said. "Colton will be in New York weekend after next to meet with his publisher, so he won't be underfoot. We'll plan it for that Saturday night."

"You guys don't have to go to the trouble of throwing me a shower," Jolie said, but Jillian could see she was delighted by the idea. Even though the six of them were friends, and had been since elementary school, she and Jolie were besties.

Jolie was the only one who knew about Jillian's crush on Brandt.

"It's no trouble," Stella said. "Alex will donate her house.

Jillian, can you be in charge of decorations? Carolyn and I will plan the food."

"You forgot me."

Stella pointed at Misty. "Games. We need some crazy fun games."

Misty plopped her elbows on the table. "I hate shower games. They're so juvenile. I'll help with food."

Stella performed her signature eye roll. "You can't warm up a can of soup. I'll plan the games. You can decorate. Jillian, will you help Carolyn with food?"

Carolyn was a pastry chef who baked perfect delicacies for Patsy's Pastries. They could count on her to come up with something spectacular for Jolie's shower. Jillian would be happy to help wherever she was needed. Anything for her best friend.

"How do I decorate?"

"Misty!" Stella thumped the table with her palms. "What do you want to do?"

"I'll help you decorate, Misty," Alex said. She passed a napkin and a pen to Jolie. "Your job is to come up with a guest list."

The waitress stopped at their table to deliver more drinks and the huge platter of loaded nachos with extra jalapeños that Alex always ordered.

While Jillian passed out plates, they went around the table, telling the news of their lives.

"I asked my students to write a sentence using the word *discuss*. Jonathan Whitaker wrote, 'I shot a Nerf bullet at my brother and had to discuss it with my dad.'"

They laughed.

Stella always had at least one student whose shenanigans kept them entertained throughout the school year. This year Jonathan had kept them laughing.

Jolie shared a funny story that happened at work,

although they all knew there were many more she couldn't share. As the office manager for an attorney, she had to keep most of the stories to herself.

Misty talked about Sophia taking her first steps, and Carolyn blushed through a story Stella told about catching her and JT making out in a corner of the library.

"Okay Jillian." Alex turned to her. "What's new with you?"

She held a hand in front of her mouth as she finished chewing and swallowing a mouthful. "The Garretts bought the vacant building next to the gym. They're going to add an indoor pool."

"Aunt Glenda told me about that," Alex said. "I'm so excited. Charlie will love being able to swim during the winter months.

"Charlie and all the other kids in Eden Falls." Jolie turned to Jillian, a mischievous gleam in her eye. "Anything new with you on the dating front, Jillie-Bean?"

The other four friends turned toward her in unison, staring expectantly. Jillian was sure her hot cheeks gave the news away. She should have told Jolie to keep that bit of information to herself until after the fact. What if Brandt cancelled the date before it happened? What if *she* got cold feet and cancelled?

"Come on, Jillian," Stella prodded. "Who's the lucky guy? Anyone we know?"

Jillian stifled a groan and glanced at Alex, hoping the mention of Brandt wouldn't cause hard feelings between them since he and Alex had dated. "Brandt Smith asked me out today."

"I knew it!" Misty exclaimed, pointing at Jillian. "Didn't I tell you? You fitness fanatics match perfectly."

Stella wiggled her eyebrows. "Good job, Jillian."

"I agree with Misty." Alex glanced around the table, wide-eyed. "Wow, agreeing with Misty. That's a first."

"Oh, shut up," Misty snapped.

Alex laughed and turned to Jillian. "I've thought you two would make a great couple since the night of Jolie's wedding."

"That was eighteen months ago." Jolie rubbed a hand over her baby bump. "Why didn't you say something before now?"

Alex lifted a shoulder. "I believe things happen when the time is right."

Jillian disagreed. She and Brandt could have been dating for eighteen months.

"I could have put a bug in Brandt's ear, but I think natural attraction rather than suggestion is nicer. Don't you?" Alex asked Jillian.

When Alex put it like that, Jillian had to agree. Brandt asking her out of his own accord was more meaningful than if he'd been prompted by someone else.

Stella lifted her glass. "Here's to best friends, girls' night out, first dates, and baby showers."

Jolie leaned close. "Brandt's a great guy. You two will have fun."

Jillian clinked glasses with her friends. *I hope you're right.*

CHAPTER 3

When Jillian arrived at church, her oldest brother and his wife, who was due with their first baby in a week, were saving seats. Her parents scooted into the pew minutes later. She struggled to keep her eyes and mind front and center during Preacher Brenner's sermon. Even if Brandt was here, he always sat in the back in case of an emergency call. She fiddled with a hymnal until her mom stilled her with a hand and a what's-up-with-you look.

When the organ signaled the end of the hour, she remained seated, eyes forward. She was a full-fledged coward. Because of what happened in college, she'd only dated a handful of times, always chickening out at the last minute. She had no reason she shouldn't trust Brandt. Everyone thought so highly of him. *There are still good guys out there and he is one of them*.

"Hey, Jill, you going to move anytime soon?"

She glanced up at her brother, who wore an impatient eyebrow-raised stare. He and Raelyn were waiting for her so they exit the church.

"Sorry." She stood and stepped into the aisle, finally

raising her eyes. If Brandt had been there, he was gone. Conflicting emotions clawed through her, vying for first place. Was she glad he'd already left, or sorry she hadn't seen him? She decided to go with being sorry, because she would have loved a glimpse of him.

An hour later Jillian dried her hands on a kitchen towel, while her mom slipped the chicken potpie they made for dinner into the oven. Jillian had helped make five, four of which her mom would freeze for a quick and easy meal.

Her dad came up behind his wife and nipped the back of her neck. Jillian watched her shiver in pleasure, turn in his arms, and give him more than a friendly peck. The look of love they shared was sweet and…enviable. She wanted what her mom and dad had always enjoyed. They'd been married for thirty-five years and their love and passion for each other still shone as brightly as when she was a little girl.

The only way she'd ever get to experience that kind of love was to take a chance. Learn to trust. "Are the snowshoes still in the basement?"

"They should be in the same corner as the skis," her dad said.

Jillian started for the door that led downstairs.

"Grab mine, too, Jill." Her dad looped an arm around his wife's neck, kissed her temple. "We'll take them out for a spin while dinner is in the oven."

She and her dad bundled up against the cold and traversed the orchard. Luckily, her snowshoeing coordination came back quickly, so she wouldn't make a fool of herself in front of Brandt. After her dad checked the trees, they threw snowballs and Jillian made a snow angel, her first in years. They spent a carefree afternoon together, something she hadn't done with him in quite a while.

Dinner was spent speculating on how the weather would affect the orchard, discussing improvements to the barn, and worrying over the price of a new tractor. There were always improvements to be made and weather to worry about. Sometimes Jillian felt left out and other times she was glad she'd chosen another career.

After dinner, Jillian's dad and brother retired to the family room to watch a basketball game, and her brother's wife went to lie down. While her mom fixed hot cocoa, Jillian finished wiping down the countertops.

"Come here, sweet girl." Her mom settled at the table with two steaming mugs. "Tell me what's new with you."

"Not much. Work is great." Jillian pulled out a chair and sat opposite her mom. She dipped her spoon, emerging a dollop of whipped cream into the chocolaty richness. "I've been working with Marty Graw. Those are the days I have to remind myself I love my job, but other than that, I really do."

Her mom laughed. "I'm sure Marty is a handful."

"It's hard to work with someone who's so unwilling. Sometimes I think he's trying to sabotage all efforts to be healthy." Jillian took a sip of the decadent hot chocolate and licked the cream from the side of her mouth. "Mmm, this is as delicious as always. Too bad it's so sinfully fattening."

"I won't lie, the calorie count is high on this one."

Jillian's friends always looked forward to visiting Saunders' Apple Orchards on cold days. Her mom could always be persuaded to make her famous hot chocolate.

"I ran into Glenda at the grocery store last week. She said you're a lifesaver at Get Fit, that you've rescued them more than once."

"Glenda and Dawson are easy to work for. Without Get Fit, I'd be driving to Harrisville, or even farther, for a job."

"I hear they bought the building next door and are adding an indoor pool. Glenda said you'll get a new office."

"I'm excited about that part. My little cubby is dreary. Especially in the winter."

"Yes, it is."

"They'll start the expansion immediately and hope to have the pool open by September."

Her mom set her mug down and leaned her elbows on the table. "Enough of the mundane. Tell me about *you*."

"There's not much to tell." Jillian lifted a shoulder. "I'm fine. The apartment's fine. Mrs. O'Malley is fine. Work is fine. Henry's fine."

Her mother raised her eyebrows. "You're not going to tell me about your date on Wednesday?"

Jillian frowned. It was bad enough all her friends knew. "Who told you?"

"Alex told her mom. Alice told me." Her mom rested her chin on her upraised fingertips. "You really weren't going to say anything?"

Jillian looked down into her cup, watching the last of the whipped cream melt. "I was so excited when Brandt asked, because I've liked him for a long time. But I'm also terrified."

Her mom dropped both arms onto the table and reached for Jillian's hands, cupping them between her own. "You have to stop living in the past, my darling baby girl. I know what you went through in college was horrific. I also know you still partially blame yourself for what happened, but you have to stop. You did nothing wrong. Proceeding with caution is fine. You are successful at business, now you have to move forward with the personal side of your life."

Jillian swallowed the urge to cry, but not before her mom noticed.

"Brandt is a good man, or Alex wouldn't have dated him. Right?"

A light flashed bright in her narrowed mind. Her mom was absolutely right. Alex wouldn't have dated Brandt or encouraged Jillian to date him if she wasn't sure of his character.

Her mom patted her hands. "Finally. A smile."

Jillian got up and hugged her mom from behind. "I love you. Thanks for always being there."

~

The anticipation was almost more than Jillian could bear. She'd never looked forward to anything as much as this date with Brandt. Or been more nervous. What was said or done could make or break a first date. She wished she knew him better, certain that would relieve some of her anxiety. A mental list of things they could talk about was tucked in a corner of her mind. Would she remember anything on that list when she was face to face with Brandt?

She set her untouched bowl of oatmeal in the sink.

Breathe.

Once Brandt showed up, she'd be able to relax. According to the clock in her kitchen, she had thirty minutes. She put a hand to her jittery stomach. He would be here in thirty minutes.

Her cell phone rang, and her stomach twisted. *Brandt is calling to cancel. It's okay. You can handle this. You even kind of expected it.* Sure, she was disappointed, but really, it was probably for the best. She could get her laundry done after all.

She reached for her cell phone, experiencing another tumble of emotions. *Not Brandt.* She connected the call. "Hi, Mom."

"Oh, honey, I'm glad I caught you. We're on the way to Harrisville Regional Hospital. Your niece is coming."

"What? Now?"

"Yes. Don't worry. Joe and Raelyn will understand if you

can't make it, but I didn't want you to feel left out. Go on your date and I'll text you updates."

All the excitement and anxiety leaked out of Jillian's body and puddled around her feet. Her first date with Brandt, and her niece decided to enter the world today. "I'll be there."

After she hung up with her mom, panic hit. She didn't have Brandt's phone number. Alex mentioned that he'd just moved from an apartment to a house, but she didn't know where. *What do I do?* She had no way to get in touch with him.

She quickly changed from winter wear to everyday clothes, wrote out an apology, and taped it to her door on the way out.

~

Brandt was tired when he climbed from behind the wheel of his truck. He hadn't slept much last night, worrying about this date. He probably should have shown Jillian his scars first, then asked her out. She'd seen the edges under his shirt and still said yes, but she didn't know the extent.

When the sun rose over the horizon, his midnight fears eased. He shoved the past behind him. Not all women were Kacie. He looked up at the clear blue sky and released a pent-up breath. Today was beautiful, perfect for snowshoeing.

Following Jillian's instructions, he rounded Mrs. O'Malley's house to the basement door. He opened the storm door to knock, but a folded piece of paper taped to the inside of the glass stopped him. His name was written on the front. He pulled it free and read

Brandt,

I'm so sorry I have to break our date this way, but I didn't

have your phone number. My sister-in-law is in labor, and I had to go to Harrisville Regional to be with my family.

Sincerely,

Jillian

Surprised by the disappointment that settled in the pit of his stomach, he stuffed the note into his coat pocket.

Now he had the whole day to wrestle with self-doubt, which began tearing away at him immediately. He'd seen Jillian in church on Sunday, sitting next to a very pregnant lady, so the story sounded legit. On the other hand, Kacie hadn't visited him in the hospital because of made-up stories. Of course he didn't know at the time that her aunt wasn't sick and her grandmother hadn't broken a hip in a fall.

He had to work next Wednesday, so rescheduling was out.

On his way to his truck, he decided he wouldn't spend the day wallowing in uncertainty. The spare bedroom was finally cleaned out. Today he'd paint.

The only hardware store in Eden Falls was still under construction after it was set on fire by an arsonist almost a year ago. The grand reopening was set for some time in March. Even though Harrisville had a chain hardware store only fifteen minutes away, he missed the convenience of having one in town. Especially when he ran out of something in the middle of a project.

He spent some time picking out a soft gray color that would run throughout the house, and crisp white for the baseboards, doorjambs, and windowsills. He also bought brushes, rollers, paint trays, and a tarp. An updated light fixture would replace the old one, something he thought his mom would like, since his parents would be using this room when they came to visit. The smaller spare bedroom would become his office.

On his way out of town, he passed the hospital and, on a whim, turned into the parking lot. He thought he knew

Jillian's car and circled the lot twice before he spotted the white Subaru. Then he was angry with himself for doubting her. Just because Kacie lied didn't mean Jillian would.

He spent the rest of the day painting and didn't stop until hunger pangs insisted.

~

Jillian cuddled her niece close, staring down at the dark-haired angel. Black eyelashes fluttered against dewy white cheeks before the baby opened her eyes and stared straight at Jillian. If her heart wasn't already lost to this little one, that moment would have sealed the deal. The baby's pink rosebud lips puckered in the cutest way and a tiny tongue appeared.

The covers on the bed rustled, and Jillian glanced over. Poor Raelyn, whose labor seemed to go on forever, was exhausted and taking advantage of the last uninterrupted sleep she'd get for a while. Jillian was left to babysit when the rest of her family went out to pick up dinner.

Brandt ran through her thoughts for the hundredth time since she'd arrived. What did he think when he saw her note? Maybe it was best not to know.

She'd considered calling the fire station to ask for his number. She'd also thought about showing up with a batch of cookies and an apology, but she didn't want to embarrass him at work.

A little voice in her head whispered, *Let it go*. She'd written a note, explained the situation. He could either understand or not. An unavoidable situation had popped up, and she'd done the best she could under the circumstances.

The door opened and her brother walked in. He stopped inches away and looked down at his daughter with an expression Jillian had never seen him wear. "She's so beautiful."

"Yes, she is." She relinquished the baby to her daddy when he held out his arms. "You and Raelyn did good, Joe. She's absolutely perfect."

"She is pretty perfect." Their eyes met. "Thanks for being here. Mom said you had plans today. A date with a fireman?"

Thanks, Mom. "She wasn't supposed to tell anyone. At least not until after the date."

"Well, I'm really glad you came today. I know Raelyn appreciates it, especially since her mom and sister couldn't be here."

She leaned forward and kissed her brother's cheek. "Family is family. I wouldn't have missed this moment for the world." *Or a date*. And she meant it.

Jillian pulled to a stop at the curb in front of Mrs. O'Malley's just as her phone rang. She connected the call. "Hi, Jolie."

"Hey, Jillie-Bean. I was scared to call. Is he there?"

"No," Jillian breathed out on a sigh.

"Good. Tell me everything."

"There's nothing to tell. Raelyn went into labor, so I had to cancel." *Ironic. I thought it would be him who cancelled.* "I spent the day at the hospital."

Since Jolie was so near her own due date, she was more interested in the delivery than the cancelled date. Jillian told her everything, smoothing over the rough edges for Jolie's sake. "They named her Ada and she's gorgeous."

"What a cute name. Nate and I are still arguing over what to name this baby. I don't think we'll ever agree."

"Maybe once she's born, you'll know exactly what to name her."

"Maybe. I am sorry about your date. Did you reschedule?"

"I don't have Brandt's phone number. All I could do was leave a note taped to the door."

"Didn't he call your cell phone to set up the date?"

"He...." She thumped her forehead with a gloved palm. Brandt's number was stored in her call history. *Stupid!* In her rush to get to the hospital, she'd completely forgotten. "I have to go, Jolie."

After hanging up, she scrolled through her recent calls and there was his number. She pressed Call before she could chicken out. The phone rang three times, then she heard his deep, surprised "Hello, Jillian."

"Hi. I wanted to call and apologize for cancelling our date with a note on the door. In my rush to get to the hospital, I completely forgot I had your number in my call history. I was just in such a hurry...." The words tumbled out as fast as her tongue allowed.

"Not a problem. How'd everything go?"

She sucked in a deep breath to settle her nervous insides. "Good. The baby is healthy and gorgeous, and my sister-in-law is fine. Everything's fine."

"I'm glad to hear that."

She heard dishes clinking. "It sounds like you're busy. I'll let you go. I didn't mean to interrupt. I just wanted to apologize, first for cancelling and then not calling." *Stop babbling!*

"You didn't interrupt. I was just finishing dinner. Since our date was postponed, I decided to paint a spare bedroom, and lost track of time."

"Oh." Her mind stuck on the word postponed like a glob of gum on the bottom of her shoe. *Postponed means delayed or suspended. Not nearly as negative or harsh-sounding as cancelled.* She loved the word postponed!

"I work next Wednesday and Sunday. How about the following Wednesday?"

"Yes." She did a mental calculation of the date. Valentine's Day. Had he meant to do that? Would he be sorry? Should she tell him or just roll with it? Her thoughts were tumbling so fast they made her dizzy. Better to be safe than sorry. "That's Valentine's Day."

A pregnant pause had her holding her breath.

"Valentine's Day isn't a problem for me," he said. "How about you?"

"Yes, it's okay with me." *Perfectly fine.*

"I should have asked what you'd like to do. Does snowshoeing sound okay for a first date?"

"Yes," she repeated for the third time. When she wasn't a bobblehead, she was impersonating a parrot.

"I'll pick you up at the same time, a week from Wednesday."

She was completely tongue-tied, scrambling to say anything that would prolong their conversation. "Okay."

"Congratulations on your new niece."

"Thank you."

"Thanks for calling, Jillian."

"'Bye." She disconnected the call before she could embarrass herself any more. She got out of her car and did a happy dance right there in the middle of the road. She had another date with Brandt. On Valentine's Day!

~

Groundhog Day dawned cold and blustery. The snow wasn't floating softly to the earth. The wind was whipping it every which way, stacking it up in drifts. Other than a few daring die-hards, the gym was dead, which gave Jillian plenty of time to clean equipment and organize the front desk and her office. She went through files, swept, dusted, and sanitized everything.

At noon, she met Carolyn and Alex at Noelle's Café to

finalize plans for Jolie's shower. Alex's first words were "How'd the date go?"

Jillian spent a couple of minutes explaining that it didn't and why.

Their first remarks were about the new baby. The next were questions about Brandt.

"But you have another date," Carolyn said. "That's so wonderful, Jillian."

Their discussion turned to the mini sandwiches, veggie sticks, and warm potato soup that would be served at the shower. Carolyn planned to make a white cake with purple accents, since purple was Jolie's favorite color. Jillian had ordered pink, white, and purple balloons. Alex would arrange a fabulous bouquet for the food table, and Stella was crafting a diaper cake, three tiers of rolled diapers and other baby necessities, as a centerpiece for the gift table. Misty sent out the invitations a week earlier. So far, everyone they'd invited was coming.

Halfway through their meal, Brandt walked in with another firefighter to pick up lunch. Jillian's heart threatened to knock right out of her chest when he stopped at their table.

Normally his gaze would have floated over her and stopped on Alex while he said his hellos, but today his eyes were on her. She was glad she'd called and apologized. And relieved she'd taken the time to apply a touch of makeup before leaving the house this morning. She wasn't able to contribute much to the short conversation, because she was so busy watching his face, the way his eyes crinkled when he laughed, the dimple that winked at them several times. He was the most beautiful man she'd ever seen, and they had a date next Wednesday—*Valentine's Day*.

She spent the afternoon thinking of Brandt, which she could easily do while resuming her cleaning spree. As the snow continued to fall, clients began cancelling appointments, until she, Glenda, and Dawson were left with an empty gym.

"You might as well head home, Jillian," Dawson said. "The streets aren't going to get any better."

After shoveling Mrs. O'Malley's driveway and sidewalk, she lit candles around her dark apartment, popped a romantic comedy into the DVD player, and cuddled under a blanket with Henry curled close.

~

Brandt's nagging doubts evaporated as soon as he saw Jillian. Her smile and the interest in her eyes were real. She'd seen his scars—or at least she'd seen a fraction of them—and still she said yes to his snowshoeing invitation.

His thoughts were cut short when the buzzer blared throughout the fire station. They had a call, an accident out on the highway. With the blizzard blowing through the state, he knew they'd be busy with emergencies all night.

When they reached the accident, he went to work. After fellow firefighters freed a man and woman whose car had skidded into a ditch, he dressed their wounds. EMT's loaded the couple into an ambulance headed for Harrisville Regional. Luckily their injuries weren't serious, just a few lacerations, bruised ribs, and a possible concussion.

Before they got back to the station another call came in, a chimney fire. They were able to put it out before it spread beyond the living room. Still, the roof had major damage.

The next call was a fender bender after one car slid through a stop sign and T-boned another. Again, no major injuries.

Between each call, he thought of Jillian. Today at Noelle's, she'd looked carefree and happy. Her big brown eyes sparkled while she laughed at something one of her friends said. Her laugh had faded when she spotted him, but the sparkle hadn't. She hadn't spoken much, but she had smiled. And blushed a pretty pink. He liked her blush. He'd also noticed a beguiling little mole near her left eye.

He'd been so intent on shielding himself from hurt that he'd overlooked what was right in front of him. Then again, maybe he hadn't been ready to notice beguiling yet. He'd needed to heal first.

He and the other men on his shift had time for grilled cheese sandwiches before they were called out on another accident. The men on his shift would spend most of the night outdoors without much sleep.

The next morning Brandt stopped as close as he possibly could to Mrs. O'Malley's front curb. With eighteen inches of fresh snow, church was cancelled. He knew he made the right choice to come when he spotted Jillian, who was bundled up tight, shoveling the driveway.

He climbed out of his truck and grabbed the shovel he'd stowed in the back. She must have heard the scrape of metal against concrete, because she stopped and looked up. He liked the wide-eyed surprise when she realized he was there. He liked the smile that followed even better. "Thought you could use some help."

She shook her head, but her expression said she was glad to see him. "After last night, you have to be exhausted."

"I have all afternoon to sleep."

Her expressive eyes glowed with appreciation.

They shoveled in companionable silence, piling snow into banks along the driveway. She did the porch and steps while he worked on the path that ran around to her door. They met in the middle.

"Would you like to come in for some breakfast, something warm to drink?"

He nodded. She looked cute in her colorful hat, her cheeks rosy from the cold. "Any other day, I'd take you up on the offer, but I'm afraid if I sit down, I'll be asleep in seconds."

"Did you get any sleep?"

"From about four to six."

She motioned toward the walkway. "Thank you. This would have taken me another two hours."

"You're welcome." He'd wanted to see her and he didn't want to tell her goodbye now. They stood for a long moment, looking into each other's eyes. "Go in and get warm," he finally said.

~

On Friday, Jillian got off work a little early and stopped to pick up Stella as soon as school let out. They were meeting Alex in Harrisville to stock up on party decorations and favors.

"How did the date go?" Stella asked as soon as she got in Jillian's car.

"It didn't. Raelyn had her baby, so I had to cancel."

"And?"

"And we're going this Wednesday instead."

"Valentine's Day?"

An irritating blush heated Jillian's cheeks. "Yes."

Stella grinned. "Like Alex, I can't believe I'm agreeing with Misty, but I do. I think you and Brandt are a perfect match."

"I wish everyone would stop saying that. I'm afraid you'll jinx us."

"Don't be silly. No one is going to jinx you. Brandt and

Jillian were meant to be."

After shopping, the three of them went to dinner and talked guys and clothes and jobs and guys. Jillian loved spending time with her friends. All of them but Carolyn, who moved to town in the third grade, had been together since kindergarten. They'd experienced births, deaths, disasters, and triumphs together. Shared clothes and shoes, laughs and tears. Jillian knew them all so well and they knew her. She could call any one of them if she was in a bind, and they would be there for her. Even Misty. And she would be there for them. They were forever friends.

Alex and Stella took her mind off Brandt for a few hours. She hadn't seen him since Sunday, which wasn't unusual. Normally they ran into each other around town every couple of weeks—though she probably saw him more often than he saw her because she was looking for him.

When their dinner conversation circled back around to guys, Jillian decided to ask a question that had been in the back of her mind all week. "Since Brandt and I are going out on Valentine's Day, do you think I should buy a gift?"

"Why don't you bake a fun treat to eat on the trail?" Alex suggested.

"Good idea. I didn't want to show up with something and embarrass him because he didn't, but I also didn't want to go empty handed if he brought something. I was dangling between cheap and presumptuous.

"Make heart cookies with pink frosting."

Jillian shook her head at Stella. "I think I'll keep it simpler than that." *And less suggestive.*

When Stella left to use the bathroom, Jillian turned to Alex. "Brandt was in the gym a couple of weeks ago and I noticed a burn scar. Do you know how he got it?"

"He got caught in a burning building when he went back in to save a woman trapped by a fire. I've only seen a little of the scar, but he said it runs from neck to knee. I think he's pretty self-conscious about it."

Information to store for later.

Her cell phone rang just as she got home. Brandt's number showed on the screen and she held her breath. *Please, please, please don't cancel our Valentine's Date.* "Hello?"

"Hi, Jillian, it's Brandt."

She put a hand to her tight throat. "Hi."

"How are you?"

She dropped into a chair and Henry jumped up onto her lap. "Good."

"I wanted to call and confirm that we're still on for Wednesday."

She breathed a silent sigh of relief. "Yes."

"Great." She heard the smile in his voice, which calmed her racing heart. "How was your day?"

"Good." *Ask him something. Show you care.* "H-how was yours?"

He chuckled. "Much slower than last Saturday."

"I'll bet. Have you caught up on your sleep?" She cringed when the question left her mouth. *Is that too personal to ask someone you haven't even gone out with yet?*

"Yes. Thanks for asking."

A long uncomfortable pause that she didn't know how to fill followed. She racked her brain for something—anything to say, but nothing from her mental list came to mind. She ran a hand over Henry's fur.

Brandt cleared his throat. "I'll see you at nine next Wednesday, if not before."

Though he couldn't see her, she nodded, caught herself and said, "I'll see you then."

After they disconnected the call she sat worrying. If they couldn't hold a simple phone conversation, how would they ever spend a morning snowshoeing? Sure they would be trudging through the forest, or wherever he planned to take her, but still, they would have to talk!

~

Jillian parked in front of Alex's house early Saturday morning. The sky was clear and the air so bitter cold, it bit through her coat. She unloaded the berry trifle and finger sandwiches she'd made for the shower as quickly as possible.

Inside, she shed her coat and helped Alex and Misty hang streamers and place balloons around the living room and dining area. Carolyn arrived with the gorgeous cake. Stella came in with wrapped prizes for the games. They finished decorating and arranging the food table, followed by picture-taking to record the occasion for Jolie. This would be a day Jolie could add to a book of remembrance for the baby.

By the time Jolie, her mother, grandmother, and mother-in-law arrived, Alex's little house looked festive and completely feminine.

Jolie had the time of her life. Thirty guests pampered her and showered her with beautiful baby gifts. They ate yummy food, and Jolie cut into the cake that was *almost* too pretty to eat. The games Stella came up with were silly and fun and Jillian laughed so hard her cheeks hurt. She was happy for her friend, who loved every minute of this special event.

Through it all, her insides danced with the knowledge that she had a date on Valentine's Day. With the man she'd been crushing on for two years.

CHAPTER 4

Brandt climbed out of his truck and made his way around the side of Mrs. O'Malley's house. Jillian must have shoveled again after the last snow, because the walk was clear. When he reached her door, he was relieved to see it was note-free.

A moment after he knocked, Jillian answered. She was wearing suspendered black ski pants and a white sweater. Her reddish-brown hair—he'd ask his Mom the name of that color —was braided, the end hanging over her shoulder.

He held out the tulips he'd picked up at the grocery store to avoid Alex cross-examining him. "Happy Valentine's Day."

Her sweet smile softened, and pink tinted her cheeks. "Oh, a touch of spring. Thank you." She opened the door wide enough for him to enter. "Let me put them in water."

He stepped inside and looked around. The kitchen and living room were one space, small, but tidy. And colorful. "You have a nice apartment."

"It's tiny, but very affordable."

He closed the space between them when she stretched for

a vase just out of reach in a cupboard over the fridge. "I'll get it for you." This close he could smell her perfume: soft, floral, feminine.

"Thank you again." After snipping off the ends of the stems, she arranged the tulips in the vase, which she placed in the middle of her coffee table. She cocked her head and flashed him another smile. "They brighten up my dark room. Thank you…a third time." She blushed as she turned toward a door on the opposite wall. "I'll get my coat."

He heard the meow before he spotted the cat. Squatting, he held out his hand, surprised when it rubbed whiskers against his fingers. He slipped his hand under the cat's chest and lifted it to eye level. "Hey. What's your name?"

"That's Henry." Jillian appeared, pulling on a purple coat. "He allows me to live here as long as I remember my place in his kingdom."

"King Henry?"

"Actually, he's named after Henry David Thoreau." She raised her brows. "I'm surprised he let you pick him up. He's usually leery of strangers."

"I have a way with cats. My sister has two of the most temperamental felines in existence."

He held Henry close as Jillian bustled around the tiny kitchen. She put a bowl of food on the floor, zipped a backpack on the counter, and slipped it over her shoulder. Last, she pulled on a crazy purple, yellow, and green ski hat that looked exactly right on her. "Ready."

As soon as he set Henry on the floor, the cat ran to his bowl. Jillian stooped to run a hand over his back. "See you later, Henry. No clawing my comforter." She glanced at Brandt. "He pouts."

"Most cats do."

Her laugh was musical and happy. He wanted her to feel relaxed and to enjoy herself today. In fact, he wanted both of them to have a really great time. He'd been looking forward to this day since he first asked her.

~

Jillian stomach was jumping like a paper bag full of grasshoppers. She glanced at Brandt behind the wheel of his truck. He seemed so relaxed, like this was any other day, rather than a day she would remember all her life.

"Did you have a nice weekend?"

"I did." She shifted in her seat. "How about you?"

"Pretty uneventful. I ran into Nate on Saturday. He said you ladies threw Jolie a baby shower."

"We did. We were in the planning stages when you came into Noelle's that afternoon."

"How was it?"

"We had a good time. Jolie loved being pampered for an afternoon."

"Did all of you go through school together?"

"All but Carolyn. She moved to Eden Falls in third grade."

He asked more questions, and she answered, feeling her cheeks quiver with the strain of her stiff smile. She hated being this nervous, hated that her answers sounded so stilted. Why couldn't she be more like Alex, who could strike up a conversation with anyone? Or Stella. She could coax a laugh out of the grouchiest person.

She was relieved when they reached the parking lot near the waterfall, which the town was named for. He ran around the truck and opened her door, then helped her fasten her snowshoes. They walked past frozen Eden Falls to a familiar trailhead. She'd hiked here many times, but never when it was snow-covered. The trail wasn't steep, but the incline was steady. Previous trekkers packed the snow, so they were only traversing about six inches of fresh powder.

Once they were on the trail, her nervousness and doubts subsided. She was in her element, and the terrain was familiar. The exercise warmed her muscles quickly, and she relaxed.

She allowed herself to focus on her surroundings, let herself be in the moment, paced her steps and her breathing. Her warm breath came out on white puffs in the crisp air while they moved between the trees, the scent of pine strong. Except for the noise they made, their world was quiet. Peaceful. The sky, occasionally appearing through the trees, was a brilliant blue, with no clouds in sight.

Brandt paused and looked back. Probably to make sure she was keeping up. She thought it was sweet he checked on her, but she was pretty confident she could keep up with any pace he set.

Brandt pointed at the ground. "Fox tracks."

Jillian bent to have a closer look.

When she straightened, Brandt took her gloved hand. "Let's see where they go."

Holy cow, he's holding my hand! She let him lead her off the trail, through deeper snow. They followed the imprints until they disappeared up a steep hill. Brandt shrugged. "I guess he didn't want to be followed."

"Or her," Jillian interjected.

Brandt grinned, and that knee-melting dimple flashed like a lighthouse beacon in the dark. "Or her."

As they headed back to the trail, a small branch snagged the bottom of her snowshoe. She tried to squelch a yelp when she fell into a puff of powdery snow. Brandt attempted to hold back a laugh, but failed miserably as he pulled her to her feet.

He took a step back and caught his snowshoe on the same

branch. With arms flailing in a desperate attempt to keep his balance, he reached out and grabbed the closest thing. Her arm. She landed on top of him with an "ooomph." The surprise on his face was so comical, she giggled until they were both laughing.

Any remaining nervousness slipped away when he pulled off his glove to brush snow from her cheek. She let him, skin against skin. His warm. Hers cold.

Farther along the trail, Brandt took a left instead of the right she always used to go higher up the mountain. After another hundred yards, the forest opened to a small clearing. The sunshine sparkled across the undisturbed, crystallized snow, glittering like thousands of inlaid diamonds. When she gasped and turned to tell him the spot was beautiful, he was watching her, his dimple carving a deep half-moon in his cheek. She wished she could hug him for guessing she'd love this magical setting. But she would never dare.

They trudged to a fallen log, removed their backpacks, and laid out lunch. He unpacked tuna sandwiches, chips, and apple slices. She contributed two thermoses, one with homemade chicken noodle soup, the other, hot cocoa. For dessert she shared sugar cookies with pink sprinkles. Lunch had never tasted so delicious.

The surrounding beauty enveloped them in a comfortable quiet, and her in a happiness she hadn't realized she was missing. She loved her family and her job and the people she worked with. She loved her friends, and counted her blessings of good health and fortunate circumstances every day. But today...today was an ultimate gift. If only she could wrap all this happiness up, tuck it in a pocket, and take it out to relive and enjoy at her leisure.

Just as important, she felt safe with Brandt, which was hugely glorious.

Birds flitted close, enjoying the crusts of bread she and

Brandt tossed out for them. A slight breeze rustled through the evergreen boughs, sending glittery showers of snow down around them.

While they ate, Brandt told stories of his childhood with brothers who hunted and fished together. His family sounded amazing. She was afraid to hope she'd be able to meet them, for fear it would never come true.

The sun started its downward descent, ending the afternoon way too soon. They packed up their lunch things and headed down the trail. On their hike out, Brandt spotted a snowshoe hare and pointed. She couldn't see it until he moved behind her and lowered his chin almost to her shoulder. She followed his arm out to the tip of his gloved finger and saw the twitch of an ear.

"Oh," she whispered. "I see it."

He straightened but left a hand resting on her shoulder. She paid more attention to the warm weight of that hand than to the hare watching them before scampering under a hollow log.

Jillian stood with her back against the door of her apartment, listening to Brandt's receding footsteps. Today was one of the best days of her life—one of the top five, for sure. And he hadn't even kissed her. She wouldn't dwell on that, or the possible reason why. She'd only think of the positive tonight. His skin against hers when he brushed snow from her cheek, the way he held her hand on the way to her door, watching her during lunch when he thought she wasn't aware.

She wished she could find a book of instructions. As the tall, skinny girls in school, she and Carolyn had always stood a head taller than any of the boys in class pictures. Boys were intimidated by their height until high school, when they finally caught up and then bypassed them.

By then her and Carolyn's reputations as socially awkward were set in concrete. Just when she'd started to feel more secure about her height, she began to notice her curveless body. Her narrow hips and nearly nonexistent breasts heaped more fuel on the embers of her self-conscious bonfire.

What she did have going for her was a penchant for physical activity. She credited her parents for her love of the outdoors and for her drive to be physically fit. As a family with an orchard to run, they'd spent many hours outdoors, mowing, moving crates, climbing trees. From early morning until late at night, they enjoyed nature. In the winter, they skied cross-country and downhill, and ice-skated at the pond on their property. They spent their family vacations in tents at national parks where they hiked trails, fished in lakes and cooked what they caught around a campfire.

She picked up Henry, who was twining around her ankles, demanding attention. In the living room, she flipped on a table lamp before falling onto the sofa, wondering how she'd tell Jolie about her day without sounding like a giddy teenager. As much as she wanted to share all, she also wanted to keep the day special and untainted by remarks that might dilute the feelings coursing through her.

Henry curled in her lap, happy to have some company and a tickle behind his ears. Jillian obliged. His pleasure reverberated through his chest.

"Maybe I should have been a cat."

"Meeeowww."

She ran her hand over his head. "Even though I tell myself I won't, I know I'll be checking my phone for missed calls, worrying about the battery or the reception. I'll become one of *those* girls, pathetically waiting to hear from him."

Henry yawned.

"Yes, I had a fabulous time. Thanks for asking."

He stretched a paw out and sank his claws into her pants.

She pulled each one of Henry's nails out individually so he couldn't snag the fabric. "Don't be jealous. You'll always be my number-one guy."

"Meeeowww."

~

Brandt wasn't sure what he'd expected, but it wasn't the fantastic day he'd experienced.

Jillian was quiet when he first picked her up, but it didn't take too long for her to loosen up. When they took a tumble together, it was as if a door opened and her inhibitions were set free. During lunch they laughingly confessed likes and dislikes, talked about books, music, and work. They discussed their religious beliefs and political affiliations with only minimum amused disagreement.

While they ate, he studied her under the guise of appreciating nature. She had the biggest brown eyes he'd ever seen, and they fairly danced with delight from the moment they reached the falls until they said good night. His attention locked on her mouth when she applied lip balm after lunch, and he didn't realize he was staring until she offered him some.

His only regret? He hadn't kissed her then, or when he dropped her off at her door. He should have. Both times. Would she have let him?

She was a little on the shy side, sweet-natured, and blushed easily. She was able to hold her own on a somewhat challenging trail and had been in awe of their surroundings. He liked all those things about her. He also liked that she'd named her cat after Henry David Thoreau, who wrote about uncomplicated life in natural surroundings.

She put thought into choosing a cat's name rather than going with the unoriginal Fluffy or Tiger. She obviously liked to read.

She'd asked about his childhood and listened with interest. He learned some things about her too. She loved her family fiercely, she never wanted to own an orchard, and she ate all vegetables and fruits except peaches.

He'd laughed at her admission. "I've never met anyone who didn't like peaches."

A blush had touched her already-red-from-the-cold cheeks. "Now you have."

She admitted to being a good student. She had a degree in physical education from Central Washington University, and a master's in physical therapy from the University of Utah.

"Why aren't you using your physical therapy degree?"

"I do occasionally. Doctor Newell sends a patient my way every once in a while, but there isn't much need in Eden Falls. Plus, I like working at the gym."

He couldn't argue with her there. After graduating from Washington State Fire Training Academy in North Bend, he was hired on with the Tacoma Fire Department. While there, he went on to earn his EMT state license, and then his paramedic certifications, from Tacoma Community College. Even though he was hired as a paramedic, he used his firefighting degree much more often.

He loved Eden Falls too much to move to a larger city. The options were endless for an outdoorsman. He enjoyed the camping, skiing, hiking, biking, fishing, and miles of trails, plus he was only a three-hour drive from Spokane and his family.

Brandt sat parked at the curb, looking at one of the illuminated basement windows. From what he remembered of her apartment, the window was in her living room. Did she like the tulips? He'd heard her say she liked Gerbera daisies, but he didn't want her to know he'd been eavesdropping on her and Marty's conversation at the gym.

What was she doing? Had she turned on the television, picked up a book? Was she starting dinner or would she call for takeout? He wished he'd extended their time together by inviting her to Noelle's Café. Not an elegant choice, but a hearty, home-cooked-style meal would have topped off his best-ever Valentine's Day. Except the one when he and his brothers tried to surprise their parents with dessert—chocolate cupcakes with flaming strawberries—and almost burned down the kitchen. Even though they'd gotten into major trouble, that was a fun Valentine's Day too.

He fished his phone out of a pocket and scrolled to Jillian's name, which now featured a selfie he'd taken of them at lunch. They had their heads tipped close, his beanie touching her bright knit hat. They looked together. He hit the Call button.

"Hello?"

Her hesitant greeting after two rings made him smile. "Hi. Sorry to call so soon."

"That's okay…."

"I wanted to say thanks again for the really nice day."

"Thanks for asking me. I had a lot of fun."

"Me too." He hesitated, but only for a moment. *It's time to take a chance.* "I was wondering if you'd like to have dinner with me Saturday night?"

He heard her intake of breath, imagined her blush. "I-I'd love to."

"Shall I pick you up at seven?"

"Seven is fine."

"Great. Goodnight, Jillian."

~

Jillian wrapped a towel around the back of her neck as she walked her spin class out of the room. After waving goodbye to the last client, she headed for her office, stopping twice to encourage, and once to answer a question. Mid-February was a slow time for the gym. Get Fit's patrons were mostly regulars at this point. Business would pick up again after the weather warmed with the promise of swimsuit season just ahead.

When she reached her office, her cell phone was vibrating across her desk, buzzing like an angry bee. She picked it up and looked at the screen. Six missed calls from Jolie. She knew her friend was anxious to hear juicy details. "Hi, Jolie."

"Jillian, where have you been? I've been calling and calling."

"I see that." She lifted the towel off her neck and wiped her forehead. "I was teaching a class, and before that I was wearing my personal-trainer hat."

"So tell me everything, and hurry, because Owen has a client due in five minutes."

"We…I had a great time." Jillian pushed her door shut and sat on the edge of her desk. "Brandt said he did too. We took the trail past the waterfall and hiked most of the day. It was beautiful. We stopped at a clearing and had lunch—"

"I don't have time for the minute details. Get to the good parts. Did he kiss you?"

"No. He did invite me to dinner on Saturday night, though." She wondered if Jolie detected the defensive tone in her voice. She'd decided, during a long toss-and-turn night, he hadn't kissed her out of respect.

"He didn't kiss you?"

"It was our first date, Jolie. I'm sure he could tell I was over-the-top nervous."

"Why were you so nervous?"

She'd never told Jolie about the date rape in college, so she wouldn't understand Jillian's apprehension about dating *anyone*. "You know I'm not great at this dating thing. I haven't been out in months."

"You did it yesterday, and you had a great time. Now you have a second date. I'm glad for you, Jillie-Bean. Did he say where he was taking you to dinner?"

"No." She was ready to move the conversation on to another topic. "How are you feeling?"

Jolie laughed without humor. "Like I'm about to explode. I can't see my feet, my ankles are nonexistent, my innie belly button is an outie, and I run to the bathroom every thirty minutes."

"Is Nate helping you?"

"He's doing it all. He's been fabulous. And he's so excited."

Jillian ran the towel around her neck. "He's going to be a cute dad. Have him call me the second you go into labor."

"He has strict instructions to call you first. Oh, I've got to go. Owen's client just walked up the porch steps. I'm happy your date went well, Jillie."

Jolie hung up before Jillian could say goodbye. She glanced at the clock on the wall. She had just enough time to splash cold water on her face before Misty came in for her workout.

She opened the door to Alex's surprised face. "Ack! You scared me."

Jillian put a hand to her chest. "You scared me too. I was just headed to the locker room."

Alex held out a small vase of colorful Gerbera daisies. "These are for you."

Jillian was sure her grin looked just as goofy as it felt spreading across her face. Her cheeks heated at the assumption they were from Brandt. Marty was beginning to see results, so maybe....

"They're from Brandt," Alex said with her own grin. "He called from the fire station this morning."

Alex set the vase on the corner of Jillian's desk, pulled a card out, and handed it to her with a flourish.

Her goofy grin was back, along with shaking hands, as she opened the flap and slid the card out.

I had a great time yesterday and look forward to seeing you Saturday night.

He must have overheard her tell Marty Gerberas were her favorite. If so, she was delighted he remembered.

Alex inherited Pretty Posies from her Grandma Garrett, who also taught Alex the Victorian language of flowers. Alex incorporated that language into the beautiful bouquets she created. "What do Gerbera daisies mean?"

"Happiness or innocence."

Jillian shook her head. "Most men probably have no idea...."

"No, they don't. Brandt said you liked Gerberas and asked if I had any. He told me he looked them up and thought they were cheerful, so it made sense they were your favorite." Alex leaned back against the wall. "I take it your date went well."

"I had the best time." Jillian sat on the edge of her desk again because her knees were quivering like she'd just finished a marathon. "He brought me tulips yesterday for Valentine's Day."

"Nice. I knew you two would have fun."

"We're going out again on Saturday night." Jillian looked down at the card still clutched in her shaking hand. "I just can't believe he asked me out. I've liked Brandt since he first moved to town, and then, out of the blue, he asks me to go snowshoeing. It's like a fairy tale come true, but I'm terrified to get my hopes up."

She glanced at Alex. "In my fairy tales, the glass slipper usually breaks."

"Like I said at Rowdy's, I've thought since Jolie's wedding that you two would make a great match. You have so much in common. Him asking you out proves he's as smart as he is handsome." Alex cupped Jillian's shaking hands. "There's nothing wrong with getting your hopes up. That's the exciting, spine-tingling part of a new relationship. Enjoy the newness of it all."

Jillian nodded.

"Don't expect everything to go smoothly," Alex added, "and don't give up if there are bumps along the way. Remember the rocky road Colton and I took?" She squeezed Jillian's hands. "If things are supposed to work out, they will. Just take one day at a time, and appreciate every moment you're given."

Jillian picked up the vase of flowers admiring them for a long minute after Alex left. The Gerberas brought a bit of sunlight to her dark, windowless space.

On a whim, she clicked a picture with her cell phone and sent it to Jolie. A moment later, her phone pinged with a message.

Nice! accompanied by a smiley-face emoji.

~

Brandt glanced at the clock on the fire station's stove. He knew it was too late to second-guess his decision to send Jillian flowers. Alex said she'd deliver them before lunch. He hoped two things—first, that he wouldn't scare her away sending flowers so soon, and second, that she wouldn't think it meant more than it did. He just wanted to thank her for being willing and adventurous, and to let her know he'd had a nice time.

He also hoped they made her smile.

He'd only dated Alex a few times, but she was the only woman he'd dated since Kacie. They'd gone to a movie once, to dinner another time, and their last date had been a baseball game. He knew early on there wasn't, and never would be, more than friendship between them, but it had been nice to have someone to go out with on a Saturday night.

One date with Jillian wasn't enough to know for sure, but he felt like this could go somewhere. One date, and he felt pretty positive something good could emerge.

No secrets. He would show her his scars early on.

His earlier thought, that he didn't want Jillian to assume the flowers were more than a friendly gesture, was wrong. He wanted her to hope for the same possibilities he was imagining.

He tucked the leftover taco fixings in the fridge. Someone else could benefit from him making too much for lunch today. Just as he finished wiping down the table, the fire alarm rang through the station. Time to go to work.

CHAPTER 5

The next two days slogged along with methodical tedium. Jillian looked at her watch or the clock on the wall more times than she ever had before. Working with Marty took every ounce of patience she could muster, and trying to motivate Misty was even more frustrating.

Her appetite was nonexistent. She felt like she'd downed a pot of coffee by herself she was so jittery, and she didn't even drink the stuff. So she pasted on a pleasant expression and tried to stay as busy as possible, hoping the hours would speed by.

At the same time she wished the world would stop spinning altogether. She was anxious to see Brandt again, but terrified her feelings would end up one-sided.

Her anxiety wasn't coexisting comfortably with her anticipation.

The night before The Night, she tried on everything she owned. Twice. Henry watched while she discarded outfit after outfit before he decided a quiet spot as far away as possible was preferable. He obviously hoped her sanity would return after Saturday night had come and gone.

She finally decided a new dress was in order.

Brandt hadn't told her where they were going, so she wasn't sure what to wear. During her lunch break on Saturday she ran to Red Barn Clothing on the square. After trying on several outfits, she finally decided on a sweater dress and boots, since the weather was still cold. The dress was casual enough if he wore jeans, and dressy enough if he wore a sports coat. She also bought a new necklace and earrings.

Jolie would laugh at her for making such a fuss, but it had been a long time since she'd splurged on something new. Other than a few dresses for church, her wardrobe consisted mostly of workout clothes, with a few jeans and sweaters thrown in for nights out with her girlfriends.

Saturday night, in front of the mirror, she stared at her reflection for a long moment and decided she was okay with who she was as a person. She was okay with the way she'd handled the situation in college. She'd done the right thing by reporting the rape and then following through to make sure Canon didn't hurt anyone else.

She added a touch of lipstick and tried to smile around the tightness in her chest.

When she sat on the edge of the bed, Henry finally came out of hiding and jumped up next to her. "Did you come to say hello finally?"

"Meeeowww."

"I know I've been acting crazy, but I'm so nervous. I really like Brandt." She ran her hand from Henry's head to the tip of his tail. "Don't look at me like that. You liked him too."

Besides Henry, no one but her parents knew about what happened in college. And they only knew because the school called them. She'd endured a year of therapy and finally accepted that she'd truly done nothing wrong. She hadn't worn suggestive clothes or said anything to lead Canon to believe she wanted to sleep with him. She said no repeatedly in the two minutes she fought him as he lifted her skirt and pulled down his pants. "I've let what happened be a part of me for too long. It's time to start trusting again."

A purr vibrated through Henry's chest.

She picked him up and cuddled him close. "Tonight's the night I let go of old hurts."

"Meeeowww."

"Okay, you caught me in a lie. I might not be able to let go quite yet, but soon." She kissed Henry on the head, then rubbed at the lipstick mark she left. "I'm afraid I'll do something stupid to mess this up. I'm afraid Brandt will notice what a novice I am, or that I'll jump away if he tries to kiss me. I don't want to look like a doof."

Henry licked his paw and jumped out of her arms. He sat at her feet staring, tail swishing.

"You're right. If Brandt doesn't like me as I am, then he isn't the man for me. I'm an okay person. I'm not exactly outgoing, but I'm nice. My friends like me. Most of my clients like me. Well...not initially, but once they start meeting their goals, they like me.... For the most part. Okay, I give you that one. Marty may never like me, but he's the only one. As far as I know."

Jillian jumped at the knock on the door. She checked her watch. After the past two days of obsessive clock-watching, she couldn't believe she'd lost all track of time while talking to a cat.

She took one last look in the mirror and walked into the living room, smoothing a hand over her anxious stomach.

~

Brandt couldn't remember ever being this nervous about a date. He and Kacie were friends before they started dating. They moved easily from having dinner with friends to it being just the two of them.

Alex was just so darned easygoing, it was hard to feel nervous around her.

Even after spending hours with Jillian three days earlier, he felt like they'd barely scratched the surface of knowing each other. Talking was hard on the trail, because she was either in front of him or behind him. At lunch, they sat side by side on a log, not facing each other across a table.

He knocked, the door opened, and his jaw dropped. Jillian had worn her hair down. Soft reddish-brown curls cascaded around her shoulders. She was wearing a dress, and he felt like an idiot for not telling her where they were going for dinner, not that she wasn't dressed perfectly, but he should have remembered that basic courtesy. He'd learned from Kacie that most women worried about those kinds of things. They also appreciated compliments, which was easy to give in this case. "You look…beautiful."

Jillian glanced down at her dress, and her cheeks pinked. "Thank you. You look nice too." She opened the door wider. "Come in while I get my coat."

He stepped inside.

"Thank you for the daisies," she said over her shoulder. "They're so pretty." Her blush deepened.

"I'm glad you like them. I hope you don't think they were too much, too soon."

"I think they were…thoughtful. They brighten my office." She held up a finger. "I'll be right back."

He squatted and held out his hand when Jillian's cat appeared. He stayed just out of Brandt's reach. "Come here, Henry. I won't hurt you."

Henry took a step closer and Brandt scooped up the cat to cuddle against his chest. He noticed the pink outline of lips on Henry's furry head. *Lucky cat.*

Jillian came back carrying a red coat. "I'm amazed that Henry comes to you. Jolie loves cats, and he won't come near her." She tickled Henry under the chin. "Jolie is going to be very jealous."

"Henry and I have an agreement. I'll be nice to him if he doesn't scratch me."

Jillian's brown eyes twinkled in amusement. "It doesn't look like that's going to be a problem."

"It's time for us to go, Henry. Don't watch too much television tonight, okay?" He set the cat on the floor, glad his stupid joke made Jillian laugh. He took her coat from her and held it out. The surprise on her face made him wink. "My mom did teach me a few manners."

After she slipped her arms in and buttoned up, she bent down and stroked Henry. "'Bye, Henry. The new throw on the end of the sofa is not for you."

He held out his arm after she closed and locked her door. The path leading around to the front of the house had been shoveled but was slippery in places, and she was wearing heeled boots. She tentatively slipped her gloved hand into the crook of his arm and held on. "Thank you."

"You should use a little salt back here."

"I usually do, but didn't have time this morning after shoveling."

"You do all the shoveling?"

She lifted one side of her mouth in a what-you-going-to-do smile. "My landlady is an eighty-two-year-old widow, and my rent is ridiculously low. The least I can do is shovel. Besides, I like the workout. We never have so much snow that I can't get it done before or after work." She flexed her arm like he might be able to see a muscle through her heavy coat. "Remember, I grew up working in an orchard."

He opened the passenger door of his truck. "That's right. I'm dating Wonder Woman."

"Not Wonder Woman, just Jillian."

He gazed down into her pretty, brown eyes. "I like just Jillian."

He took her to an Italian restaurant in Harrisville. She asked so many questions over lunch when they were snowshoeing that he ended up dominating the conversation. Tonight he encouraged her to do the talking.

Over salads, he learned that, like his, her family was close. She spoke sweetly of her parents and their wonderful marriage. She told stories of her childhood, of hiking and camping with her family, who seemed to love the outdoors as much as his. While he and Jillian enjoyed their main course—lasagna for him, penne with sun-dried tomatoes for her—she described springtime in the orchard when the trees were in bloom. Her descriptions carried him to a place where he could see the variegated blossoms and smell their heady fragrances.

The longer he spent in her company, the more he wondered why it had taken him so long to notice her. They had a lot in common. He hadn't grown up on a farm, but his family loved the outdoors, and still spent as much time in nature as possible.

He could easily imagine camping next to a lake with Jillian, or spending a day in the mountains hiking and picnicking, sitting under a blanket of stars while they watched the campfire flicker, highlighting the red strands in her hair.

He could easily imagine Jillian as a permanent part of his life.

~

"Would you like to come in?"

Brandt glanced from her to the door of her apartment. "Yes. For just a minute."

Jillian unlocked the door and they stepped inside. Her heart was pounding so hard she was afraid it would bruise her ribs. She reached up to unbutton her coat, but Brandt caught her hand and pulled her close. They stared at each other for a long, time-stopping moment.

The quiet was finally too much for her. "I…I had a wonderful time tonight. Dinner was delicious."

"I should have asked if you liked Italian before I took you there."

"I love it." *For future reference.*

He nodded, his gaze dropping to her mouth. He was going to kiss her. This was the moment she'd hoped for since he asked her out. A first kiss with someone was special, a moment to always remember. And she would.

But…what if, in this defining moment, Brandt realized how rusty she was and walked away disappointed?

If this was to be their only kiss, she would remember the feel of his lips, his woodsy cologne with its hints of citrus… and maybe lavender. She'd memorize the green flecks in his eyes, and his dark lashes, his beautiful nose.

His lips touched hers, and she didn't move, couldn't breathe. She relished the feel of his arms as they pulled her closer. Even with her coat on, his palms spread reassuring warmth up her back. The kiss was hesitant at first, as though he was asking permission, which she gladly gave.

This moment was the most perfect, most memorable moment of her life.

He turned his head slightly and she followed his lead.

Soon they were giving and taking, tasting and testing, like the slow rising of the sun lighting the sky until it reaches the horizon, then shooting fingers of gold high overhead. If she hadn't been clutching his coat she would have dropped to her quaking knees. The kiss lasted three seconds...or three minutes. She only knew she'd been waiting for this moment her entire life.

He drew back just enough to look into her eyes, and then he smiled. She amended her earlier thought. Their first kiss was fantastic, but this—his smile afterward—was the most perfect, most memorable moment of her life.

She swallowed, hoping her voice didn't sound shaky. "Thank you again for dinner, Brandt. I had a nice time."

"I had a nice time too." He sounded surprised, as if he hadn't believed a nice time with her was possible.

She took a step back. His tone instantly filled her with self-doubt. She didn't want her insecurities to ruin the evening—not when her lips still tingled from his kiss. She didn't want to spend a sleepless night second-guessing and questioning every minute of the last three hours they'd spent together.

But now she would.

As they stood gazing at each other, she wondered if she should invite him to take off his coat. She wished she was better at this. Maybe if she wasn't so insecure, he wouldn't be so surprised he'd had a good time. Yep, uncertainty was taking hold.

"I'd better go. I have to be at the station early tomorrow." He bent like he was going to kiss her again, then grimaced. "Ahh...."

"What?"

"Henry has decided I've taken enough of your time," he said through gritted teeth. He bent, extracted the cat's claws from his pant leg, and scooped Henry up.

Jillian shook her finger. "Henry, you should be ashamed of yourself."

"Meeeowww."

"Sorry, Henry, but you're going to have to share." Brandt held him at arm's length and dropped another kiss on her mouth before handing her the cat.

Then he flashed his devastating, dimpled grin. "I'll see you soon."

She closed the door with a mixed sense of relief and anxiety. *I'll see you soon. Does that mean he'll see me around town or call for another date?*

~

Their second date and the second time he sat in his truck at the curb, stalkerishly watching the lights in Jillian's basement apartment windows. He wasn't quite sure what he'd expected from the night, but it wasn't this dizzying euphoria. He felt like a kite soaring on a breeze that lifted him higher as the night progressed.

The ease between them over dinner was as natural as breathing. They fit together so nicely when kissing, and he enjoyed his pounding-heart excitement when she kissed him back. He liked that short-of-breath feeling when things were new. The starting of things, the first day of college, the beginning of a career, the excitement of moving to a new town, the discovery of a new relationship.

Possibly his last first kiss.

Again, it was too early to be considering long-term, but his thoughts were already spinning in that direction.

From their conversation, he knew they loved to be outdoors and enjoyed physical activities. They liked the same music and loved to read. Her movie choices were on the girly side, his geared toward action, but that was something they could work around. He knew these few commonalities weren't enough to build a relationship on, but they were a starting point.

He owed that Boy Scout troop a thank-you. If they hadn't taken over the fire station's training room to work on merit badges, he wouldn't have gone into Get Fit for his workout. Fate. Destiny. He didn't care what name people put on a chance meeting, but he was glad he noticed Jillian Saunders three weeks earlier.

Her sweet patience with Marty Graw grabbed his attention. Soon he was watching the way her lithe body and toned muscles moved while she showed Marty the correct way to use the leg press. His gaze had passed over the curve of her back and the shape of her calves more than once during that hour.

It was too soon to think about introducing her to his family, but it was exactly where his thoughts traveled. He already knew that his parents would love her. They hadn't loved Kacie, but he didn't know of their reservations until after his accident.

He was so ready to settle down. The dating game was old, and he was tired of playing. He was ready to find the right girl and get married, and, not too far down the road, start a family.

He shouldn't compare Jillian with Kacie. They were nothing alike, but it was hard not to notice the differences and evaluate.

He started his truck and pulled away from the curb, immersed in possibilities. Already anticipating the next time he'd see Jillian.

CHAPTER 6

Jillian got to hold her beautiful baby niece for the entire hour of church. From the little bit of peach fuzz on the top of her head, it looked like she'd have red hair like her mama. Jillian ran her finger along the baby's cheek and under her chin, basking in the miracle of soft, sweet-smelling perfection.

Her thoughts drifted to her kiss with Brandt, and she slid her knuckles over her mouth. She went to bed happy, woke up happy, and was still happy. How could a simple kiss make her feel so different? Was the change obvious? If she felt so different inside, she had to look different on the outside.

"Where are you?" her mom whispered close to her ear.

"I'm here."

Her mom ran her hand over the baby's cap of hair. "You haven't been here since you walked through the chapel doors."

Jillian looked down at the angel in her arms. "I'm here now."

"I'm making your favorite for dinner."

Jillian enjoyed cooking, but didn't very often. Living

alone, she made simple meals for herself. Maybe she should get a few recipes from her mom and invite Brandt over for dinner. Her dad always teased that Mom's stuffed pork chops were what convinced him to get married. Jillian knew he didn't propose because of pork chops, but maybe there was something to what he said. Not that she and Brandt were anywhere near that point. They'd just shared their first kiss, and she looked forward to perfecting that for a while.

After a dinner of chicken enchiladas and salad, Jillian offered to do kitchen cleanup. Halfway through, her mom touched her arm. "I'm still wondering where you are. I called your name twice with no response. You hardly said anything through dinner. Is something bothering you?"

"No. Everything is fine." Jillian rinsed the dishcloth out under hot running water. "More than fine." She turned to her mom. "Brandt took me to dinner last night."

"Where did you go?"

"The Italian place in Harrisville that you and Dad like."

"Portelli's? I love their food."

"The penne with sun-dried tomatoes was wonderful."

"Mmm, I've never tried that. I'll have to talk your dad into dinner out next weekend."

Jillian wanted to talk to her mom about her date. At the same time she wanted to keep the details all to herself. A blush heated her cheeks at her mom's continued scrutiny. "What?" she finally asked.

"Two dates in three days." Her mom sat and patted the chair next to her. "That's moving quickly."

"No. Really?" She dropped into the chair. *How would I know?*

"You must have had a good time on the first date or you wouldn't have said yes to the second."

She knew her mom was saying she must feel safe with Brandt or she wouldn't have gone out a second time. "Other than being nervous because it was Brandt, I felt completely safe. I had the best time. He's easy to talk to." She lifted her gaze and noticed her mom's pleased expression. "We have a lot in common."

"All important things."

"We got to know each other better with that 'which do you like best, sunsets or sunrises?' game."

"Fun idea. Did he open the door for you?"

"Yes. He also held my coat and offered his arm so I wouldn't slip."

Her mom patted her hand over her heart. "I love a gentleman."

"Henry likes him."

"Also important, because Henry is pretty particular about who he likes. How does Brandt feel about Henry?"

"They get along fine." Silly that they were talking about whether Henry and Brandt liked each other. "He's given me flowers twice. Gerberas and tulips."

"Two of your favorite flowers, very thoughtful," her mom said. "Did he know, or was it a lucky guess?"

"I think he overheard a conversation between me and Marty about the Gerberas."

Her mom laughed. "You and Marty were talking about flowers?"

Jillian waved her hand. "It's a long story."

"Are you going out again?" her mom asked, pushing back from the table when her dad walked into the kitchen, signaling it was time for dessert.

"Going out with who?"

Her mom patted his chest. "Our Jillian is dating Brandt Smith."

"The fireman?"

Jillian stood, too, noticing the concern around his eyes. "We've only gone out twice, and he was a perfect gentleman."

"You didn't answer my question," her mom said, opening the fridge. "Are you going out again?"

"He said he'd see me soon." She sneaked her phone out of her jeans' back pocket—completely unnecessary, since it was also set to Vibrate when silenced. No missed call. "He had to work today."

Her dad pulled her into a hug. "I've heard good things about Brandt."

Her mom wrapped her arms around both of them. "We're happy for you, sweetheart."

Jillian, still riding on her cloud of bliss, smiled.

~

"What put you in such a good mood?"

Brandt looked up from the breathing apparatus he was checking. The crew chief stood in front of him, hands on his hips.

"Hey, Jeff. I'm a...." He glanced around, unsure if he'd already checked his turnouts, radio, and flashlight. Checking equipment after a call was the first thing he did every shift. Forgetting what he'd already checked was definitely new. His mind was on Jillian, not his SCBA. He was sorry he'd been on a call and couldn't see her at church this morning.

Usually his doubts resurfaced after dark, but they didn't last night. If anything, his belief that something great could develop between them was stronger than ever.

"Hello, you in there?" Jeff waved a hand in front of Brandt's face. "You were whistling. Now you're beaming like you won the lottery."

Brandt chuckled. “Not the lottery. I had a date last night, and it went…well.”

Jeff raised a brow in question.

“Jillian Saunders.” Brandt picked up his radio and wiped at a smudge of soot.

“I went to school with Jillian’s oldest brother.”

“Yeah?”

“How long’s this been going on?”

“Not long.” *Okay, no more waiting*. He pulled out his cell phone, scrolled to Jillian’s number, and quickly texted the first thing that popped into his head.

Thinking about you.

He didn’t expect a response and was surprised when his phone pinged less than thirty seconds later.

Good.

So…she hadn’t exactly responded that she was thinking of him, too, but it didn’t mean she wasn’t. He knew she was on the shy side. It might take a while for her to get comfortable telling him that kind of thing. Was he pushing too hard, moving too fast for her? Only one way to find out.

How about dinner and a movie on Tuesday night?

Sounds wonderful came back immediately.

He started whistling again.

~

Brandt felt a little more relaxed this time when he picked up Jillian. She’d mentioned she liked Chinese, so he decided to take her to East Winds, which was on Town Square. He hoped she wouldn’t mind going public as a couple, because they would be seen together tonight. Eden Falls was a small town and word would spread quickly.

Afterward, he’d take her next door to watch the romantic comedy playing at the cinema.

She opened the door and took his breath away yet again. Not that she was dressed fancy. She wore jeans, a purple sweater, and boots. Her hair was down, all soft around her face. Her beautiful smile and her bright eyes indicated she was glad to see him. He loved that she wore her feelings out in the open. Kacie liked to keep him guessing; was she happy, sad, angry with him for some reason? Jillian was authentic. "Are you ready?"

"I am." Jillian slipped her arms into her coat and picked up her purse.

After they were outside, he pulled her door shut, made sure it was locked. "How was your day?"

"Busy. Dawson and Glenda were with an architect all day, so I—"

"An architect?" He held out his arm and she tucked her hand into the crook like she'd been doing it for years.

"Didn't I mention? They're buying the vacant building next to the gym so they can add an indoor pool and a few more classrooms. They're also making room for a physical therapy area."

"So you can use your degree."

She lifted a shoulder. "Doc Newell is pushing for it, but I really enjoy what I'm doing, so...we'll see. Harrisville has a great physical therapy building right next to the hospital."

"I used it when I broke my leg last year in the hardware store fire. It's a great facility, but one in town would be more convenient."

Over salads, she told him a little more about her childhood. She was such a sweet person, he had a hard time believing some of the stories of trouble she and her siblings got into.

"Of course, being the baby, I was seldom punished."

"I, on the other hand, always got punished, but I also came up with most of the ideas."

She laughed, her eyes dancing with merriment. He decided he liked making her laugh.

They went back and forth revealing their favorite color—his green, hers purple. Their favorite food—his was ribs, hers pizza. Her favorite memory was Christmas at her grandparents' house. His was the same.

He wanted to know everything about Jillian Saunders.

"Do you like the snow or prefer the beach?"

She sat back in her chair. "I don't mind the snow. I like winter sports and warm fires and cuddly sweaters, but I like summer and sunshine more, so I guess the beach."

Brandt glanced out the window at the dirty snow piled around the square. He loved to watch big, fat flakes floating down from a dark sky and he enjoyed winter sports, too. But, like Jillian, he liked summer and sunshine more. "City or country?"

"Definitely country. You?"

"Country, but I do like my hometown."

She picked up her glass of water with long, slim fingers. She had pretty hands. "What do you like about it?"

"Have you ever been?"

She nodded. "A couple of times for concerts with friends. My sister used to be an artist and my family would go there for her art shows."

"I like Spokane because it's clean and close to nature. It isn't too big. I love that the city is built around the Spokane River." He took a chance and reached for her hand. She let him intertwine their fingers. Their hands fit together nicely. "What do you like about Eden Falls?"

"Everything. It's small, quaint. We never have to worry about traffic jams or noise and pollution. You?" she asked again.

He ran a thumb over her knuckles. "I visited Eden Falls when I saw the ad for firefighter and fell in love immediately.

It's close to Spokane, so I can see my parents on days off. In fact, I'm driving over tomorrow for a long weekend." *And I want to take you with me.*

"Tell me about your family."

Family was an easy subject for him. "As I said, I'm second of five. My sister is the baby. We grew up riding bikes and building tree houses and forts. We skied in the winter and camped in the summer. Everyone still lives in Spokane but me. We get together as often as possible."

She put a hand to her chest as he spoke, her smile soft around the edges. "Sounds idyllic."

He nodded, because most of the time, it was. He felt extremely lucky that they were so close and loved spending time together. "Does your whole family get together often?"

"With a brother in the Gulf of Mexico and a sister in Texas, we don't see each other, except at Christmas. Everyone tries to come home for that holiday. Only the marine biologist couldn't make it this year." She paused to sip from her water glass. "Do you have a favorite holiday?"

"Hum, not sure I have a favorite. I guess if I had to choose, I'd say Thanksgiving, because I love turkey with all the trimmings." He also loved watching her changing facial expressions. One minute she was smiling, the next her eyebrows were raised over her expressive eyes. When she was thinking, she pursed her lips in an innocent, yet completely alluring way.

"I like Christmas best, because of family. We play a lot of board games when we're together."

One more thing we have in common, he thought as the waiter brought their entrees. When they ordered, they chose different dishes so they could share. The idea sounded fun to him. Kacie didn't mind swapping spit but thought sharing food was disgusting.

Stop comparing.

Jillian dished some of the kung pao triple delight onto her plate, then passed the dish to him. He did the same with his spicy beef and mushroom.

He watched her take a bite and slowly draw the chopsticks through her pink lips. His stomach clenched in a nice way.

"Your choice is spicy, but delicious," she said.

"This kung pao is pretty spicy too." He popped a shrimp into his mouth. "Do you like spicy food?"

"I do unless it's so hot my taste buds blister."

He pointed his chopsticks at her. "I'm in agreement there. My oldest brother likes things so hot his ears turn red."

She laughed.

They continued sharing information about themselves, stopping only long enough to greet any Eden Falls' residents who paused at their table.

"We're going to be the talk of the town by tomorrow morning," she said.

"Do you mind?" He was sorry he asked as soon as the question left his mouth, worried at what her answer might be.

She looked down when her pretty blush pinked her cheeks, and she shook her head.

Good.

He held her hand throughout the movie. And when he dropped her at her door, he kissed her until they were both breathless. She was perfect for him. They were perfect for each other. For the first time since he found Kacie cheating on him, he believed he could be truly happy again.

Events fell into place for a reason. His accident, Kacie with another man, the ad for a firefighter in Eden Falls, his trip here to check out the town…had they all happened so he could find Jillian?

He was grateful he'd only recently noticed her. He might not have been ready for a relationship when he first arrived in town. The hurt from his broken engagement was too fresh then. He had to learn to trust again, to know not all women were like Kacie. Now the time was right, and he was crazy about Jillian.

She looked up at him, the overhead light near her door reflected in her pretty, brown eyes.

"I'll call you when I get home from Spokane."

"Promise?"

"I promise." He lowered his mouth to hers in a kiss that was different from any other he'd ever experienced. It touched him in places never touched before, which didn't speak well of him, since he'd been engaged. That was something he'd have to work through in private.

Sometimes life threw a wrench into your well-laid plans. And sometimes the disruption was for the best, though you couldn't see it at the time. He wasn't going to question his good fortune. Instead, he'd enjoy every kiss they shared.

~

Jillian closed the door, love niggling her heart while doubt rattled through the rest of her. Things like this happened to her friends. Sure, she'd already had a huge crush on the guy, but tonight.... Tonight couldn't have been more perfect.

She picked up Henry when he came out to say hello, running a hand over his soft fur. No doubt angry because she'd worked all day and then gone out with Brandt, he turned his head away. She tickled him under the chin. "I'll stay home with you all day tomorrow. We can do laundry. I know how much you love warm towels just out of the dryer."

Henry continued to ignore her.

"Please don't be mad. I'll make it up to you." She settled

into the sofa cushions and pulled a throw over her legs, then placed Henry against her chest.

"Can I confide in you? I'm a little scared about losing my heart to Brandt. The really scary, wonderfully awful, toe-tingling, sick-to-my-stomach part is"—she sighed—"I already have. I love him, Henry. He's sweet and kind. And gentle. We have fun together. I can imagine marrying him and having his children and raising them together. I can see us going on vacations and sitting on the porch watching sunsets. With you on my lap, of course."

She raised Henry's head so he was looking at her. "Best of all, I can imagine a happily ever after."

Henry blinked. "Meeeowww."

CHAPTER 7

Jillian grabbed her cell phone from the nightstand before realizing it wouldn't be Brandt at just a little after two in the morning. "Jolie?" she said when she connected the call.

"It's Nate. Jolie's been in labor for about three hours. I'm taking her to the hospital now."

Jillian was already stumbling out of bed. "I'll be there right behind you."

"Hang on. Jolie wants to talk to you."

Jillian reached for a clean pair of jeans from her closet.

"Jillie?"

"Hey, girlfriend. How are you feeling?"

"Tired. Will you come?"

The thermostat in her bathroom said it was just below freezing outside, so she went back into the closet for a sweatshirt. "Of course. I'll be there as soon as I can get dressed and brush my teeth."

"No, I mean, will you be with me in the delivery room?"

Jillian stopped in surprise. "What about Nate?"

"He'll be there, but he's a little squeamish about me being

in pain. My mom faints when her own blood is drawn. Remember what happened when I broke my arm? She couldn't be in the emergency room with me, but you were there. Please, Jillie-Bean?"

"Whatever you want, Jolie. I just don't want to step on anyone's toes. Is Nate okay with this?"

"Yeees—" Jolie gasped and the phone dropped onto something hard.

"We're headed to the hospital, Jillian."

"Nate, tell her I'm on—" Jillian didn't get out a complete sentence before the call was disconnected.

Three short weeks and Jillian was back in Harrisville Regional Hospital for another birth. She was impressed again by the soothing colors and cozy feel of the maternity wing. The nurses changed her into pink scrubs and led her into Jolie's room. Jolie was bent forward, groaning in pain. Nate, a mechanic, was a genius with engines, but the poor guy looked frantic, in as much agony as his wife, and completely out of his element as he rubbed her back.

Jillian moved to Jolie's other side. "Hello, gorgeous."

After her contraction eased up, Jolie fell back against the pillows. "I don't feel gorgeous."

Jillian set a cool cloth on her friend's forehead. "Want me to braid your hair, so it's out of your way?"

Jolie nodded.

"Why don't you take a quick break, Nate? Maybe go down to the cafeteria and get a cup of coffee?"

Nate looked at Jolie as if asking permission. Eyes closed, Jolie nodded again "Yes, babe, take a break."

After Nate left, Jillian brushed and braided Jolie's hair just the way she used to do when they were little. A nurse came in and said Jolie could have ice chips, which Jillian spooned into her mouth. When Nate came back, they worked side by side to ease Jolie's discomfort by wiping her brow and rubbing her back when her contractions subsided.

"Thanks for planning this on my day off," Jillian said to Jolie's stomach. She glanced at her friend. "It would be much easier if I knew who I was talking to. Have you decided on a name?"

Jolie flashed the radiant smile of a mother as she gazed into her husband's eyes. "Riley Jean Klein."

"I love it." Jillian bent close again. "Hi, Riley Jean. I'm Auntie Jillian."

~

Jillian was exhausted but euphoric when she got home after dark.

Riley Jean made her grand entrance into the world an hour earlier, complete with well-developed lungs. Nate was almost as tired as Jolie, who'd kept her husband running for ice chips and rubbing her feet and back all day. He held up well, and was so proud when he finally got to hold his sweet baby daughter. Riley herself was as gorgeous as her momma. A darling button nose and big, round eyes accentuated her adorable, heart-shaped face. She had tufts of hair as dark as her momma's, and a dimple in her chubby little chin that matched her daddy's.

Jillian grabbed her cell phone, which she'd left on the charger in her rush to get to the hospital, and flopped down on the sofa, too tired to fix dinner. Three missed calls from Brandt, but no voice mails. Still, seeing that he'd called shifted her pulse into high gear.

Henry hopped onto the sofa and curled up in her lap.

"Well, Riley is here. Jolie was a trooper, and Nate a knight in shining armor."

Henry's satisfied purr assured her she was missed and all

was well with the world. She stroked his back and glanced at her phone.

"Brandt called me three times, Henry. Should I call him back? I don't want to bother him while he's visiting with his family, but...what if it's an emergency?"

Henry's you're-an-idiot look made her laugh.

"You're right. He wouldn't be calling me if he had an emergency." She scratched the cat's head. "So you think I should just wait until he calls back." *Hope he calls back.*

Jillian quickly texted all her friends about the birth, then answered several responding texts. She was just about to set her phone aside when it rang. She jumped, launching Henry from her lap. "Hello." She hoped her voice didn't sound as breathless to Brandt as it did to her.

"I was afraid you were avoiding my calls."

Did she detect the tiniest bit of worry in his tone? "No. Jolie had her baby. I've been at the hospital since about three this morning."

"You've had a long day."

She settled back against her pillows. "I did, but it was wonderful. Jolie wanted me to be in the delivery room with her and Nate. I've never...." A sudden threat of tears clogged her throat. She'd never witnessed anything so beautiful in her life. The second Riley was born, Jillian was choking on sobs of joy. She, Jolie, and Nate spent ten minutes crying, laughing, and snapping pictures together. Then she left the room so husband, wife, and baby daughter could have a bit of privacy before their families converged.

"Are you okay?"

She managed a shaky yes.

"I know the emotions can be overwhelming. My first time out as a paramedic, I delivered a baby. The dad was traveling on business, and the mom was home with no family close.

The baby came so quick, we couldn't get her to the hospital in time."

"You delivered a baby?"

"I did. It was pretty awesome. Are Jolie and baby okay?"

"Everyone's perfect, even poor Nate. He was pretty nervous during labor, but did great with the delivery." Since she was so close to tears, she changed the subject. "You obviously made it to your parents' house safely. How is your family?"

He laughed. "The same as always, good-natured, teasing, and bickering over dinner. My oldest brother brought his fiancée, which was a surprise to me. I had no idea he was engaged."

"No one told you?"

"Nope. It was a well-kept secret."

"How much older is he?"

"Just eighteen months. I miss you," he added after a short pause. "I know we've only gone out a couple of times, but—" He cleared his throat. "I don't know… I mean, I hope me saying that doesn't scare you away."

Him saying that set her heart pounding so hard she put a hand on her chest to keep it from leaping out of her rib cage. She was afraid to hope, but wanted this to work with Brandt more than anything. "It doesn't scare me."

Her cheeks burned making her glad the conversation was over the phone instead of face-to-face.

"I'd better let you go," he said, after they talked for several minutes about mundane things that didn't matter, but kept them both on the phone a little longer. "I just wanted to hear your voice."

She sucked in a shaky, happy breath. "I'm glad you called."

~

Jillian, Alex, Misty, and Stella met at Carolyn's house the next night to make a few freezer meals for Jolie and Nate. They each brought the ingredients for one dinner, which they'd cook and assemble together, then wrap them for freezing, ready for Jolie and Nate to heat when they were needed.

"I have to go to Harrisville tomorrow night to pick up spring decorations for my classroom. Anyone want to come with me?" Stella asked. "We can drop the meals off with Jolie and see the baby on the way."

"I wish I could go, but JT bought tickets to a concert in Seattle months ago," Carolyn said.

Misty shook her head when Stella looked at her. "I have to work tomorrow night."

"I can't go, either. I have to speak at a function in South Bend," Alex said.

"Can you go, Jillian?" Stella waggled her eyebrows guy-style. "Or do you have a hot date?"

Jillian covered her cheeks so her friends wouldn't see her ridiculous blush. "No, I don't have a hot date. Brandt's in Spokane visiting his family."

"You know what we should totally do when Brandt gets back? Date night! I don't think we've all been dating at the same time before." Stella glanced at Alex and Misty. "You married women can come too."

Alex laughed. "Misty and I appreciate being included. For your information, even though we're married, we still do go on dates with our husbands."

Jillian wasn't sure date night was a great idea. She and Brandt were too new. She didn't want to push him into feeling like he had to take her somewhere or meet with a whole gang of people.

Stella rolled her eyes dramatically. "Stop being a worrywart. I can see the wheels in your head turning, thinking up every bad scenario that might happen if you ask Brandt."

"We've only been out three times. I don't want to seem too forward by inviting him out with friends already. It might seem like I'm implying we're a couple."

"You are a couple," Misty said. "Everyone in town saw you at East Winds."

"We could keep it casual. Something like sledding on that hill just past Glenwood," Alex said. "If JT asked him, it wouldn't be coming from you."

"Yeah, and what if he invites someone else to go with him?" Jillian asked.

"Oh, come on." Stella shook her arm. "Sledding would be a blast. We could roast hot dogs on an open fire and bring a big thermos of hot chocolate."

"I'm going to need something stronger than hot chocolate if we're going sledding and roasting hot dogs," Misty said.

"Maybe after the next snow," Jillian replied, hoping to buy some time. Though, she had to admit, even if only to herself, sledding sounded like another perfect date idea.

~

Jillian's phone vibrated in her pocket just as Stella pulled away from the curb after dropping her off. She connected the call and pressed a hand to her chest as if that would slow her breathing. "Hello."

"Hi, Jillian."

She decided a long walk in the cold air while she talked with Brandt would keep her grounded. Large, fat flakes floated through the night air, settling on everything around her. Except for the soft scrunch of her footsteps in the new-fallen snow, the world was quiet. "How are you?"

"Full. My mom hasn't stopped cooking since I walked through the door. Is it snowing there?"

She looked up into the night sky, snowflakes settling on her face. "Yes. It just started."

"How was your day?"

While she rounded the block, they talked about unimportant things. She told him about her shopping trip to Harrisville with Stella and listened while he talked about helping his dad install new garage doors. Her dad and both brothers could fix almost anything, and Brandt sounded just as capable.

She wasn't ready to hang up when she reached her door, so she let herself in and sank onto the sofa with Henry cuddled close.

"I'm leaving after lunch on Sunday. I thought I'd stop by your house, if that's okay."

Would her heart ever stop pounding a mile a minute when she heard his voice? Would her lungs ever have enough air, or would she always feel light-headed when he was around? "Yes. I'd like that."

~

Brandt was a goner. He hadn't spent this much time thinking about a woman since…well, ever. Jillian was on his mind all the time. While at his parent's' house, he couldn't wait to get a minute alone so he could call her and talk without interruption. Last night she described the snow falling around her. She used words that put him there with her, walking down the sidewalk side by side, hearing the crunch under their feet. He imagined her big brown eyes, her hand in his, and their breaths mingling in the white clouds they exhaled.

They had talked late into the night, and she was on his

mind first thing this morning. He and his family had gone skiing today, and when he stood at the top of the mountain looking over the beautiful valley below, he thought of her and how in awe she would have been of the view

After dinner, when he was anxious to escape to his room to call Jillian, his mom stopped him with a hand on his chest.

"I think you've met someone."

He looked into her wise eyes. *Obviously it shows.* He inhaled a long breath. "I've known Jillian since I moved to Eden Falls."

"I've never heard you mention a Jillian before."

"I didn't actually know her, but I knew who she was. She and Alex are friends."

Her nod encouraged him to continue.

"She works at the gym as a personal trainer. I went there for a workout. We had a brief conversation, just a few sentences, mostly about her job, but that's all it took. I went back the next week and asked her out. We've only been out a few times, but...."

"You think about her constantly, can't wait to see her again." His mom leaned a hip against the kitchen counter, eyebrows raised. "Am I close?"

Brandt chuckled. "Yes."

"Sounds like you've fallen for this girl pretty fast."

"I have." He held up a hand. "I get your worry, but she's different, Mom. We went snowshoeing for our first date and had a great time. She's sweet, and you wouldn't believe the patience she has for a couple of ornery clients." *She has this adorable blush.* He raised his eyebrows to match his mom's. "And she is the complete opposite of Kacie."

"Family?"

"Her parents own a big apple orchard just outside of town. You've probably seen the signs when you've come to visit."

"I do remember the signs. What's her last name?"

"Saunders. Her family is a lot like ours, outdoorsy."

"She sounds nice."

He leaned next to his mom. "She has reddish-brown hair. What's the name of that color?"

"Auburn."

"Auburn." He pulled his cell phone out of his pocket and scrolled to the picture of them together. He held it out for her to see.

"Very pretty." Her smile was the knowing one of a mom, the one that said everything was right with the world for the moment. "You two make a cute couple."

"I like spending time with her. She's a little shy, but easy to be around. She's a down-to-earth, I-am-what-I-am kind of person. I'm not sure why it took me so long to notice her."

"Maybe you weren't ready."

He released a huff of air. "I came to the same conclusion the other day."

"Are you in love?"

He shook his head. "It's too soon." *Though it feels an awful lot like love.*

"Does she know about your accident?"

And my scars. His mom was worried Jillian would discard him the way Kacie had. "We haven't talked about it."

She handed his phone back. "Don't you think you should? Before you get serious?"

Too late. At least for me. "I'll talk to her, but I don't think it will matter. Jillian is not Kacie."

~

Jillian ran to the door when Brandt knocked. She didn't care if she appeared anxious anymore. She'd been on pins and needles since he said two days earlier that he would stop by before going home.

He kissed her the moment he stepped inside the house. The quick action surprised her, but she happily reciprocated, wanting to warm his cold lips with her own, warm his cheeks with her hands.

He laughed, his blue eyes alight with something she decided was happiness, and hoped seeing her had put it there. "Can you tell I missed you?"

She ran the pad of her thumb over his dimple, something she'd wanted to do since he first asked her out. "I've missed you too."

She stepped back so he could come in far enough to close the door and take off his coat. "I made some popcorn and noticed an action movie was on tonight. Can you stay for a little while?"

"Absolutely." He kissed the tip of her nose, which she found oddly intimate. And endearing. "Three of my favorites, popcorn, an action flick, and you."

She led him into her tiny living room and turned. He was unbuttoning his shirt. Her stomach lurched. "Wh-what are you doing?"

After releasing the cuff buttons, he shrugged his shirt off. "I want to show you something."

No. No, no, no. She took a step back and grabbed her cell phone off the coffee table. *This can't be happening. Not again. Not Brandt.*

He lifted his white undershirt over his head and turned to reveal a burn scar down his right side. "It runs from my neck to my knee."

His skin was puckered and still looked raw in places.

Before she could stop herself, she reached out and ran a finger along the edge of skin and scar.

"I think you already saw part of it at the gym, but I thought you should know the extent. I got caught in an industrial fire. Chemicals caused an explosion and I was too close."

Her gaze met his and she realized why he was showing her. He was scared she'd be repulsed. Or worse. "How long ago?"

"Three years."

She moved her finger over another area. "How long were you in the hospital?"

"Three weeks, then I was moved to a rehab facility."

"You were worried the scar would bother me?"

He nodded as he put his arms back in his undershirt and pulled it over his head.

She'd been so worried about what he was doing, she hadn't taken the time to appreciate his physique before he covered it up. "It doesn't."

"I still suffer from PTSD a little. That fire at the hardware store, when I fell through the roof and broke my leg…."

She set her phone on the coffee table. "We all carry a past, some baggage."

His brows wrinkled over his nose. "What's your baggage?"

She debated for thirty seconds. No one knew but her parents. Would telling be freeing or folly? She might be sorry, but Brandt had trusted her with his secret. She'd trust him with hers. "Date rape."

Shock washed over his expression, replaced by horror, then sympathy. He lifted the hem of his undershirt. "You grabbed your phone because you thought I was going to…. I'm sorry, Jillian."

"I shouldn't have assumed."

"Do you want to talk?" He took a tentative step toward

her, reached for her hands. "About what happened?"

She shook her head.

"Maybe another time we can share."

She knew her smile wobbled at the corners. "Another time."

They settled on the sofa with a bowl between them, but before long Jillian was enjoying every kiss they shared, every tingle that shimmered through her when his lips touched hers. He found several sensitive spots on her neck that sent shivers of delight though her. She wasn't experienced, but kissing Brandt came naturally and her anxieties soon fled. Brandt made her feel safe and at ease. More so than she'd ever felt before.

He was also very good at kissing, which meant he probably had a lot of practice. She pushed the jealousy aside. The past was the past. But her uncertainty blossomed bright. She just hoped he didn't find her inexperience boring.

"When can I see you again?" he asked while shrugging into his coat at the end of their evening.

She laughed, not because of what he'd said, but because she felt the same urgency she heard in his voice. She didn't want their leisurely night to end, but they both had to be at work early tomorrow.

He shook his head as if trying to loosen a thought. "I sound crazy, don't I?"

"No, not crazy."

"You have Wednesday off, but I have to work. What about Tuesday night?"

This time she shook her head. "I promised Glenda I'd teach her nutrition class that night. She had something come up."

"And I teach a CPR class on Thursday."

"Maybe Saturday night?" she asked, hopeful.

"Saturday it is, though it sounds awfully far away. I might

have to stop by Get Fit to see you sooner."

"I hope you do."

"Let's plan a ski day for our next free Wednesday."

She nodded.

He kissed her again.

There are too many days between now and Saturday.

"I'll call you tomorrow."

She wondered if her eagerness was flashing across her face like a neon sign.

~

How was it possible that she'd fallen in love after only four dates? Yet Jillian knew she had.

She was in love for the first time in her life. There was no use denying her feelings, but she wasn't going to shout them from the rooftops, either. And she certainly wasn't brave enough to say the words to him, even if he said them first. Not yet. She couldn't allow her hopes and dreams to take charge—which made her angry, because she wanted to enjoy every second of these new, amazingly beautiful sensations surging through her. She was on a roller-coaster ride of emotions—one minute at cloud level, the next plunging straight for earth at the speed of destruction.

She looked up at a knock on her open office door, disappointed to see Glenda rather than Brandt. Already Tuesday and he hadn't stopped by to say hi yet.

"I have good news."

Jillian set down her pen and folded her arms on her desk. "I love good news."

"You have the night off. I was supposed to babysit Sophia tonight, but Misty's dad offered, so I can teach that nutrition class after all."

Brandt immediately popped into her mind, not that he'd

been absent for longer than a second. She had his number. Did she dare call? "That is good news."

Glenda grinned. "It's still early. Why don't you take the rest of the afternoon off and make a date. Maybe with a cute firefighter?"

Jillian's mouth dropped open. "How did you…?"

"Misty told me Sunday after church." Glenda put a hand on her hip. "Why did I have to hear it from my daughter-in-law?"

"We're still too new."

"I can't think of two people more suitably matched." Glenda flapped a hand. "Get out of here. Go spend some time with your man."

Your man bounced around Jillian's mind while she shut down her computer and gathered her things. She'd never had a "your man" before.

She walked out of the gym, searching for keys in the bottom of her purse, and jumped when someone put their hands over her eyes from behind.

"Guess who?"

"Sam!" she squealed in delight, recognizing the voice immediately. "What are you doing here?"

As soon as her big brother removed his hands, she catapulted into his arms. He picked her up and swung her around in circles, just as he'd done when she was little.

~

Brandt stood still, paralyzed by the sight of Jillian in another man's arms. He'd come to the gym to work out while she taught her nutrition class. After she got off, he'd planned to take her to his house. He wanted to show her the work he was doing. But it didn't look like there was a class.

Had there ever been a class, or was she using that as an excuse?

Memories splashed over him like a bucket of ice water thrown in his face. He'd gone into downtown Tacoma to surprise Kacie and caught her in a similar situation. Holding hands with a man as they left her office. Then kissing on the street corner like she wasn't wearing his engagement ring.

I showed her my scar.

How could he have been dumb enough to let the same thing happen again? How had he been so blind to any signs that Jillian might be seeing someone else?

When the man set Jillian on her feet, she took his face between her hands and kissed his cheek. Then they were hugging again. A moment later they climbed into a sports car and sped out of the gym's parking lot.

Brandt yanked open his truck door and climbed inside. After stabbing his key at the ignition a couple of times without success, he finally dropped his hand and leaned his head back against the seat. *I'm an idiot. When am I going to learn?*

Slowly he sat upright, shook his head once, started the truck, and followed the sports car. They turned onto Main and circled the square, parking in front of Noelle's Café. He pulled into a spot in front of Patsy's Pastries and turned in the seat to watch them walk in, arms around each other. They sat in a booth in the front window, looking happy to be in each other's company. Jillian was doing nothing to hide that she was with the guy. Why hadn't anyone told him she was seeing someone else? Why hadn't Alex told him?

Brandt was tempted to go in and confront Jillian, but why bother? He'd done that with Kacie and she confessed everything, but her confession hadn't changed the facts. Or made him feel any better.

To be fair, he'd just assumed he and Jillian were seeing

each other exclusively. They'd never discussed it or made any commitments. They certainly weren't engaged.

He sat for a long time, watching the comings and goings of Eden Falls. The streets began to clear as dinnertime neared. JT Garrett went inside Patsy's Pastries. A few minutes later, he and Carolyn West came out hand in hand. The police chief took the keys from her and locked up for the night. They kissed, spotted him and waved before heading to JT's truck.

The lights went out at Pretty Posies. He knew Alex would be leaving by the back door. He thought about talking to her, asking why she hadn't told him Jillian was seeing someone else. Again, what did it matter now? Jillian was sitting in the front window of Noelle's Café having an early dinner with another man.

~

Jillian was thrilled to be hanging out with Sam. He'd been stuck in the Gulf of Mexico for the past seven months. Now he was here and safe and would be in town for less than a week. The whole family had missed him, especially over the holidays.

While Sam told her about what he'd been studying and how they were working so hard to protect the environment, she tried to pay attention, but her thoughts floated to Brandt more often than she'd ever admit to her brother.

She'd been so excited about having the night off, but everything changed when Sam surprised her. She'd actually planned to step into the world of the brave, call Brandt, and invite him over for a home-cooked dinner. Now she wished she could invite him here, but she wouldn't do that to her brother. He was only in town for a short time. They'd have dinner together, and she'd see Brandt on Saturday like they planned.

~

Brandt scrolled to Jillian's number and hit the Call button. He wasn't looking forward to this conversation, but might as well get it over with rather than dragging things out.

"Hi."

"Hey, Jillian, it's Brandt." *Just in case you're unclear about which guy is calling.*

Her laugh was light. "I know. How are you?"

"Uh…." He didn't want to prolong the conversation with pleasantries. "I had something come up and won't be able to make our date on Saturday."

"Oh…I hope it isn't anything serious."

She was going to play this to the hilt. "Nope, nothing serious."

"Okaaay. So—"

"I have to go. I'll…see you around, Jillian."

He hung up before she could respond. Not exactly his proudest moment, but one that would save him from saying something he might regret.

CHAPTER 8

Six days had passed since Brandt had kissed her good night at her door. Three days since he'd called to cancel their date. He'd stood at her door and told her Saturday seemed too far away, yet he hadn't called to reschedule or come by the gym or her apartment. He'd stood at her door and made her think he was just as excited to see her as she was to see him. Then nothing. No follow-up call or visit to set up another date.

And just like that her tall-girl-flat-chested insecurities escalated, growing to overwhelming proportions. She felt foolish to have believed Brandt Smith was actually interested in her.

Now she stood stone-still on the sidewalk while her nightmare grew. Of course she would run into Brandt around Eden Falls. How could she not in a town this size?

Forgetting to breathe, she watched him cross the square, jog up the stone steps of the library, and disappeared inside.

Should she follow, wander among the shelves like she was searching for the perfect book to spend the night with?

They'd accidently bump into each other, and Brandt

would say, "I'm so glad I ran into you. I haven't called because I was in the hospital having an emergency appendectomy."

She'd say, "Oh my gosh! I'm so sorry."

"I kept my phone near the bed, hoping you'd call me."

She'd blush at her stupidity. "I thought about it so many times, but was worried you didn't want to see me anymore."

He'd reach for her, pull her close. "Are you crazy? I thought about you every second we've been apart."

"Are you feeling okay now?"

He'd flash one of his dimpled grins and set her heart palpitating. "Everything is fine now you're here."

Then he'd kiss her.

Or....

She'd walk down the same aisle he was in, so preoccupied searching for that perfect book that she wouldn't notice him.

He'd glance up and say, "Jillian."

She'd look up with a you-look-vaguely-familiar-do-I-know-you? glance.

"I'm sorry I haven't called. I dropped my phone in the river and lost your number."

A distracted shrug, a wave of her hand would follow. "I've been so busy, I hadn't noticed."

"How about a movie this weekend?"

"Mmm...." She'd frown in thought. "I'll have to check my schedule."

Someone touched her shoulder and she almost fell off the curb. How long had she been standing here, rooted to her spot on the sidewalk, gazing longingly at the library?

JT, his police parka zipped to his chin, grabbed her arm to steady her. The crests of his cheeks and the tip of his nose were red from the cold. "Jillian, are you okay?"

"I.... Yes, I'm fine. I just got...." She put a hand to her

racing heart. "I was so caught up in a thought...but I'm fine." She tried to sound convincing, but the concern on JT's face told her she'd failed.

"The weather sure turned cold, didn't it?"

She shivered, as if his words brought a northern gust of wind skittering down her back. "Yes. I haven't watched the news in a few days, so I wasn't expecting this."

"I was at the gym this morning and noticed they started the renovations."

"Yeah, an indoor pool will be great."

"Where are you headed?"

She thumbed over her shoulder in the direction of Pretty Posies. "I was going over to order a bouquet for my mom's birthday."

His glance moved from Pretty Posies to Patsy's Pastries and back to her. "Are you good at keeping secrets?"

Who am I going to tell? My cat? She nodded.

He took her elbow again and pulled her into the vestibule of The Roasted Bean, where they were sheltered from the chilly air blowing off the mountains. He glanced around as if making sure no one was nearby before he pulled a velvet box out of his pocket. "I have to tell someone and it can't be Alex. I'm afraid she won't be able to keep quiet."

Jillian's heart flip-flopped when he opened the box to display a gorgeous three-stone, emerald-cut engagement ring. "Ohhh, JT. It's beyond beautiful."

"I was going to propose on Valentine's Day, but"—he shook his head—"I remembered that was Alex and Colton's anniversary, so I'm going for this weekend instead."

She, too, had high hopes for this coming weekend. She glanced at the library. Those hopes fizzled three days ago. "Carolyn is going to be.... I have no words for how excited and happy she will be." She hugged him. "Congratulations. I truly am thrilled for you both."

JT grinned. "Don't congratulate me yet. She hasn't said yes."

Jillian swallowed threatening tears. "She will. There is no doubt in my mind."

JT closed the box, slipped it into his pocket, and put a finger to his lips.

"Don't worry. Your secret is safe with me." She turned to leave their shelter. "I better get home."

"I thought you were going to Pretty Posies for flowers."

"I…forgot I have to get home to…feed my cat."

"Stay warm."

"You too," she said, then made a mad dash for her car.

Once she was inside her little she-cave, her insecurities crashed over her like a tidal wave, leaving her struggling for air. She should have known better. Instead, she'd let her guard down, allowed herself to believe.

What remained were shattered dreams and a fragmented heart.

She was born into an encouraging household. Her parents fostered their children's aspirations, encouraged them to dream big. Anything was possible if you worked hard and had faith in what you were doing. They urged goal setting, cheered achievements, and were above and beyond supportive.

Despite that, she was the insecure, tall, gangly girl no one wanted to date. She could beat any guy at school in a foot race. She was always the first girl picked for a team rather than the last, but not because of her popularity.

Henry rubbed against her boot for attention. She picked him up.

"Hello, sweet Henry. How was your day?"

"Meeeowww."

"No, Brandt still hasn't called. I've run our Saturday night conversation through my mind a thousand times and can't think of anything I said or did that would have insulted or hurt him." The only out-of-the-ordinary thing that came to mind was mentioning the date rape. Did that sully her? Was she the instigator in his eyes?

She ran a hand from Henry's neck to tail. "I saw him today."

A purr rumbled through Henry's chest.

"He was going into the library."

Henry blinked gray eyes at her.

"No, he didn't see me." Her laugh sounded hollow, lonely to her own ears. "I actually thought about following him inside. Pathetic, huh?"

"Meeeowww."

"Luckily JT stopped me from doing anything stupid. Speaking of JT, he showed me a gorgeous engagement ring be bought for Carolyn. He's going to propose this weekend. Love was shining in his eyes. He's so excited and nervous, worried Carolyn might turn him down, but she would say yes if he offered a pebble mounted on a gumball-machine ring. That's how it is when you fall in love. The simplest thing makes you happy. And sad."

She carried Henry into the bathroom and stared at her reflection in the mirror. Her eyes were probably her best feature. She'd learned in college how to play them up with touches of eye shadow and liner. Her lips were more full than not. She wasn't beautiful by any means, but she wasn't unattractive, either.

Henry pushed paws against her chest, so she set him down at her feet.

Her cat's simple rejection was the last straw. Tears just under the surface spilled down her cheeks. She'd been here before, wondering what she'd done wrong. She just wished she knew the answer.

~

Brandt walked out of the library with an armful of books to help keep his mind off Jillian. He glanced around the town square. Darkness had fallen, and the streetlights lit empty sidewalks. No doubt the cold had chased everyone indoors.

He turned toward Noelle's Café. The warmth of the heater hit him in the face as soon as the door closed.

"Hi, Brandt." Noelle moved around the counter. "Table for one?"

"Yeah, it's just me tonight."

She led him to the same booth where Jillian and her mystery guy sat while having a delightful meal together. *Great.*

"We have plenty of comfort food on the menu tonight, along with our usual fare. Albert made chicken and dumplings, tuna noodle casserole, and pot roast with mush-room gravy. The gravy is out-of-this-world yummy."

"I'll have the pot roast and a cup of coffee."

Coffee would keep him up, but he hadn't slept well since he saw Jillian four endless days ago. He didn't have to work tomorrow, so he'd read all night if his mind wouldn't shut off.

He opened the book on top of his pile, but his gaze wandered out the window. What was Jillian doing? Was she with the guy, or alone with Henry? Had she even thought about the date they'd planned for tonight? He rubbed his eyes with thumb and forefinger, wishing he could erase the image of her with someone else. On the flip side, if he hadn't seen them, he'd still be following her around like a puppy, completely in the dark.

When would he learn to read people? He'd always thought he was a pretty good judge of character, but he was just as far off with Jillian as he'd been with Kacie. His mom called last night, and he lied, told her everything was great with Jillian, because he was too embarrassed to admit he'd been duped again.

When he saw Jillian Tuesday night, he told himself he was never going to date again, but never was a long time. He knew he'd date. Instead, he now asked himself how he could ever trust his choices. Maybe he should look into one of those dating sites. He'd never joined one before, but his older brother met his fiancée online, and a younger brother was dating a girl he'd met online.

"Why the long face?" Noelle asked as she set a cup of coffee in front of him.

"Long day."

"I'm a good listener, if you need an ear."

After reaching for a packet of sugar, he shook his head. "I'm good, but thanks for the offer."

"I'm here if you change your mind." She patted his shoulder. "Your dinner will be out in a minute."

After telling Jillian something came up, would word that he'd eaten dinner at Noelle's get back to her? He wasn't sure why lying to her, of all people, bothered him, but it did. His mom would say he was raised better than that. He should have just told Jillian he'd seen her and been done with the incident.

He sat over his dinner for a long time, staring out the window, knowing the temperature was dropping, but hating the idea of returning to his empty house.

~

Brandt got out of his truck at Eden Falls Sports Park, more than ready to begin his annual Little League coaching stint. He'd asked for the same team he'd coached for the past two years. The boys, six- and seven-year-olds this year, were a great group, and the parents were always willing to step in and help when necessary.

Although a few daffodils were popping up around town, the air was still chilly for early March.

After greeting the other coaches, most of whom he knew, he picked up a copy of his schedule of practices and games. He'd spend the rest of the afternoon contacting boys and dropping off uniforms.

On his way through town, he stopped at Pretty Posies. Alex was in the walk-in cooler selecting flowers from buckets. Tatum waved from behind the counter.

"Hi." Alex flashed her infectious smile when she stepped into the showroom. "Are you here for flowers?"

He didn't want to get into the subject of Jillian and why he wouldn't be buying flowers for a while. "I came to deliver Charlie's baseball schedule and uniform."

"Oh, you are a lifesaver. Charlie is driving me crazy asking when baseball starts."

"Tell my star player"—*and the heart of our little team*—"the first practice is in two weeks."

Alex gave her armful of flowers to Tatum so she could take the uniform and schedule from him. "Are you sure I can't interest you in some tulips? The ones I have coming in are really beautiful."

"No. Would you be willing to take care of the after-game snack signup again?"

"I'd be happy to." She glanced at the list of Charlie's teammates then back at him. "No Gerberas?"

He turned for the door. "I have more uniforms to deliver. Have a nice night."

~

Three days later, Brandt pulled out of the station's parking lot and headed for Town Square. Today was the first of four days off, and he wasn't sure how to spend it. His initial plan had been to spend one of these days off on the ski slopes with Jillian. He could go alone. A snowstorm had rolled through last night and dumped several inches of fresh powder at the nearest ski resort.

Or he could gut the hall bathroom in preparation for a complete renovation.

Or empty the kitchen cupboards and raise them to better suit his six-foot-four height.

He'd paid more for the fixer-upper than he should have, but something about the Craftsman bungalow spoke to him. The place, with its gabled roof, dormer windows, and inviting porch, felt like home before he even set foot inside. He'd planned to start renovations right away, but winter sports, and then Jillian, had seemed more important. Now he was back to just winter sports, which would be winding down soon. Spring was all about baseball.

He glanced up at the heavy snow clouds rolling in. On Monday, Mother Nature lifted her skirts for a teasing peek at spring; now snow was in the forecast. He decided to save skiing for another day and get to work on the hall bathroom. Other than ripping out the carpet and refinishing the wood floor, the spare bedroom was done.

Decision made, he rounded the square on his way to Harrisville's hardware store.

When he passed Patsy's Pastries, the impulse to indulge in an unhealthy breakfast grabbed him. He hadn't stopped for a sweet treat in a long time. Brandt found a parking space a few doors down and climbed out. The scent of sugar hung in the air even before he pushed through the door. He took a step inside, then froze in his tracks. Jillian stood at the counter laughing with the pastry shop owner, Patsy Douglas.

He knew he'd run into Jillian sooner or later, but had hoped for later. The bad thing about dating someone who lived in the same small town was if things went south, you both still lived in the same small town.

The cold from outdoors swirled into the warm shop behind him, and Jillian looked over her shoulder. Her laughter faded away.

"Good morning, Brandt." Patsy's glance bounced from him to Jillian.

"Morning, Patsy. Hi, Jillian."

"Hello." Jillian turned back to the counter and picked up a white box. "Tell Carolyn thank you for the rush order, Patsy."

"I sure will, hon. Wish Dawson a happy birthday for me."

"I will." She walked to the door, and Brandt pulled it open for her. She didn't raise her eyes to meet his when she passed. "Thank you," she said, so quietly he almost missed it.

She slid behind the wheel of her car, which was parked right in front of Patsy's. How had he not noticed? She bent sideways to set the box on the passenger seat, then backed out of the parking space without a glance his way.

"You got any brain cells in that handsome head of yours?"

Brandt turned, not sure he'd heard Patsy right. "What?"

"I swear every man in this town is as dense as a Washington forest. What's *wrong* with you?"

He glanced outside. Jillian was driving around the other side of the square, probably heading to Get Fit. She didn't seem bothered that they hadn't talked in ten days, which stung his pride. He'd sure missed the mark with her. He shook his head at his own stupidity.

"I thought you two were a couple—at least that's how it looked at East Winds a couple of weeks ago. You looked quite cozy over dinner."

He pulled a gray beanie off his head and ruffled a hand through his hair. "Looks can be deceiving," he said, wondering when his relationship with Jillian had become any of Patsy's business.

Patsy stared at him like he'd grown an extra eye in the middle of his forehead. "After all the food-sharing I saw, that's a little hard to believe. Things don't usually go from hot to cold in a matter of days."

"Things were never hot, Patsy." *At least not in public.* "We only went out a few times." He'd been so certain something good would develop. *What do I know? Obviously not enough.*

"So what happened? Are you digging your heels in because you feel something more than just lust?"

Brandt's face heated at Patsy's casual use of the word. He glanced around, glad there was no one in the shop to hear their conversation. He stepped to the pastry case. "I saw Jillian with another guy, and they were...more than just friends." *And why am I defending myself to Mrs. Busybody?* The answer was simple. He liked Patsy. She was down-to-earth, even if she was all up in his business.

Patsy moved from the cash register to stand in front of him, resting her arms on top of the pastry case. "You said you had a few dates with Jillian. Where did you take her?"

He tapped his fingers on the glass top hoping Patsy would detect his impatience. "We went snowshoeing."

Patsy nodded thoughtfully. "Sounds like something Jillian would enjoy."

"I thought we had a good time. Our second date was a restaurant in Harrisville, and our third was East Winds and a movie. We also watched a movie"—*but not really*—"at Jillian's house."

"I've never seen Jillian with another guy."

"This isn't coming from a third party, Patsy. No one told

me she was with someone else. I *saw* her." He turned from Patsy's steady gaze. "I just wish she had told me. I don't like being lied to."

"Did you ask her if she was seeing someone else?"

"No."

"Then technically, she didn't lie."

He snorted out a breath of frustration. *In my book, omission is as bad as a lie.*

Patsy raised dramatically arched brows. "Are you sure you didn't misunderstand?"

"How exactly would I misunderstand when I saw her hugging and kissing another man?"

Patsy narrowed her eyes and lifted her chin defiantly. "Jillian Saunders is one of the sweetest girls I know. She would never mislead anyone intentionally."

"I'll have one of those maple twists and an orange juice," he said, to end a conversation he wasn't sure why he was having in the first place.

Patsy tsked under her breath as she flicked a white paper bag open with a crisp snap. She put a maple twist and a glazed donut inside, then grabbed a bottle of orange juice from the refrigerator case. When he held up a ten-dollar bill, she planted both hands on the counter and leaned forward until they were almost nose-to-nose.

"Keep your money, but take some advice. You call that girl and straighten things out, because anyone watching could tell there was some mighty strong chemistry buzzing between the two of you. It would be a shame to ignore something that beautiful because you *think* you saw her with another man."

"I told you I saw—" He shook his head, picked up the bag, and headed for the door. "Thanks for breakfast." He was done listening to the advice of a woman who'd been through as many husbands as Patsy. If he hadn't seen Jillian himself, he might question the information. But he knew what he saw

—an instant replay of Kacie. Fool me once, shame on you. Fool me twice, blah, blah, blah. He wasn't that stupid—though clearly he had been. Twice.

He sat in his truck while dark clouds began to drop their snow, glad he'd decided not to go skiing, but wishing he hadn't gone into Patsy's Pastries for a donut, either.

~

Jillian contemplated turning around and asking Brandt to his face what she'd done wrong, but assertiveness wasn't in her DNA. The mere thought of questioning him made her skin prickle and her stomach lurch uncomfortably. She'd never been good at confrontation.

She'd watched her phone, checked the reception, and waited for Brandt's call. After spotting him going into the library—obviously not in the hospital from a burst appendix—she knew their short time together was over. Still, until she saw him face-to-face and he'd barely acknowledged her, she'd held on to a small ember of hope. *Stupid on my part.*

She swallowed back her foolish tears before she walked into the gym. She was through crying over men, through with self-doubt and recriminations. She'd had a wonderful time with Brandt, and she'd told him so. Just as he'd been open about showing his scars, she'd admitted to her date rape. If the knowledge offended him, that was his problem.

If she'd insulted him in some other way, she was sorry, but he'd have to tell her what she did wrong if he wanted an apology. And if all he wanted to do was humiliate her...well, he accomplished his goal. Her friends all knew they'd gone out, and soon enough they'd know she and Brandt weren't dating anymore. She felt about as low as was possible after her college experience, but she'd survived then, and she would again.

She set the cake Glenda had ordered for her husband's birthday on the break-room table amid paper plates and Happy Birthday napkins. She'd come in earlier and strung crepe paper streamers and balloons across the ceiling.

When everything looked just right, she walked into her office, hung up her coat, and braced herself to meet her most unenthusiastic client. Marty's wife called a few days earlier to tell her how much more energy he had, that his pants were getting loose, and he'd actually chosen a salad over a hamburger the last time they ate out. Yet here he was, leaning against a treadmill as if scoffing at her in silence.

"Hello, Marty. Did you warm up?"

"No."

The same answer she'd gotten for the past nine weeks. "Three minutes on the stationary bike. I'll be timing you."

"I still don't like you."

Her smile didn't come as easily today. "I know, but I'm going to remain hopeful."

When he walked away, she turned to the wall of mirrors. *There is nothing wrong with you. You are a kind person. When the time is right, you will find a wonderful man, fall in love, and live happily ever after. Stay true to yourself. This is just a small pothole in the road of life, and you made it through without a flat tire. Yay, you.*

CHAPTER 9

Brandt waved to Rance and left The Fly Shop with a new tackle box. Opening the door of his truck, he noticed Jillian coming out of Renaldo's Italian Kitchen with a bag of takeout. He didn't have to wonder who she was having over for dinner. His imagination took him to her apartment, candles flickering on the table while she and Mystery Man shared lasagna or spaghetti and meatballs and Renaldo's famous buttery breadsticks.

He shook his head to clear the thoughts.

Though he wanted to, it was unfair of him to think badly of Jillian. Patsy was right. Jillian hadn't lied...possibly because he hadn't asked, but that was his problem, not hers. He just wished she'd told him she was dating someone else at the same time. But they'd made no commitments to each other. They weren't engaged as he and Kacie had been. They'd been out less than a handful of times. She was free to date whomever she wanted, as was he.

Thus the date he was meeting in Harrisville tonight. He was showered and shaved and ready to get to know someone new, to try once more, because *never going to date again* had been a stupid thought. Two days earlier, after seeing Jillian in Patsy's, he'd gone home and joined a dating site. Lena was an instant match. They were having dinner at a new restaurant overlooking the river just outside of Harrisville. Lena said the food was good, and she loved the romantic atmosphere.

There was only one road to Harrisville, and he couldn't ignore the lurch of his heart when he found himself following Jillian's car out of town. So she wouldn't be eating lasagna in Eden Falls. She must be taking the food to Mystery Man's place.

Brandt ended up following her through town. She turned left off Harrisville's Main Street into a residential neighborhood. For a split second he considered following her, but glanced at the clock on his dashboard. *Idiot! You'll be late for your date because you're following another woman.*

~

The back door opened, and Jolie stood, jiggling a pink bundle. Jillian held up the bag of Italian. "Time for dinner."

Jolie pushed the door wide. "Thank goodness. I'm starving."

"I'll trade." Jillian shut the door, set the bag on the kitchen table, and dropped her coat on the back of a chair. "You eat. I'll cuddle."

Jolie set the baby in Jillian's outstretched arms. "She's been fussy all afternoon. Maybe you can get her to sleep."

Jillian looked into Riley's cherubic face. "Are you testing Mommy's boundaries today, sweet girl?" Riley's little lips puckered adorably. "Oh, no crying is allowed while Auntie Jillian is here."

"Ha-ha." Jolie pulled plates down from the cupboard and

silverware from a drawer. "We'll see how long she minds that request."

"How are you feeling?" Jillian asked as she stuck her nose in Riley's flyaway dark hair. *Mmm, lavender and vanilla.*

"Pretty good, other than being so tired I can't think straight. I don't think I'll ever catch up on my sleep. Poor Nate's up half the night with me, then has to get up for work. He fell asleep on the sofa last night with Riley on his chest." She scrolled to a picture on her cell phone and held it out.

"Adorable. You need to frame that one." Jillian pulled napkins from a holder on the countertop and set them on the table.

Jolie walked toward her purse. "What do I owe you?"

"Absolutely nothing. This is my treat. When will Nate be home?"

Jolie glanced at the clock on the stove. "He should be here any minute. Thank you for dinner. I've been craving Renaldo's."

"Me too." Jillian slid into a chair, trying not to disturb Riley, whose eyes were drooping. "How's this little sweetie doing?"

"She's hungry all the time, but good. Today is her first fussy day. Nate is so cute with her. We've scheduled a family photo session next week."

Jillian nodded when Jolie held up a container of tortellini.

"So tell me how are things with you. Any more dates with Brandt?"

"Nope. We had a tentative date set up for last Saturday. He called and said something had come up. I haven't heard from him since."

Jolie glanced up, concern crossing her face. "Maybe he had to go out of town for something."

"No, I saw him going into the library that day, then

Tuesday he came into Patsy's just as I was leaving. He didn't say a word other than hi." She stabbed a tortellini with her fork and shoved it in her mouth.

"What happened?"

"I have no idea." Jillian lifted her shoulder in a half shrug before covering her mouth, blinking hard to keep her tears at bay. "What's wrong with me?"

"Nothing." Jolie reached across the table and squeezed her arm. "Don't you dare think something's wrong with you because Brandt Smith broke your date."

"I hate that I got my hopes up, you know? I've liked Brandt for so long…." Jillian bit her lip and tried to force her trembling lips into a smile. "I'm so tempted to call him and ask what I did wrong. What I might have said or done to offend him."

"I could talk to him if you want."

Jillian laughed the tears away. "You're a wonderful friend, and I appreciate the offer, but no." She bit into a breadstick. "I'll be fine."

With some time, I'll be perfectly fine. And she believed it.

Jolie nodded toward Riley. "You're a natural. You got her to sleep."

Jillian looked down at the sleeping angel. "She's gorgeous, Jolie. And she smells divine. I could cuddle and smell her all day."

Jolie tried to stifle a yawn.

"Go take a nap."

"What if she wakes up? She usually doesn't sleep long."

"If she wakes up, I'll come get you."

Jolie looked skeptical for about five seconds before she stood. "I promise to return the favor."

Jillian was tempted to laugh at the thought of her ever having a baby, but didn't want to wake Riley. After Jolie disappeared down the hall, she walked into the living room and sat in a rocker. Suddenly she could see herself in this very position with her own baby. The thought made her smile through more tears. She rocked, humming softly, until Nate arrived.

"Hey, Jillian. Jolie said you were coming by." He glanced around. "Where is she?"

"I sent her to take a nap. There's a plate of Italian in the kitchen, or you can join Jolie before Riley wakes up."

She read the gratitude in his eyes. He kissed his daughter's forehead and disappeared down the hall.

She got to hold Riley Jean for an hour and fifteen minutes before the baby woke up, and another ten before she began to fuss. Jolie was next to her in seconds. She wrapped her arms around Jillian's neck from behind. "Thank you."

"Anytime." Jillian ran a finger over the baby girl's cap of downy hair. "In fact, I'll come back Wednesday so you can get another nap."

"You don't have to do that."

"What else am I going to do? Laundry?" Jillian placed Riley in her mom's arms.

"Everything will work out for you, Jillie-Bean. You'll find someone, get married, and have babies. We'll both live our happily ever after just the way we planned. We'll meet at the park, and our kids will play while we gossip about the crazy things Misty does."

Jillian actually laughed. Misty would always give them something to talk about

"If it's not with Brandt, it's because he wasn't the perfect one, but there is someone who is just right. And he's looking for you too. One day you'll say, 'Man, I'm glad that Smith guy broke that date. If he hadn't, I might not be here right now. This is where I'm supposed to be.' It's Brandt's loss. One day he'll be walking by, see us in the park and think, 'What a dope I was.'"

Jillian liked Jolie's fantasy.

On her drive back to Eden Falls, she decided Jolie was right. When the time was right, she'd find her perfect match. She'd be patient until that time came.

~

Brandt drove away from the Harrisville restaurant, glad he'd met his date there rather than pick her up, because he didn't think he could have spent one more minute with Lena Knox. The dating site was wrong. They were not a perfect match. In fact, they had very little in common. She was arrogant and rude and contradicted everything he said. She even challenged what he did for a living, saying firefighters really didn't have to know much to aim a hose at flames.

Who says things like that on a first date?

No one he knew except maybe Misty before her great change into a nicer person.

By that time, he was ready for the date to end, and their dinner hadn't even been served.

Lena was studying psychology, and decided to analyze why "a hunky man like him" was still single. She asked about his past dating history and wouldn't quit badgering until he told her about his broken engagement. Then she tried to analyze that. He didn't go into his scars. She told him he should have ordered the halibut rather than salmon, and reprimanded him when he over-tipped. In his opinion, the waitress earned every dime of the twenty-five percent he left, for patiently listening to how she refilled water glasses incorrectly, served the dinner without any flair for the extravagant, and didn't clear their dishes away fast enough.

Lena got up on tiptoe to kiss him goodnight and he turned his head so she hit the corner of his mouth. There wouldn't be a kiss on the second date, either, because there wouldn't be a second date.

He chided himself when he drove past Jillian's house. It was only eight-twenty-one and her car was in the driveway. Even though his awful night had lasted longer than her date with Mystery Man, tonight was obviously a bust for both of them.

~

After only a few hours of sleep, Jillian got dressed and went for a run. She seldom ran outdoors anymore when the gym's track was so convenient, but the morning air was in the high thirties, so she bundled up and worked her muscles until they burned. Maybe she'd sleep better tonight.

As she circled Town Square, she spotted Brandt's truck turning onto Main Street. He must be headed into work early. Hard as it was, she kept her breathing steady. In and out and in and out—*I will get past this.*

She ran for so long, she barely had time for a shower before work. Mechanically she moved through her day teaching classes, working with clients, and helping at the front desk. At lunch she called Jolie to see if she was feeling more rested and to check on Riley. She had one small thing to look forward to, her Wednesday afternoons as an unofficial auntie. She'd spoil Riley as much as Jolie and Nate would allow.

Thinking of Jolie's little family helped keep her mind off Brandt. She knew getting over him would take time, and she would have to exercise patience. Luckily patience came pretty naturally for her. And so did exercise.

She left the gym later than planned, and was surprised by the soft, warm breeze. Mother Nature working her magic. Frigid early morning hours gave way to the gentle brush of warmth by evening. But just as the idea of spring settled in, Mother Nature would pull the rug out from under them with a foot of snow. A reminder of who was in charge.

The full moon lit the mountains with their snow-white caps, and stars winked down on Eden Falls. She stared up at the black sky, taking a moment to wish on a star. It wasn't the first one she'd seen tonight, but it was the brightest. Then she hurried to her car, because she was late.

The girls were already at a table helping themselves to a huge platter of loaded nachos sitting in the middle when she arrived at Rowdy's. She took the empty chair between Stella and Misty and helped herself to a chip. As usual, Rowdy made sure the order was nice and spicy for his cousin Alex.

"Sorry I'm late. I had a new client who took a little longer than usual."

"You didn't miss anything. We just got started, and tonight I want to go first." Carolyn held out her left hand, the diamond JT gave her sparkling under the dim overhead lights.

They all squealed with pleasure and congratulations, took turns hugging their friend and gawking at the beautiful ring. Jillian marveled at how happy all her friends looked. Alex was a cheerful person anyway, but since her wedding a year ago, she glowed. Misty, who'd never been a cheery person, was radiant with love for her husband and daughter. Now Carolyn was engaged to her high school crush and beaming in delight. Even Stella looked happy. Len must have kept his date last night.

"When is the wedding?" Stella asked.

Carolyn blushed. "We haven't discussed dates yet. We've only been engaged for twenty-four hours."

"You should be with him tonight," Jillian said.

"I would be if he wasn't working."

They discussed wedding venues and dresses, cakes and flowers for several minutes. Jillian didn't mention she and

Brandt weren't dating anymore. Her friends would find out soon enough.

"How is Jolie doing?" Alex asked.

"Other than being exhausted, she's doing great. I went over last night and watched Riley so she and Nate could take a much-needed nap."

"Bet that's not all they were doing," Misty said.

"Misty." Stella performed her signature eye roll.

"What? Once you have a kid, there's no time for sex, and when there is, you're too exhausted."

"I didn't care what they were doing while I held Riley. She's a doll." Jillian picked up another chip. "She has Nate's eyes and nose."

Misty frowned. "Exactly what every little girl wants to hear."

Jillian shrugged. "She does. She might have Jolie's chin, but she looks a lot like Nate."

"She's adorable," Alex said. "Nate had me deliver flowers last week and I got to hold her for about fifteen minutes."

"Jolie said to apologize for not making it tonight," Jillian said to her friends. "She'll be here for our next girls' night out."

Through nachos, short ribs, and drinks, Jillian immersed herself in the conversation and laughter. It wasn't until Colton came in to collect his wife that she noticed Brandt at the bar, talking with Rowdy but watching their table. He obviously hadn't been headed in for one of his twenty-four hour shifts this morning.

Don't get your hopes up, girl. He's only looking this way because we're being loud. She turned her attention back to her friends, who were razzing Colton mercilessly, which he didn't seem to mind a bit.

Alex stood to leave but leaned close. "How're things between you and Brandt?"

Jillian shook her head. She really didn't want to get into a discussion about Brandt with her friends tonight, and especially not with him sitting just yards away.

Alex's eyebrows drew together. "No more dates?"

Jillian shook her head again.

"What happened?"

Jillian shrugged. *I'd love to know.* She'd commiserated with Jolie, and that was pity party enough. Jillian just wanted the situation to die a peaceful death. Over and done. No real damage or casualties. "We weren't really the match everyone thought we'd be."

Alex reached up and intertwined finger with the hand Colton had laid on her shoulder. "Men are such dorks."

Colton circled his arms around his tiny wife. "She's right. We are."

A look of determination crossed Alex's face, and Jillian reached for her arm. "Don't say anything about this to Brandt. Or anyone. Please, just let it go."

Alex studied her a long moment, then nodded. "Okay, but I am sorry, Jillian. I really thought you two would be ideal together."

Jillian was beginning to think a match was impossible, at least for her. Though, confirmed bachelor Colton had found love with Alex and her son, Charlie. Mean girl Misty was happily married. Jolie and Nate had a few bumps along the way, but they'd also found their happily ever after.

It is possible for you too.

Jillian liked who she was, felt comfortable in her skin. She loved her job, loved helping people realize their dreams and achieve their goals. She liked to watch the transformation of a body as it gained strength. With strength, people gained confidence and became proud of their accomplishments. When her clients met their goals, she enjoyed a sense of satisfaction right along with them. Maybe that's all life would hold for her.

Sure, she wished she had someone to go to the movies or on hikes with, but she was far from old-maid status. *Does that even apply in this day and age?*

Thirty minutes later, she walked out of Rowdy's Bar and Grill arm in arm with Stella, proud that she didn't glance Brandt's way again.

Not even once.

~

Brandt tried not to watch Jillian at a table with all her friends. They were laughing one minute and in deep conversation the next. Only once during that time did Jillian's eyes meet his. She was the first to look away and hadn't looked at him again. Not even when she left with Stella.

He'd seen her early this morning, jogging around Town Square and wondered if she did it often. Jogging outside of the gym wasn't something they'd ever talked about. Actually, as much as they'd talked, there was a lot they hadn't covered.

"Trouble in paradise?"

Brandt turned on his stool to face Rowdy Garrett, who was watching the door Jillian had just disappeared through.

"We never really got to the paradise stage." *Or did we? I was pretty happy for a couple of weeks.*

Rowdy planted his hands on the bar. "Women."

Brandt picked up his drink and swirled the liquid in the bottom of the glass. "Why don't I ever see you out with anyone?"

"I made it a habit never to date anyone local. Eden Falls is too small for breakups."

Yep, it is.

"Sorry, man. I shouldn't have said that."

Brandt waved the apology away. "You ever going to settle down?"

Rowdy glanced toward the door, an almost wistful expression on his face. Brandt raised his brows. "Ha! There is somebody. Who is she?"

Rowdy nodded toward Brandt's almost-empty glass. "Can I get you another?"

Brandt laughed. "Nope, I'm good."

CHAPTER 10

Jillian arrived at the Eden Falls Library early Saturday morning. She'd volunteered at the semiannual book sale, held in the basement, since she was a teenager.

Lily Johnson—the librarian who'd opened the building's doors at the age of eighteen—her husband, Rance, and their police officer son, Mac, already had most of the tables and shelves set up and organized. Several boxes of books had arrived late, and Jillian was in charge of getting those in place before Lily unlocked the doors at nine. The event was widely publicized and always drew a crowd, usually raising enough money to fund the summer reading program and the additional employees needed for that program.

Before becoming the library, the stone structure Jillian loved so much was Eden Falls Town Hall. After town hall moved into a new structure next door, the decaying building was restored. The library was now a historical landmark, and had been photographed for magazines and newspaper articles across the country. As a teenager she worked there after school and on weekends. While her friends were out on their

Friday and Saturday night dates, Jillian manned the checkout desk and restocked shelves.

She'd just finished organizing the last of the books when the first customers came down the stairs. Before long the large room buzzed with chatter while people sorted through the shelves, checked smartphones for reviews, and added to their stacks. She wandered the aisles, answering questions, directing the ones she couldn't answer to Lily, and offering suggestions.

The sale wasn't an hour in when Jillian noticed a big red fire truck pull up outside one of the basement windows. Four men climbed out. Ironically one was Brandt. She considered ducking into the bathroom but decided against the coward's way out. She had nothing to be embarrassed about. She and Brandt went on a few dates. He decided not to further the relationship. Since he hadn't told her otherwise, she was going to believe she'd done nothing wrong. They lived in the same town and would inevitably run into each other, so she would face him, be nice, and move past the awkwardness.

Her rationalization didn't alleviate the furious beat of her heart or the trembling of her knees. She hadn't seen him in a week, not since the night at Rowdy's Bar and Grill. She wished she had more time to prepare, to think of something she could say that wouldn't sound practiced. Nothing came to mind.

Holding grudges wasn't her style. They dated. Things didn't work out. Sure, it hurt. And for her it would be uncomfortable for a long time, because she'd fallen in love. *Something I'll have to work past.*

Now she just had to figure out a way to fall out of love. If only there was a pill or some neutralizing spray....

She turned when Lily called her name, happy for a diversion. At least she wouldn't be standing near the door looking expectant when he walked down the stairs. She went to the other side of the room to help Lily with another late-arriving box.

In spite of straightening books, answering questions, and ringing up sales, Jillian was hyperaware of where Brandt was in the room. As hard as she tried not to look, her traitorous eyes kept him in her periphery. He visited with people he knew while he moved around the tables and perused the shelves.

A woman Jillian didn't recognize stopped him. A flip of her hair and a giggle enticed him to flash his dimpled grin. A sharp pinch of jealousy hit her in the chest and she turned away.

A few minutes later the hairs on her arms prickled and she knew someone was watching her. She didn't have to look up to know who, but she did, and her gaze collided with Brandt's. Her stomach dropped in a sickening way, but to look away and not acknowledge his presence—well, she'd done it before and felt juvenile, so she smiled. A moment of indecision crossed his face, and an uncomfortable thought formed. What if he didn't want to be on friendly terms? Maybe he'd rather go back to looking through her as if she didn't exist.

Then he smiled, not enough that his dimple appeared, but enough that she could breathe again.

There. The awkward meeting is done. She put a hand to her stomach to still the mass of hummingbird wings beating at her insides.

Alex's son Charlie and his uncle JT were in the children's corner. They were looking over the Magic Tree House series, so she crossed the room to see if she could help.

"Hi, Charlie. Hi, JT."

"Hi, Jillian!" replied the little boy with his usual wide-eyed eagerness.

JT dropped a hand on his nephew's shoulder. "Here's the person who can probably answer your question."

Jillian squatted down to eye level with the seven-year-old. "I'll try. What's your question, Charlie?"

"How come you don't have all the Adventures of Jack and Annie books? It's called *Night of the Ninjas*."

"These books are donated, and we only have the books people want to give away. Are you reading the series?"

"Yup, and we're up to five—huh, Uncle JT?"

"We finished number four last weekend."

"Ms. Lily probably has number five upstairs in the library. You could check that one out and buy number six."

"Can we, Uncle JT? Hey, there's Coach Smith." Charlie dodged around Jillian in a mad dash to speak to Brandt.

"He clearly loves reading."

"And has the attention span of a gnat." JT held out his hand and pulled Jillian to her feet. "That kid has enough energy to fuel a turbine."

Jillian watched Brandt crouch to Charlie's level, as she had. He coached Charlie's baseball team last summer, and the boys loved him. "What I wouldn't give to have half that energy."

"You and me both."

She glanced up at JT. "Congratulations on your actual engagement. Carolyn showed us the ring last Saturday night. She said you haven't set the date yet."

JT picked up a book and turned it over to read the back. "I'd get married tomorrow, but Mom and Alex talked Carolyn into a June wedding. They said it would take that long to plan a decent one, which I think is crazy, because Alex planned Mac and Noelle's wedding in three or four days."

Jillian loved that JT was in such a hurry to marry Carolyn. "June is only…what? Ten weeks away?"

"Ten weeks," JT groaned.

"Carolyn's first wedding was in a judge's chambers. I imagine Alex wants everything to be magical for her this time." *Do I sound as wistful as I feel?*

"I know, and that's why I'll be patient." JT set the book down with a smile.

Jillian straightened a few books that were threatening to fall off a table. "You have Charlie today. Is Alex working?"

"Colton had to go to Los Angeles on business and wanted Alex to go with him. They haven't had a chance to get away since their honeymoon, so I told her I'd take Charlie for the weekend."

"You're a nice brother."

"Now Alex and Colton are married, he picks up the slack. I don't get to see Charlie as often as I used to, and I miss spending time with him." He picked up another book.

Charlie rejoined them, and Jillian said her goodbyes before moving to the opposite corner of the room to help a couple searching through the travel books. Then she was off to ring up sales at the small register, where a line had formed. She appreciated being busy enough to have lost track of Brandt, but it didn't last long. While she was bagging a purchase for another customer, she heard, "Hi, Jillian."

Time to step out of your comfort zone. She took a very deep breath and met his gaze with resolve. "Hi." *Short, to the point. Possibly a little breathless, but not too noticeable.* "How are you?"

"Good."

She handed the bagged purchase to the customer in front of him. "Thanks for your support. Have a nice day."

Brandt set his stack of books next to the cash register. "The library received some great donations this year."

She felt a stab of annoyance. He couldn't say more than "Hi Jillian," in Patsy's. Now he wanted to have a conversation. "I think Colton McCreed might have had something to do with that."

He picked up the top book. "I figured it was about time I read one of Colton's books."

As another volunteer started ringing up Brandt's selection, Jillian pulled another bag from a box under the table, trying to keep her shaking hands busy.

"Have you read any of his books yet?"

"No. Alex says they're pretty gruesome."

He rubbed at the corner of his mouth with his thumb. They both smiled—his looked as tight as hers felt—and glanced around, her searching for anything else to say. Him, possibly the same. Both came up empty.

The volunteer told Brandt his total. Jillian bagged his purchase while he paid. She met his gaze long enough to say the words she'd repeated numerous times. "Thanks for your support. Have a nice day."

"You too."

She looked out the window moments later to see him waiting next to the fire engine while the other firemen finished with their purchases. That he'd rather stand out in the cold to wait for his buddies stung, but she gave her mental self a shake. She was proud of the conversation she'd managed. She was proud she hadn't run like a scared rabbit. She deserved a gold star. She'd looked him straight in the eye, and without blushing.

A tiny victory for blushing women everywhere. Yay, me!

~

Lounging in a recliner in the fire station rec room after dinner, Brandt had one eye on the flat-screen where a basketball game was in full swing, the other on the Colton McCreed novel in his hands. But his mind was on

Jillian. She'd looked pretty today in her jeans, sweater, and knee boots. He'd taken in every detail, down to the scarf around her neck and her big brown eyes.

He also noted her mystery man wasn't in the room.

In fact, he hadn't seen her around town with the guy again, but he had seen her around. She was at Rowdy's with her friends last Saturday night. He'd seen her in the produce section at the grocery store, where he turned tail and slinked to Frozen Foods like a chicken. He also saw her in East Winds Chinese Restaurant with Stella last night.

He felt torn between what she said after their last date, what he'd seen, and Patsy's advice. If she was dating someone else, why had he only spotted them once? They'd seemed very familiar, as if they'd known each other for quite some time. She'd been excited to see the man. First showing surprise, then jumping into his arms.

He wished he understood how a woman could tell a man she'd had a great time on a date, that she couldn't wait to see him again, and then be with another man two days later.

The kisses they'd shared baffled him further. Her lips had burned a memory in his brain that he wouldn't soon forget. Hesitant, like she hadn't been kissed often, yet she'd done just fine keeping up. Were her innocent streak and shyness artificial? No, because the blush that frequently tinged her cheeks certainly wasn't fake.

Except today…she hadn't blushed. She'd appeared confident, so maybe her innocence *had been* an act. How could he have misjudged her so completely?

He closed the book when the commercial ended and the game resumed. He was spending too much time dwelling on her. Time to let the idea of him and Jillian fade away like it never existed.

CHAPTER 11

Brandt and the other four firefighters on his shift returned to the station after dousing a small grease fire. The kitchen had sustained enough damage to warrant a remodel, but they'd confined the blaze to one room, thanks to quick acting residents. He loved his job, even if some days all he did was rescue a scared kitten from a storm drain or extinguish a grass fire. He also enjoyed the crew he worked with. They worked well together, and got along in spite of living together for days at a time in a fairly confined space.

They took turns making dinner, and it was his night, so while the other men cleaned and put away the equipment, he went to the kitchen. He slid the lasagna he'd assembled at home last night into the oven. Then he added sautéed garlic to melted butter and drizzled it over a loaf of French bread, which also went into the oven. For a salad, he chopped a head of lettuce, added cherry tomatoes, and topped it with crumbled bacon.

He set the table with plates, utensils, glasses, and two jugs of milk. Everything was ready when the troops filed in with "I'm starved!" and "Man, that smells great, Smith."

Conversation was suspended as the men dug in like they hadn't eaten in a week. Brandt's mom taught her son's to cook, insisting it was a valuable skill, even for boys. He was glad he'd paid attention. He was the best cook at the station, and often took over kitchen duty because he preferred his food edible rather than charred.

Jeff reached for another slice of garlic bread. "I talked to the other two crew chiefs. Our first practice for the annual Gunslingers-Smoke Eaters baseball game is this Saturday at six o'clock at the sports park." He glanced at Brandt. "You going to pitch again?"

"Sure, unless someone else wants the position." Brandt poured more milk in his glass and passed the jug down the table.

"We need to recruit a new player. Our left fielder is seven months pregnant," Greg Schneider said.

"You're not going to let your wife play?" Brandt teased, followed by a round of laughter.

"Nope. Sheee's out!" Greg said umpire fashion, to another bout of laughs.

"I was at my stepmom's for dinner last night. She suggested Jillian Saunders."

Brandt glanced toward Jack Frazier at the mention of Jillian's name.

"She's a personal trainer at Get Fit. I bet she can swing a bat," Jack added.

"Why didn't you think of her?" Jeff nudged Brandt with an elbow. "You and she are dating, aren't you?"

Yep, this is just what I want to discuss at the dinner table. Brandt took a swig of milk and set his glass down harder than he intended. "We only went out a couple of times."

Greg lifted a brow. "Does that mean you can't ask her?"

"One of you guys can ask her." Brandt stabbed at the last bite of lasagna on his plate.

A collective “Ooo” was followed by a third round of laughter.

“I’ll ask her,” Jack volunteered—a little too enthusiastically, in Brandt’s opinion. Jack held up a hand in surrender. “Unless you have a problem with that.”

“Nope.” Brandt pushed away from the table, picked up his plate, and set it near the sink.

Jack also stood. “Patsy said Jillian played baseball on the high school team.”

Jeff slapped the table with his palms. “Why didn’t we know this years ago? She could have been playing for us all along.”

Since he’d cooked, Brandt was off cleanup duty, so he grabbed his jacket and headed outside to sit on a bench in front of the station. He hoped his gesture looked casual and not bursting with the frustration he felt. He’d heard all he wanted to about Jillian.

The day was winding down, staying light a little later now that spring was on the way to Eden Falls. He liked watching the town slip from bustling to calm.

Blowing out a deflating breath, agitation settled in his stomach. He didn’t like feeling out of sorts about Jillian. And he didn’t like that Jack’s apparent interest bothered him so much. He had no one but himself to blame for the way he ended things. Cancelling their date with no explanation hadn’t been right. They should have discussed what he saw that night, but it was too late now. He’d let too much time pass.

He shook his head to clear his tumbling thoughts.

Jillian would be great at baseball. Memories of their day snowshoeing flitted through his mind. From her glowing brown eyes to her pink-from-the-cold cheeks, she’d radiated happiness that day. Kacie would have whined the whole time they were outdoors.

The sun dipped behind the mountain peaks, softening the world around him. He zipped up his jacket as the temperature dropped with the waning light. The sky changed from swirls of blues and pinks to deep indigo. A few stars appeared, winking at him in the early twilight.

Beam Garrett came out of the hardware store across the street and locked the door. Brandt had watched workers install the new Eden Falls Hardware and Lumber sign just this morning. A year earlier, the lumberyard was set on fire. Before Brandt and his crew could get the fire put out, it spread to the hardware store and burned it to the ground, adding more stress to Beam's already stressful move back to Eden Falls from Seattle after his daughter's birth.

The grand reopening was scheduled for tomorrow. After more than a year of driving to Harrisville for their hardware needs, a lot of people in Eden Falls would be thrilled.

He'd fallen through the roof during that fire, rekindling nightmares of the fire that had burned him so badly. After falling two stories, he was lucky to come out with only a broken leg and wrist. He rubbed a hand over the edge of the scar on his neck. Maybe he should have waited to show Jillian.

He shook his head again. If she couldn't accept him as he was, then she wasn't the girl for him.

Beam stood back on the sidewalk and looked up at the new sign.

"Looks great."

Beam turned, spotted him, and jogged across the street. "You said those same words to me a year ago." Beam sank onto the bench next to him. "Last time we sat here, we actually might have seen the arsonists days before they set the fire."

"Yep. If only we'd known. Are you ready for the grand reopening tomorrow?"

"Everything's set." Beam stretched out his legs. "It's been a long time coming."

"Yes, it has. I'm sure I'm not the only one looking forward to the celebration. Harrisville isn't that far away, but just down the street is way more convenient."

Beam chuckled. "Believe me, I'm just as ready as everyone else."

Brandt thumbed over his shoulder. "The crew was discussing baseball at dinner tonight."

Beam and his brother, Rowdy, also played for the Smoke Eaters. Their dad, a firefighter years ago, founded the Gunslingers-Smoke Eaters annual game and the good-natured rivalry had become a Memorial Day tradition.

"Rowdy and I were talking about the same thing earlier today."

"We're going to need a new left fielder."

"Male or female?"

Beam asked because the only rule making this game different from regular baseball was that each team had to have at least three women on the roster, and one of those women had to play in every inning—which wasn't a problem, because Eden Falls had some fine female baseball players. The winning team didn't receive a trophy, just the privilege of strutting around town for a year, holding the victory over the losing team's head.

"Female. Patsy suggested Jillian Saunders. Jack said he'd ask her."

Beam raised his eyebrows. "Great idea. Now you mention it, I'm surprised the Gunslingers haven't already nabbed her."

"Our first practice is Saturday night at the ballpark. Six o'clock."

"Sounds good. I'll tell Rowdy." Beam stood. "I've got to get home and read a story to my baby girl before Misty puts her down for the night. I'll see you around."

"Yep. Take it easy."

Brandt gazed up at the sky. Along with the grand reopening of the hardware and lumber store, tomorrow was St. Patrick's Day, and spring was right around the corner.

The station door behind Brandt opened. "We're starting a game of poker. You in?" Greg hollered.

"Yep, deal me in." Brandt pushed up from the bench. He needed to win back the sixteen bucks Jack won off him last week, and a game of poker would keep his mind off Jillian. A win-win situation.

~

Jillian walked to Eden Falls Hardware and Lumber from Get Fit. Today was the grand reopening, and all her friends were meeting here to support Beam, and Misty's dad, Mason. Patsy was standing just inside the door holding a tray of shamrock-shaped cookies, since it was also St. Patrick's Day. Patsy and Mason were married seven months earlier, and Patsy still carried the glow of a newlywed.

"Welcome, hon."

Jillian accepted a frosted cookie, a weakness of hers, and glanced around. "The store looks wonderful."

"It sure does." Patsy held the plate out when another couple entered. "Welcome," she said to them, then turned back to Jillian. "Mason and Beam did a great job, didn't they?"

Jillian's glance stopped on Brandt. He was near the cash registers talking to Beam and Misty. Sophia was in Misty's arms reaching for her daddy. Beam took her, snuggling her close.

Brandt hid his eyes behind his hands. When he moved

them away, Sophia giggled. The sight melted Jillian's heart. He would make a great dad.

"Jillian!"

Brandt glanced her direction when Stella hollered her name. Their eyes connected, which meant he'd caught her staring a third time.

Get used to it, pal. Just because we aren't dating doesn't mean I'll stop appreciating a handsome man.

She smiled at him and then waved to Stella and Carolyn, who were standing next to a display of flowerpots.

A man joined her and Patsy. He took a cookie and dropped a kiss on Patsy's cheek.

"Jillian, have you met my stepson?"

"No, we've never officially met."

"Nice to meet you, Jillian. I'm Jack Frazier from Patsy's fourth marriage." He added the last part like it was a normal extension of his name.

Patsy gave him a playful swat to the chest. "You don't have to tell her that part."

The pastry shop proprietress's marriages were as talked about as the Seattle sports teams. Or the weather. But Jillian was convinced Mason Douglas would be Patsy's final husband.

"Jack works for the fire department."

The mention of the fire department made Jillian think of Brandt. She was tempted to glance around but kept her eyes on Patsy and Jack instead.

"I'm glad you're here. I was actually going to stop by Get Fit after this to talk to you," Jack said.

"To me?" she asked in surprise.

"Would you be interested in going to Noelle's Café to talk? She's serving corned beef and cabbage for St. Paddy's."

Suddenly questions bounced through Jillian's mind. Why would a stranger want to talk to her? Jack was a fireman. Had

Brandt sent him for some reason? If so, why couldn't Brandt talk to her himself?

Her reluctance must have been evident, because Jack held up his hands, palms out. "I'm completely harmless, and I think my proposal will interest you. We could go somewhere else if you don't like traditional St. Patrick's Day food."

"I can vouch for him, Jillian. He's a tease, but a good guy. I know what he wants to talk about, and I think you will be interested." Patsy turned to offer Rance and Lily Johnson cookies when they stepped inside.

Jillian had planned to drive out to her parents' house tonight. Her mom always cooked corned beef and cabbage, but she hadn't called to say she was coming, so she wasn't expected. She didn't know Jack, but she knew Patsy well enough. They'd certainly be well chaperoned in Noelle's. The place would be packed with customers tonight.

And, she had to admit, she was intrigued to hear his *proposal*. "I do like traditional St. Patrick's Day food, so…." She shrugged. "Okay."

Since they were only a block and a half away, they walked. They were early enough that they didn't have any trouble getting a booth by the front window, the same booth she shared with her brother a few weeks ago. The night she'd planned to shed her protective turtle shell and ask Brandt out. She couldn't help but wonder, would they still be dating if Sam hadn't intercepted her?

Jack waited until she sat before he slid into the bench on the opposite side of the table. They both ordered the special. Over idle chitchat and a house salad, Jillian studied the man in front of her. She liked the contrast between his blond hair and the black brows above friendly blue eyes, and his engaging manner made it easy to respond in kind. His long-sleeved dress shirt was strained enough to emphasize his well-defined biceps.

As a personal trainer—and as a woman—she noticed.

He set his salad bowl aside. “I’m sure you’re familiar with the Memorial Day baseball game between the firemen and police.”

“The whole town is. I’ve watched it every year since I could walk. Possibly before then.”

“So you know each team has at least three female players.”

A faint light began to dawn. “Yes.”

“Do you know Greg Schneider?”

“Sure.”

“Then you probably know his wife, Jeanine, is pregnant, and Greg won’t let her play this year.”

“Bummer,” she said with a smirk.

He chuckled. “Yeah, that’s what we all said. Anyway, the Smoke Eaters are looking for a new female player.”

And the sun rose over the horizon.

“Patsy tells me you played softball on the high school team.”

And college.

“Would you be interested in playing for the fire department?” He waited a moment, eyebrows raised, blue eyes intense.

She wasn’t sure she wanted to play on the same team as Brandt. At the moment, she’d rather be the woman on the other team who caught his fly ball, basking in glory when the umpire yelled, “Out!” She frowned at herself for such a mean thought—not like her at all.

“Our first practice is scheduled for this Saturday night at six.”

She looked down, pushed a sliced carrot around the bottom of her almost-empty salad bowl.

“We hold all our practices at the town sports park. We

usually meet kind of late because of Little League. The school-age kids need the fields before dark."

"What days do you practice?"

"Practice isn't set in stone. Since firemen work twenty-four-hour shifts, we have to alternate days so the guys on all three shifts get a chance to practice. Would that be a problem?"

She raised her brows. "You're assuming I'm going to say yes."

"No." He flashed his easy smile. Judging by the sun crinkles at the corners of his eyes, she imagined he smiled often. "Hoping, but not assuming."

Curiosity spurted words out of her mouth before she could bite them back. "Will the other team members be okay with me playing?"

"When I mentioned your name to the guys on my shift, they were all in favor of me asking you."

Patsy had mentioned her name to Jack, and he'd brought it up with his teammates. More questions swirled around in her head. Was Brandt there? Would he be okay with her playing on the team? Or would he think she said yes because she still had feelings for him?

Because she did. Still have feelings for him. If she played with the team, she'd have to keep those feelings in check. She'd kept her fantasies to herself for a couple of years. She could do it again.

Jillian wanted to laugh at the irony. Why couldn't the Gunslingers be the team that needed the female player? Why did it have to be the Smoke Eaters?

"Are you lost in thought or are you considering?"

Lost in thought, quagmired in questions, take your pick. She couldn't believe she *was* actually considering.

"Sorry." She pushed her salad bowl away. "Alternating days wouldn't be a problem. I'm usually off work by six."

Jack set his salad bowl in hers and placed them at the edge of the table. "We do have a couple of Saturday practices."

"I won't be able to make those. I work Saturdays."

"Not a problem. With firefighters rotating shifts, we all have to miss a couple of practices." He leaned his forearms on the table, his expression hopeful. "Does this mean you'll play?"

There was only one reason keeping her from saying yes, but it was time to stop living in fear of running into Brandt, or worrying about what he thought. "It's been a while since I've played on an organized team."

"Piece of cake—like riding a bike." He threw out the clichés with a grin.

She had to admit she loved the idea of being included, but she wasn't quite ready to commit yet. "I'll think about it over my corned beef and cabbage."

~

Brandt followed Jack and Jillian—how ridiculous did that sound?—out of the hardware store. They walked down the street side by side to Noelle's Café. For the second time in his life, jealously reared its ugly head. He didn't identify the emotion immediately. It took him several long minutes of examination before he realized what he was feeling. Then he took a few more minutes to analyze why he was feeling jealous. The realization hit hard.

Because he thought Jillian was the one. Because maybe, just maybe, he'd already been on his way to falling in love.

Jealousy was an ugly emotion. He'd been overcome with hurt, then anger, when he spotted Kacie with another guy. The jealousy didn't come until he confronted her. He had the same reaction with Jillian—hurt, then anger. Now, seeing her with Jack…jealousy burned bright.

He wondered if he should warn Jack that she was already seeing someone.

Why hadn't he seen her around town with her mystery man? Plenty of people would have seen them together that day in Noelle's. If she was trying to hide it, she should have gone somewhere else. Yet no one had mentioned anything. There were no rumors floating around town about her with another man. At least none that made their way to him.

He'd planned to go to Noelle's for St. Patrick's Day meal, but now it would look like he followed her. When he walked past the café, he saw Jillian and Jack at the same table she shared with her other date. Yep, he should probably warn Jack.

When he walked into Rowdy's, the smell of corned beef and cabbage surrounded him. He hadn't realized he was so hungry until that moment. The place was busy, but he found a stool at the bar. Rowdy approached as soon as he took a seat.

"You here for the special?"

Brandt nodded. "I just left your brother's place. It looks great."

Rowdy grinned. "Yeah, I was there earlier. He and Mason did good."

"I'm glad they decided to rebuild. Eden Falls needs a hardware store."

It was Rowdy's turn to nod. "I'll get that special right out."

Brandt listened to the recorded country music in the background. Of course the lyrics mentioned big brown eyes, and he thought of Jillian. Had Jack asked her to play for the Smoke Eaters? Is so, had she agreed? Would Mystery Man be at the games?

Enough.

CHAPTER 12

Brandt pulled his Little League equipment out of the bags in anticipation of his team's arrival. He had coached the five-year-old tee-ball team two years ago, and asked to move up with the same kids each year. He'd built a comfortable camaraderie with them, and hoped it would continue through this baseball season. He had nine boys and four girls on his roster.

A warm breeze ruffled the evergreen branches surrounding the park, bringing the scent of spring with it. He took a brisk jog around the field to warm up his own muscles before the team arrived, finishing just in time to greet his most enthusiastic team member. "Hey, Charlie."

"Hi, Coach Smith." Charlie ran over to him, the McCreed family dog, Barney, hot on his heels. Colton McCreed brought up the rear.

Charlie resembled his Native American father, with his bronzed complexion, dark hair and eyes, but his grin was his mother's. Alex's smile was joyfully contagious, and Charlie's was always just as infectious. His excitement for baseball made him the heart and soul of their little team.

Brandt rested a hand on Charlie's shoulder. "You ready for a new season?"

"Yes!" he shouted, pumping his fist in the air.

Brandt exchanged a handshake with Colton before he bent to scratch Barney behind the ears.

"Look at the new mitt I got for Christmas, Coach Smith."

Brandt inspected the mitt carefully for Charlie's benefit. "This is great, and it looks like you've already broken it in."

"I've been practicing with Colton and Uncle JT."

"Good for you. Here comes Zeke. Why don't the two of you throw the ball to each other while we wait for the rest of the team?"

"Okay." Charlie gave his dog a hug around the neck, and his stepdad a high five. "'Bye, Colton."

"Have fun. Your mom will be here to pick you up in an hour."

Fifteen minutes into practice, Brandt could tell that at least half the boys were more serious than they were the year before, and the girls had them beat. Keeping a five-year-old's attention through an entire game was hard work. Working with six-year-olds was only slightly better. As their practice progressed, Brandt was certain this year would move along more smoothly.

Charlie had enthusiastically carried the team on his shoulders the past two years, but he'd have some help this season. At least two of the other boys had been practicing too.

Alex showed up to collect her son at the end of their hour. The boys crowded around her when she pulled out baggies of orange slices and juice boxes. She handed Brandt the last bag of wedges with her usual smile. "How'd it go?"

"A year makes a huge difference in a little kid's attention span."

She laughed. "Yes, it does."

Brandt looked down at the cheerful faces as they

munched on their treats, juice running down their chins. Their happy chatter lightened his heart. "They're a good group of kids."

"They have a good coach."

He popped an orange slice in his mouth, appreciating the compliment. Alex was always good about throwing them out, and you never had to wonder if they were genuine or not. She meant what she said.

"I've always liked working with kids." He held out an orange slice and she bit it in half. He popped the rest in his mouth. "Thanks for this. I didn't think to bring snacks."

"It's a female thing. Maybe if you had one in your life, she'd remind you to bring treats or get a mom to delegate it out."

He frowned. "Ouch."

She shrugged innocently. "Just making a suggestion...."

"Yeah, well, I'm not having much luck in that department lately." He bit into another orange wedge.

"Really? I thought you were dating Jillian?"

The mention of Jillian conjured images of her and Jack at a table at Noelle's three nights earlier. "I don't like dating a woman who's dating someone else at the same time. Been there, got the T-shirt."

"Jillian isn't dating anyone else." Alex reached into his baggie and helped herself to another orange wedge. "Who told you that?"

"No one. I saw her."

Alex stared at him just as Patsy had. He almost reached up to check the middle of his forehead for an extra eye. "You must have been seeing things, because I'd know if Jillian was dating someone else."

"I know what I saw, Alex."

"Where?"

"At the gym. Some guy came up behind her and covered

her eyes. Then she was in his arms kissing him. I saw them a little while later in Noelle's having dinner." He wasn't going to admit he'd followed them.

"Did you ask Jillian about it?" Her tone was that of a parent lecturing an errant child.

"No."

She widened her stance, hands on hips. She was a tiny thing, but could make her presence big when she wanted. "You just assumed what you saw was Jillian dating some other guy and didn't bother to ask?"

"I told you, I've already lived through that nightmare once. I found out my fiancée was cheating weeks before our wedding. I'm not dumb enough to repeat the mistake."

He held the baggie out, and she looked as though she was sorry she'd given it to him. "What you're saying doesn't make sense. Jillian isn't the type of person to do something like that. She is honest to a fault. She would have told you if she was dating someone else. She would have told me."

"Like I said to Patsy when she lectured me—the same way you are—the information didn't come secondhand. I saw Jillian with another man. They kissed. They ate dinner together."

"But you didn't ask her about it."

"Hello! Been there, done that. Not going to a repeat performance."

Brandt thought about what Alex said while waiting for his own baseball team to arrive. He wasn't alone is his dislike of being played for a fool. From what little he knew of Jillian, she didn't seem the type to hurt anyone intentionally, but he also knew what he saw. There was no mistaking Jillian hugging and kissing a man. Though…they hadn't kissed like lovers. No mouth-to-mouth. More like he'd kissed her cheek and she'd kissed his. Maybe he hadn't seen…

He shook his head. It was bad enough that Alex and Patsy were questioning him, now he was questioning himself.

He knew Jillian had accepted the invitation to play for the team, but not whether she would be here tonight. Silly boyhood anticipation settled over him at the thought of seeing her. When he spotted her friends at the hardware store celebration, he knew she'd come and felt the same anticipation.

He wanted to believe she was discussing baseball the whole time she was with Jack, but maybe they'd been on a date. Maybe they'd planned to meet at the hardware store all along. He'd noticed Patsy's satisfied expression while they talked by the door. Maybe Patsy set them up by mentioning Jillian to Jack, hoping he'd ask her out.

The eagerness he'd felt died a quick death when she arrived with Jack.

During warm-up Jillian held her own. She threw straight and true. She could scoop up a grounder as well as race for a fly. She was agile, had quick reflexes, and was perfect as their third female. They played her in several different positions, and she did well in all of them. She spoke to him when necessary, but no more.

She was wearing the kind of figure-hugging black pants women wore when exercising, and a formfitting jacket. He glanced her way often enough that he missed a couple of balls he should have caught. She never glanced back.

After two hours of hard work, they scheduled the next practice, then headed to Rowdy's for another type of team-building exercise. They pushed several tables together and, by design or not, Jillian sat as far away from him as possible. He'd hoped for a seat near her so they could talk, but Jack took the chair to her right. Beam sat on her left.

He tried not to look in her direction, tried to keep his

attention centered on his end of the table, but every time she or Jack laughed, or someone said her name, his glance shot her way. If she and Jack were dating, Brandt would keep his distance. Hard-and-fast rule—never encroach on another man's territory. Twice their gazes caught and held; both times she was the one to look away first.

They left Rowdy's in groups, and he made sure he left before Jillian and Jack. He didn't want to see Jack help her into the car, or let his imagination take him to her apartment door.

~

Jillian knew she'd see Brandt tonight, thought she'd prepared herself, but she'd been sorely mistaken. He still set her heart pounding. She had to force herself not to look his way, because she would never have been able to play tonight if she did.

She felt good about practice. Several times Jack, Rowdy, or Beam had called out, "Good catch" or "Great play," which bolstered her confidence. She hadn't played on an organized team since college, and the stretch of muscles felt fabulous.

Her heart muscle was a different story. It was extremely fragile. She still wondered what she'd done to make Brandt stop calling, but she didn't dwell on it like she had at first. Still, the thought drifted in and out occasionally, but life was too short to drag along things she couldn't change. And she'd dragged this on long enough. Brandt had decided he didn't want to date her, so.... *You had a few dates with the man of your dreams, Jillian. Now, it's time to move on.*

She'd embrace the last lines of Alfred, Lord Tennyson's "In Memoriam" 'Tis better to have loved and lost...," and was glad she could finally laugh at her melodramatic self.

~

Jillian loved the exertion and the stretch of the different muscles she used while playing baseball. She enjoyed the Smoke Eaters' camaraderie. After only a few practices, they read each other's skills, actions, and reactions well, and responded to them quickly.

She'd never been on a team where the players were so in tune with each other. It was exhilarating. She chalked it up to maturity. In college, the girls had been fighting to keep their spot, not only on the field but on the team. Playing for the Smoke Eaters was pure fun. Even though they took the game seriously, there was a great deal of laughter and joking.

The only times she felt the least bit uncomfortable were when she was working with Brandt. Playing on the same team was like playing Russian Roulette with her heart.

She waged a battle to keep from looking his way and often lost, unable to resist his magnetic pull. She marveled at how fit he was despite his obvious burns and the rehabilitation that followed. She loved to watch his muscles at work and admire the power behind his pitches. He flashed his dimple often, because he also shared a solidarity with his teammates. They'd been playing together for several years and knew each other well. She was the newbie, but they treated her as though she'd been with them forever.

Jillian got ready for work and said goodbye to Henry, who meowed mournfully at her departure. She carried a change of clothes for the movie she and Stella would see later tonight. They were both in need of a comedy. Stella was feeling blue because her elusive boyfriend Len called with another lame excuse for breaking a date. Hopefully they could cheer each other up or at least support each other through their shared pain.

Jillian's day at the gym was routine. She spent her first

hour on the computer, tweaking the schedule and classes for the next month. Then she spent two hours wearing her personal-trainer hat working with clients. After teaching a spin class, she tackled a pile of paperwork while eating lunch at her desk. She finished her day by training a new employee on the front desk.

The movie was the perfect antidote for both her and Stella's wounded hearts. They laughed until their sides hurt, while sharing a bucket of popcorn for dinner. After the movie, Jillian suggested a piece of homemade pie was needed to top off their night out. When they walked through the door of Noelle's Café, Jillian stopped so suddenly, Stella ran into her.

Stella snorted out a laugh. "What are you doing?"

Brandt sat on one of the red vinyl stools at the counter. Her first instinct was to run, but he turned to see who'd entered. Stella waved. Jillian's chest constricted painfully along with her stomach.

Why? She saw him at least twice a week at practice, and had endured their "team-building" social times at Rowdy's. So why couldn't she have a great night out with a friend without running into Brandt?

Of all the open seating in the café, Noelle led them to the booth directly behind him. Jillian saw the wheels turning in Stella's head, and knew the moment she made the decision, but was helpless to stop her.

"Want to join us, Brandt?"

He turned with plate and glass of milk in hand, as if the whole scene had been previously orchestrated.

She wanted to kick Stella under the table or reach out and smack her. She probably would have at least punched her in the arm if Brandt wasn't already standing next to her.

Really? He had two sides of the table to choose from and he chose hers. She *really* wanted to smack Stella now.

"Do you mind?"

What choice do I have? She scooted over with a nod. *And the bobblehead is back.*

"What have you got there?" Stella asked, scrutinizing his piece of pie.

"The mixed berry à la mode."

"My favorite is the coconut cream, but Jillian always orders the berry pies."

Brandt turned to her, and Jillian felt certain he was staring at the chin zit she popped earlier in the day. *Stress.*

"Why the berry pies?"

"She saves fifty calories by ordering the berry pies." Stella winked at her. "It's the health nut in her. She can't help herself, even when she's off duty."

"Are health nuts ever off duty?" Brandt asked. His adorable dimple made its appearance.

"I'm not a health nut always on duty. I just happen to like berry pies better than cream pies." Her tone was harsher than she'd intended. Heat blossomed over her face. She knew Brandt noticed, because he looked from her eyes to her cheeks.

She glanced at Stella, who flashed a scheming grin. "Jillian tells me she's playing baseball with the enemy this year."

"You consider the fire department the enemy?" Brandt asked on a chuckle.

"In baseball, I do." Stella tipped her head toward Jillian. "She any good?"

Jillian felt Brandt's eyes on her, but studied the menu as if she'd never seen it before.

"I'm not giving any secrets away. You'll just have to wait until Memorial Day and see."

"She was really good in high school."

"Stella." Jillian wanted Stella to shut up. She wanted

Brandt to leave. She wanted out of the booth, but knew none of those things were going to happen.

Noelle took her and Stella's order and took Brandt's empty plate away. Jillian expected he'd say his goodbyes at that point, but instead he leaned against the red vinyl and stretched his arm along the back of their seat. Jillian was too edgy to enjoy her pie, and frustrated with herself for allowing him to unnerve her. She sat like a third wheel, not participating in the conversation unless specifically addressed.

Stella and Brandt discussed the weather, her second-graders, and a garage fire some boys started while experimenting with firecrackers. Stella ate more slowly than she'd ever eaten in her life, and Jillian was ready to strangle her by the time her "friend" pushed her plate back.

Neither Stella nor Brandt seemed in any hurry to leave, but she was. She didn't like that his knee touched hers when he turned to look at her, or that his cologne reminded her of their kisses on her sofa. She didn't like the way he showed interest when she added anything to the conversation.

When Noelle placed their check on the table, Brandt reached for it at the same time Jillian did. Their hands collided and she jerked back like she'd been burned.

Brandt raised an eyebrow before he picked up the bill. "I'll get this."

"No." Her tone was sharper than she'd intended. She swallowed. "You don't have to do that."

He grinned, as if he'd had the best time. "Consider it a thank-you for letting me join you." He pushed to his feet and touched a finger to his brow in a cheery salute. "You ladies have a nice night."

"You too," Stella said.

Jillian nodded.

"Thanks for the pie," Stella added.

As soon as he was out the door, Stella treated Jillian to her signature eye roll. "Ohmygosh! What is up with you?"

"I'll ask you the same question. Did you plan this"—Jillian waved her hand in the air—"this 'innocent' meeting?"

Stella laughed. "You think I told Brandt to meet us here? Pie after the movie was your idea."

Stella had her there. Pie had been her suggestion.

"I thought you two were dating. What happened? I could almost feel the electrical current running between your bodies."

"We only went out a few times, and there was no electrical current."

Stella laughed again, which irritated Jillian to the core. "If there was no electrical current, why did he keep looking at you?"

"He didn't."

"How would you know? You were looking everywhere but at him. The only time you talked was if one of us asked you a direct question."

"He stopped calling me for no reason, Stella! He just stopped. Now you expect me to sit at a table and have an everyday conversation with him like nothing happened. Something happened." Jillian stood, took a deep breath, and grabbed her jacket from the booth. "In four stupid dates, I fell in love. And now I'm supposed to act like nothing happened."

"I'm sorry. I had no idea, Jillie." Stella, a contrite expression on her face, scooted out of the booth. "Why didn't you tell me before? I wouldn't have invited him to sit with us."

"It doesn't matter." Jillian shook her head, angry she'd allowed her emotions to show like a blinking neon sign. "I'm sorry, I shouldn't have said anything. I know you didn't know."

Stella put an arm around her waist. "I really am sorry."

Jillian shrugged, still shaking her head. She was embarrassed by her outburst, and sad she blamed Stella for something that wasn't her fault. "I'll run into him all the time as long as we both live in Eden Falls. Heck, I run into him more now than I ever did before."

She turned toward the door, her good mood gone.

When Jillian got home, Henry was waiting by the door. She set her purse aside, plugged her cell phone into the charger on the counter, and picked him up. "Hi there, handsome. I'm so glad to see you."

He ran the top of his head under her chin. "I know. I know. I shouldn't have left you alone for so long, but Mrs. O'Malley said she checked on you and you hid under the bed. Next time, come out and say hello when someone visits."

He purred loudly, the sound rumbling over her in a wave of contentment. "I'd be lonely without you, my furry friend. Thank you for loving me."

She sat on the sofa, Henry cuddled against her chest. "Yes, the movie was funny. It felt good to laugh." She stroked Henry's back until he arched against her hand. "You wouldn't have liked it, but it was just what I needed."

"Meeeowww."

"You're right. I should have come home right after the movie. Stella and I went to Noelle's for pie and ran into Brandt. He sat at our table and talked with Stella like nothing had happened between us. I didn't understand why it bothered me at first, but on the drive home I realized that his behavior hurt my feelings"—she swiped at a tear that leaked from the corner of her eye—"because something did happen…at least for me."

Henry jumped out of her arms to the back of the sofa.

"Sorry. I know you're tired of hearing about him. I thought I was past all this. I think I've let it go, then something like tonight happens and...it just hurts. I feel so... demoralized that something so huge slipped through my fingers. Everyone else seems to find love so easily. When am I going to get my chance, Henry? When is it my turn?"

"Meeeowww." Henry jumped off the sofa and headed toward the bedroom, letting her know he'd had enough and was ready for bed.

She put her hands over her face and let the tears fall unchecked for the first time in a very long while.

CHAPTER 13

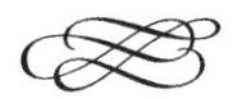

After leaving Noelle's Café, Brandt drove around Eden Falls, not ready to go home to his lonely house with nothing more than his thoughts to occupy him. And those thoughts lingered even after he'd left the lights of town behind.

He pulled off the highway onto a dirt road and drove for a few miles before parking. Through the open window he could hear the rush of the river and see the water glistening under the moonlight. With spring runoff, the river would soon reach the limits of its capacity, overflow, and fill creeks, streams, and ponds along its path.

Despite the distraction, his thoughts never left Jillian. As they'd sat side by side tonight, her perfume floated around him every time she moved, like fingers of soft fragrance reaching for him. The gold flecks in her big brown eyes sparkled under the lights even though she tried to look anywhere but at him. Was it embarrassment or something else?

Sitting there in the dark, listening to the river rush past, he decided he'd handled everything all wrong. Alex was right.

Even though he'd seen her with someone else, he should have asked her about it.

He *would* ask her.

Five weeks had passed since he saw her with Mystery Man and there'd been no gossip about her seeing anyone. The man hadn't made an appearance at any of their baseball practices. So who was he? Where had he come from? Were they still seeing each other?

~

Jillian loved visiting Pretty Posies. As soon as she walked in, she closed her eyes and was surrounded with not only the different floral fragrances, but also the rich scent of soil and the earthiness of peat moss. Pretty Posies had been a fixture in Eden Falls her entire life. Her eyes fluttered open, and she took in all the pretty displays, the bright colors, and Alex's unique way of arranging flowers.

One of the things she loved best about this town was the sameness, even while the people themselves evolved. Alex was now married. She and Colton were building a home and would eventually have more children. Those children would grow up coming into Pretty Posies after school, just as Alex had done when her grandmother owned the shop, and the tradition would continue.

"Hi, Jillian."

Tatum stood behind the counter. She was as colorful as the shop, with her pink-and-purple-streaked hair. Her black leather skirt was topped with a T-shirt in a kaleidoscope of colors and designs. Even though Jillian knew they were beads, the eyeballs hanging from her ears looked real. Jillian admired Tatum's defiance of convention and applauded Alex's belief in her. She'd shown up in town a few years earlier driving a car on its last leg. Alex hired her, found her a place to live, and now Tatum was as much a fixture in Pretty Posies as Alex.

"Hi, Tatum. How are you?"

Tatum leaned forward, resting her elbows on the counter. "Fabulous. This warm weather puts me in such a good mood. I have a hard time staying indoors."

Jillian touched a wind chime just enough to hear the sound. She'd been lulled to sleep at night by wind chimes hanging from the fruit trees around her childhood home, but Mrs. O'Malley said the noise was annoying. "I know what you mean. I guess I was more ready for warm weather than I realized."

"I hear you're going to be playing for the Smoke Eaters this year."

"I am."

"It's about time they got some new blood on the team."

"Let's just hope my blood mixes well with the old blood." Jillian glanced around. "Is Alex here?"

"She's out being a mayor this afternoon, giving a speech for Career Day at the high school."

"She could give two speeches, one as mayor and one as a business owner."

Tatum laughed. The carefree sound made Jillian wonder when she'd last felt as untroubled as Tatum.

They both turned when the bell over the door jingled and Tatum straightened. "Here's Superwoman now."

"Sorry I'm so late. The Q and A ran long. Hi, Jillian." Alex gave her a quick hug before walking around the counter. "I have the perfect arrangement for your mom's birthday."

Jillian was always amazed how Alex remembered so many birthdays, anniversaries, and special celebrations. She must have an extraordinary calendar program on her computer.

Alex waved for Jillian to follow her into the back room. Jillian pulled out a stool and sat at Alex's scarred worktable while Alex moved over to a wall of vases. She pulled a pink one off a shelf and held it up for Jillian's approval.

"Mom will love it."

"I thought of your mom as soon as I unpacked it last week." Alex set it on the table. She pulled a piece of paper from a file folder and handed it to Jillian.

The flower arrangement in the picture was the most unique she had ever seen. "Wow, this is gorgeous. Mom will be blown away."

As Alex reached for an order form, she looked at Jillian through a veil of lashes. "I've been meaning to come by the gym and talk to you."

"About what?"

"Brandt. I asked him why you two weren't dating anymore."

Jillian's stomach dipped precariously.

Alex held up a hand. "Please don't be mad. I asked the question as *innocently* as possible without bringing your name into the conversation."

Since Jillian had asked Alex not to say anything, she wasn't sure how she felt about her interference. "How could you ask *that* question without my name being mentioned?"

"I mean, I asked in a way that sounded like the question came from me, not you. I said something like, 'I thought you and Jillian were dating.'"

Mad or not, Jillian's curiosity got the better of her. "What did he say?"

"He said he saw you kissing a man."

Jillian laughed, then stopped when she realized Alex was serious. Sad but true, she could count on two fingers the number of men she'd kissed since college. Her thoughts bounced like a toddler on a trampoline. Brandt must have seen someone who looked like her. "When?"

"He didn't say."

"Did he tell you where I was?"

"He said he saw you kissing some guy at the gym, then later having dinner at Noelle's."

Jillian's thoughts bounced some more, then suddenly landed on the day Sam surprised her in the parking lot at the gym. She closed her eyes and pressed two fingers to her forehead where a headache began to thump. "You've got to be kidding me," she muttered. She opened her eyes. "You have got to be kidding me."

Alex raised a brow. "So…there was a man?"

"Yep. There was a man." Such a simple mistake that could have been explained away with two words—*my brother*—if only Brandt had asked. "It was Sam."

"Sam, your brother?"

"He came into town for a few days and surprised me. I jumped into his arms and kissed his cute face. We went to dinner at Noelle's." She dropped her head into her hands. "Brandt saw me with my brother."

"Whew," Alex said, exaggerating a swipe of her forehead. "That's easy enough to explain. All you have to do is tell Brandt."

Jillian tugged her credit card from her wallet. "He assumed I lied to him, didn't ask me or give me a chance to explain. He simply cancelled our date and didn't call back. Why should I tell him anything?"

"He jumped to conclusions because he caught his fiancée cheating on him. When he saw you with Sam, he thought you were doing the same."

Her heart twisted slightly, then hardened. "He should have come to me and asked if it was true."

A crease appeared between Alex's brows. "Don't let your pride—"

"It has nothing to do with pride, Alex. He assumed—"

"He assumed what he saw was the truth, just as you would have if you'd seen the same thing."

Possibly. Okay, yes, she probably would have assumed just as Brandt had, but she also believed she would have tried to talk to him. Self-doubt nudged her with a finger. Wasn't she just as guilty for not confronting him?

"You need to talk to him."

Jillian nodded, only half-heartedly agreeing. "Thanks, Alex." At least she knew why Brandt stopped calling.

~

Brandt watched Jillian and Jack at every practice. They talked and laughed together often, but, since that first practice, they didn't arrive in the same car, and they never left together. If the group had a team-building exercise at Rowdy's, they only sat next to each other by chance. He didn't like that the thought of them together bothered him enough to keep watch, but it did.

In fact, he found Jillian popping into his mind at the oddest times, and the more she did, the more he questioned what he saw weeks ago. What if the mystery guy had been an old friend or relative? He'd already determined their kisses had seemed more friendly than romantic.

He should have talked to her.

The team was practicing on a Saturday morning, and Jillian couldn't be there because of her job at the gym. Just as they finished up, Patsy sauntered across the field carrying two boxes of donuts.

"I just want you to know I'm not taking sides because my stepson is a Smoke Eater." She opened the top box when the team gathered around her. "I have too many Gunslingers frequenting my shop, and I'm not going to blow that business, so I delivered two boxes to your enemy at their practice last night."

Brandt moved toward the donuts, but Patsy handed off the boxes, took his arm, and hauled him the other direction.

"I haven't seen you out with anyone lately."

The comment surprised him. He crossed his arms over his chest and blew out what he hoped sounded like an annoyed breath. "Why have you taken such an interest in my personal business?"

"When I see someone who needs help, I usually step in. It's a habit I— "

"I don't need any help."

She raised an eyebrow. "Are you sure about that?"

Brandt glanced around to see if anyone was paying attention to their conversation. The team was too busy digging into the donuts. "Yeah. I'm positive."

"How's Jillian doing?"

"Good."

Her gaze took a quick survey of the team. "I don't see her here today."

"She's at work."

"When I heard Greg's wife was pregnant, I immediately thought Jillian would make a great replacement." Patsy crossed her arms over a T-shirt that said, *I'm Blond and I'm Smart. Deal with It*. "Since she hasn't played with the team before, I thought it would be nice if Jack kept an eye on her."

Suddenly his cloud-filled brain allowed a few rays of light to filter through. He saw the twinkle in Patsy's eyes a second before she winked. She had set this whole thing up. Suggesting Jillian play for the team, then telling Jack to stick close. She'd been trying to make him jealous. To his complete embarrassment, her scheme worked.

"When you told me things hadn't worked out between you and Jillian, I immediately thought of Jack. Jillian would be perfect for him. She's sweet and friendly—not to mention gorgeous. Everyone likes her. Have you ever noticed her thick auburn hair? I love how the sun brings out the red highlights. And those big brown eyes of hers…." She shrugged. "I thought she and Jack would make a beautiful couple. Imagine the darling babies they'd have. Can you tell I'm ready to be a grandma?"

Brandt shook his head and wondered if he should warn Jack about his stepmom, because Patsy was good. "Is Jack your next project?"

"My next project? I have no idea what you're talking about."

She turned on her heel, leaving him alone to feel like a fool. She waved goodbye to the cheers of the team, threw him one last happy little smirk, and sauntered back across the field.

He should have approached Jillian rather than jumping to conclusions. He should have walked up to her right there in the gym parking lot. Confronting her would have eliminated all this guessing and jealousy. And wasted time. Because suddenly he was questioning what he'd seen.

~

Jillian arrived at the church early Sunday morning to help hide hundreds of plastic Easter eggs she and about ten other volunteers had stuffed with stickers, ice cream coupons, candy, and novelty toys the night before. Luckily Eden Falls was still bathed in the warmth of spring and not the rain showers that cancelled the event last Easter.

She took a large bag of eggs to the area roped off specifically for tiny tots. These she hid in easy-to-find places.

The Easter egg hunt was always followed by a potluck lunch in the fellowship hall. Jillian had taken her time with makeup and hair this morning, and wore a new dress. She knew a fire engine and a patrol car would be there for the kids, which meant Brandt would come. Determined to find time to talk, Jillian didn't care about the results. She just wanted him to know she wasn't like his fiancée.

As soon as the fire engine arrived, kids flocked to the parking lot.

"Sorry I didn't get here earlier to help," Alex said, approaching from a different direction.

"Not a problem. We had plenty of volunteers this year."

"Brandt's here."

Jillian's cheeks heated and her pulse pounded, just two of the silly little ways her body responded when he was close. "I see that."

"Are you going to talk to him?"

Brandt climbed down from the truck, his eyes on her.

"If there's time. I'm sure he'll be busy with kids for a while." At Alex's stern look, she added, "I intend to talk to him."

"Good."

Jillian nodded while watching Brandt and the other firefighters being mobbed by children. She still wasn't sure why *she* had to clear the air when he was the one who'd jumped to conclusions, but she knew she'd feel better after she told him the truth.

"I know what you're thinking. Brandt should have talked to you and I agree, but wouldn't you rather he knows the truth?" Alex said as if she were reading Jillian's mind.

"Yes."

~

As soon as the fire truck pulled into the church parking lot, Brandt was searching for Jillian. He finally spotted her in a roped-off area talking to Alex. She wore a pink dress, her hair curled down past her shoulders. A moment later, she was pointing out bright Easter eggs to Sophia Garrett, who was also dressed in pink. The little girl sported a bow in her raven-black hair that was almost as big as she was.

When kids swarmed the truck and him, he lost track of Jillian. He and the guys on his crew handed out jelly beans, chocolates, and little red helmets. They played games with the kids, and let them explore the truck and turn on the lights.

An hour after he arrived, Brandt spotted Jillian near the corner of the church talking with Stella. He headed in that direction, fully intending to ask her about what he'd seen. Halfway there, his radio beeped to life as a call came in. Disappointed, he turned, jerking the radio off his belt, and sprinted for the fire engine as the other firefighters leapt aboard and parents hurried over to collect their kids.

CHAPTER 14

Brandt couldn't sleep. Jeff was snoring loud enough to wake the dead. After tossing, turning, and trying to put himself to sleep with a book, he finally dressed in his uniform pants, grabbed his jacket and radio, and went out into the night. Maybe a walk down Main would clear his mind. Free it of thoughts of Jillian in her pink dress, helping children hunt for Easter eggs. The nagging conviction that he needed to talk to her about that night wouldn't leave him alone.

The chilly air held the scent of pine. His footsteps echoed, keeping him company as he walked toward Town Square. All the shops and restaurants were closed, their windows dark. Soon the baskets hanging from the lampposts would hold cascades of summer flowers, and the air would smell of cut grass and sunshine.

A slight movement to his left caught Brandt's attention. He squinted, staring hard in that direction but saw nothing. Maybe a darting dog or cat, which made him think of Jillian's cat. Henry. Jillian said he didn't like people, but Henry liked him.

The niggling feeling that he should look around persisted. He did, and caught more movement in his periphery.

Was the darkness playing tricks on him, or were there two people wearing black, standing near the entrance of the alley running between Kimball's Dry Cleaning and Patsy's Pastries? A low whistle on his right made him turn in the other direction, but he couldn't see anything. He glanced back toward the alley. The figures were gone.

The hairs on the back of his neck stood on end. Something wasn't right. He looked to the right again, searching for the source of the whistle, but saw nothing. His instincts, now on high alert, told him to move toward the alley.

Before the lumberyard fire burned the hardware store to the ground, he and Beam Garrett saw two boys in trench coats walking down the street. They'd seemed to disappear into thin air too. He knew JT still suspected them for that fire and two others, one that burned down the town's Christmas tree and the one started in a dumpster pushed up against the back wall of Noelle's Café. Luckily it snowed heavily that night, preventing anything more than charred siding.

He jogged across the square, trying to keep his footfalls as quiet as possible. He wished he'd been able to distinguish whether it was two people or one, male or female. The sky was overcast and the streetlamps weren't much help. What little light they gave off was flat. He wasn't going to call 911 at this time of night on a hunch.

Compelled to investigate, he started down the alley. Probably kids. He expected to find them rolling joints or breaking open a bottle of alcohol. What he didn't expect was a sudden explosion of light that sent flames shooting skyward.

He broke into a run and reached the parking lot behind Patsy's in time to see two kids wearing black coats and ski masks disappear around the corner of Kimball's. A stack of pallets, pushed up against the back door of Patsy's, blazed, flames licking at the soffit. Someone must have been here earlier to stack the pallets and douse them with an accelerant.

The fire was burning too hot to kick at the pallets, so he jerked his radio off his belt and started after the kids.

When he rounded the same corner they had, his left leg buckled as a sharp pain shot up the back from calf to butt. He hit the ground before he could catch himself. His radio skidded out of reach. He fumbled for his cell in his jacket pocket and pressed 9-1-1. He recognized Phoebe Adams's voice immediately. "Phoebe, this is Brandt Smith. Get the fire department to the parking lot behind Patsy's—fast. Tell the crew I'm already here. Then call JT and tell him the arsonists struck again."

He tried to stand, but fell again when a sharp pain seared through his leg. Less than a minute later a police cruiser screeched into the back lot and JT jumped out. Brandt waved him past to see if he could do anything before the fire department arrived, but the fire was too big now, the heat too intense.

JT walked backward until he was even with Brandt. "You okay?"

"I tried to chase the kids, but the leg I broke last year gave out."

"The kids?"

"Looked like two teenagers in black trench coats. I was taking a walk and spotted them near the alley. Something didn't feel right. They disappeared and I followed. The fire exploded before I reached the back of Patsy's."

"Which way did they go?"

Brandt heard the pumper's engine before it pulled into the parking lot. "Around the building, but they're long gone by now."

"Can you stand? We need to get you out of the way."

Brandt held out his right hand, pushing himself up with

his left, and JT helped him stand on his good foot. With JT's support, he hobbled far enough to the side that the fire truck could get by. They watched from the sidelines while his crew put out the fire. The walls weren't burned through, but the shop would definitely require repair work.

"Sometimes arsonists like to see the damage their work caused," JT said.

Since the crew hadn't turned on the siren, there were no spectators. Brandt strained to see past the darkness but it was no use. Those kids wouldn't stick around tonight.

After the fire was out and Patsy had been alerted, JT told Brandt's crew chief he'd take Brandt to the hospital.

The fifteen-minute drive to Harrisville Regional jostled his leg enough that he knew he'd done some serious damage. He'd missed the Memorial Day baseball game last year because of this same leg, and here he was, on his way to the ER again.

A doctor walked into the exam room a short time later. Brandt described the pain while the doctor felt along the back of Brandt's calf and thigh.

"What you're describing sounds like a ruptured hamstring. We'll do a musculoskeletal ultrasound to make sure."

"An ultrasound can determine that?"

"Ultrasound imaging will allow the tech to dynamically test the tissues, to view how the hamstring changes during movement, and to determine severity. It can be extremely accurate and precise at finding the location and extent of a hamstring injury."

"If it's torn?"

"Depends on the severity. You may need surgery."

"Any chance it's just a strain?"

"There is always a chance. But from the fall you described, I'm guessing it's more." The doctor ran fingers through his curly hair, making it stand on end. "Let's get that ultrasound. Then we'll discuss it further."

Brandt watched the ceiling tiles pass while his bed was wheeled from the ER to Radiology.

Two long hours later, the doctor came in, images displayed on a tablet. "We're in luck. You definitely have a strained hamstring with only a slight tear, which should heal without surgery."

But it would be weeks before he could work, coach, or play baseball.

JT filled his pain medication at an all-night pharmacy, then drove him back to Eden Falls. Whatever the ER doctor gave him for pain had wiped him out, and he dozed off and on during the short drive home. All he wanted to do was crawl into bed and sleep. For days.

"Sorry you had to spend your night at the hospital, JT."

"Not a problem," the police chief replied as he pulled into Brandt's driveway. "I'm sorry you hurt your leg, but I'm glad you couldn't sleep tonight. If you hadn't caught that fire when you did, Patsy's, and possibly several other buildings, might have burned to the ground."

"Glad to be of service."

JT helped him inside and got him settled on the bed. "Let me know if you need anything. Between me and Alex, we can get you around until you can drive."

"I appreciate your help tonight" was the last thing he remembered saying.

~

Jillian tried not to laugh when Stella smooshed her face against the window outside her spin class. Stella had always been the silly friend, the one who could make you laugh and lighten your mood. She was also the messy friend. You could find her by following a trail. The apartment she shared with sister Phoebe was a catastrophe.

Ten minutes later, after congratulating her class on their hard work, she slid onto the stool next to Stella at Get Fit's snack bar. "What're you doing here so early?"

"I have some news." Stella pushed a green smoothie toward her. "Want some?"

"No, thanks." Jillian held up her water bottle. "What news?"

"This is pretty yummy and only has one hundred and forty calories." Stella sucked on her straw hard enough that her cheeks concaved.

Jillian nodded, waiting.

"It's filling too. I should come over here and have one of these for lunch every day. Instead I had a peanut butter and jelly sandwich. I'm almost thirty and still eating like I did when I was a kid. Maybe that's why I'm fat."

"You're not fat."

Stella pointed at her hip. "That's more than curvy."

"I wish I had a few of your curves. I'm built like a boy."

"Ohmygosh! I would trade you bodies in a heartbeat."

"Isn't it funny how we're never satisfied with what we're given? I've always wanted your curves. And your confidence." Jillian leaned her elbows on the snack bar. "I'd love to have Misty's hair, Alex's smile and built-in happiness, Carolyn's poise, and Jolie's glowing skin and teeth. She has perfect teeth."

"And I want your hair and healthy body, Alex's gorgeous green eyes, and Jolie's laugh."

Jillian nodded. "Jolie does have a great laugh. Along with her perfect teeth."

"I'd love to have Misty's sense of style"—Stella raised

her eyebrows—"and Carolyn's ability to make grown men weep over a muffin."

Jillian laughed, which made Stella laugh until she snorted. Then they were both in tears they were laughing so hard. She wished she had Stella's ability to make people laugh.

"Oh, I forgot to tell you the news," Stella said when she finally got her giggles under control. "Did you hear about the fire behind Patsy's?"

"Yeah, Janie mentioned it just now in spin class. She said the back wall and roof were burned, but there was only minor damage inside."

"Did she also mention that Brandt hurt his leg trying to chase the arsonists?"

Jillian sat a little straighter at the mention of his name. "No. Is he okay?"

"JT spent the night in Harrisville's ER with him. He's home now. According to JT, he ruptured a hamstring."

A ruptured hamstring would have him down and out for a while, depending on how severe the tear was.

"I thought you'd want to know. Maybe you could go over there, take him a nice casserole and ask him what his problem is."

Jillian shook her head. "Don't go there, Stella."

"Don't go where?" Stella asked, feigned innocence oozing from her pores. "I have no idea what you're talking about."

Jillian glanced at her watch and slid from her stool. "I have a client in five minutes."

"I bet he'd love that broccoli-chicken thing you make."

"'Bye, Stella."

"Or a hearty beef stew," Stella called out before Jillian turned the corner.

~

Brandt hobbled to the front door on the same crutches he used last year for his broken leg. He'd slept hard through the rest of the night and most of the day, and the pain pills he took around nine this morning kept the throbbing at bay. He was following the ER doctor's advice—protect, rest, ice, compression, and elevate, until he could see Doc Newell.

Another knock sounded.

"I'm coming as fast as I can," he mumbled, swinging the door open.

Alex stood on the porch holding a box. "JT told me what happened. I have all kinds of goodies for you." She maneuvered inside. "Turkey noodle soup, homemade cookies, snacks, and roast beef with mashed potatoes for dinner. Oh, and Colton sent over one of his books. He said it's too gory for me, but you might like it."

"You didn't have to do this, Alex."

"I wouldn't have to if you had a nice woman to take care of you. I couldn't stand the thought of you here all alone, shriveling away with hunger."

He raised a brow. "How do you know I'm alone?"

She looked him up and down. "Because no woman in her right mind would allow that awful T-shirt into her house."

He wasn't in the mood for the bright sunshine Alex loved to spread. Or her chiding. "I can cook for myself."

She lifted a corner of her mouth and narrowed her eyes, a look of irritation playing over her features.

He struggled to keep up when she walked into the kitchen and started to unload the box. "Thanks for this."

She turned to him and looked down at the leg he had bent behind him. "When do you see the doctor again?"

"I have an appointment with Doc Newell tomorrow."

"Are you going to be able to drive?"

"Since it's my left leg I hope so, though I haven't tried yet."

"What time is your appointment?"

"Nine."

"I'll send Colton over to take you." She pulled a plastic container full of what he assumed was soup out of the box and put it in his fridge.

Just one look at Alex's determined expression, and Brandt knew it was fruitless to argue. "Thanks. I would appreciate the ride."

"There's enough food to get you through to Wednesday. Give Colton a shopping list tomorrow and I'll pick up anything else you need." She pulled more containers from the box. "Mom is bringing over a ham with all the trimmings tomorrow. I'll tell her to add a loaf of bread so you can make sandwiches with the leftovers."

"I have bread."

"And Aunt Glenda is bringing something for your dinner on Wednesday."

"That's really nice, Alex, but totally unnecessary. I don't want to put anyone out."

She patted his chest, completely ignoring his objections. "Don't eat all those cookies at one sitting."

He situated the crutches under his arms again.

"I can let myself out. You need to heal quickly." She smirked. "I'd sure hate for you to miss the baseball game."

He chuckled at her sarcasm. "Yeah, I just bet you would."

The next time Brandt answered the door, JT and State Fire Marshal Chet Roberts were on the front porch. Chet had questioned Brandt after the hardware store fire, so they were acquainted. Brandt invited them in and went through the handshake and "Yes, I remember you."

"How's the leg?" JT asked.

"Sore. I see Doc Newell tomorrow."

"Do you need a ride?"

"Alex already volunteered Colton." Brandt gestured for them to sit, and lowered himself into a chair opposite Chet. "Would you like some water or a soda?"

"No, thank you," Chet said. "I'm here—"

"I know why you're here, and I'll probably be even less help than the last time."

After taking a seat, JT leaned forward, elbows on knees. "You saw two teenagers."

"I'm guessing they were teenagers by their build. Because of the distance between us, I couldn't testify to that. I didn't see their faces. They were wearing ski masks and dark clothing. The only thing I can say for certain is one was shorter than the other, and they both wore black trench coats."

"With the ski masks, you couldn't see their hair."

"No."

"Where'd you first see them?" Chet asked.

"On the square between Patsy's and Kimball's. I was trying to focus on them through the dark, but turned my head when I heard a whistle from the opposite direction."

Chet leaned forward, mimicking JT. "What kind of a whistle?"

"A low human whistle. It wasn't like the whistle you'd use to call a dog, rather like a warning or signal. It came from the opposite side of the square, but I didn't see anything. When I glanced back, the two figures were gone. The only place they could have disappeared so quickly was the alley. I crossed the square and started down the alley just as flames shot skyward. When I reached the parking lot behind Patsy's, the two boys were running around the corner where the driveway enters the parking lot."

"Are you sure they were boys and not girls?" Chet asked.

"No, I'm only guessing by the way they ran."

"What were you doing out there at that time of night?"

Brandt glanced at JT. "I couldn't sleep and thought some fresh air might help."

"If I showed you a picture—"

"Even with a picture I couldn't identify them, JT. I'm sorry. I know you want to get these guys. I wish I could help."

Chet leaned back on the sofa. "Tell me more about the whistle you heard. You said it was low, like a warning. Do you think whoever made the noise saw you?"

"I have no idea. I didn't see anyone." Brandt inhaled with a hiss when he tried to reposition his leg. "It might have been a third person signaling, but it could have been completely unrelated. Someone like me, out walking and whistling." *Though I don't think so*. "The only thing I feel certain of is the pallets had already been set in place and, based on how quickly the fire flared, gasoline or some other accelerant had already been poured on that wood."

He was at the door, again, an hour later. Patsy bustled inside, carrying another box. On tiptoe, she kissed his cheek. "I can't thank you enough for saving my shop."

"It was nothing, Patsy."

"Well, it's something to me. You saved my baby, my livelihood."

He hobbled into the kitchen after her. She set the box on the counter and started unloading the contents. "Carolyn made a special cake for you, and I brought a chicken casserole. It'll freeze until you're ready to bake it. The instructions are here." She placed a piece of paper on the countertop. "You also have free pastries for life."

He chuckled, feeling a little overwhelmed by everyone's generosity. "I have to say, that is tempting, but not necessary."

She turned to him and put her hand on a cocked hip. "Colton would snap that offer up in a heartbeat."

"Colton has a sweet tooth the size of Texas."

"That is true." She went back to unloading the box. "Have you apologized to Jillian?"

And we're back to my personal life. "I haven't talked to Jillian. Yet."

"The men of this town are so darned stubborn. Anyone with eyes can see you two belong together. I'm not sure why you're fighting it."

"I am a little stubborn, but I plan to talk to her." Patsy opened her mouth, but he held up his hand to stop her. "My love life isn't up for discussion."

"You don't have a love life."

He blew out a breath of frustration. "Thanks for the food, but my leg is killing me. I really need to prop it up for a while."

"Okay, okay. I'll get out of your hair, but, just so you know, I think you need to fix things before it's too late."

In reply, Brandt hobbled out of the kitchen. He needed a nap.

CHAPTER 15

After much prodding, poking, and many questions, Doc Newell pushed his glasses up his nose. "I'm just repeating what the ER doctor said, you ruptured your hamstring. I also agree that you shouldn't need surgery. By tomorrow try getting around without the crutches. I'll have Nan come in and fit you with a brace."

Brandt accepted the doctor's help sitting up on the exam table. "The ER doctor didn't tell me much besides the diagnosis and that I should see you. How do I heal a ruptured hamstring?"

"Rest, cold compresses, and elevation, stretching and strengthening exercises." Doc Newell sat at the desk in the exam room and opened his laptop. "I'll print out some information for you, but the quickest way is physical therapy. Jillian Saunders doesn't have an office, but Glenda and Dawson let her use a room at the gym when I send someone to her."

Jillian.

Doc Newell turned on his stool and pulled off his glasses, polishing the lens with a cloth retrieved from the breast pocket of his shirt. "I'd recommend doing what you're doing for the rest of the week. Relax, ice, and elevate. Then let Jillian set up a schedule for you. She'll have to help you with some of the exercises and stretches, and some you can do on your own."

"I went to Harrisville for physical therapy when I broke my leg."

"Why go all the way to Harrisville when Jillian is here in town?" Dr. Newell slid his glasses back into place. "I sure wish Get Fit had that indoor pool finished. Aquatic therapy would be ideal for you."

"How long?"

"Judging from the amount of pain you're in, I'd recommend working with Jillian for about three weeks. Then you can start working on your own." Doc Newell stood. "I hear you hurt it chasing our arsonists."

Brandt chuckled. "In a sorry attempt to chase our arsonists."

"Sounds like you were in the right place at the right time. You saved Patsy's shop and possibly more."

"I did what anyone in the same place would have done. I'm just sorry I couldn't catch at least one of them." *And mad that my leg gave out trying.*

An hour after his appointment, Brandt sat on the sofa, leg elevated, thinking about Jillian. Dr. Newell was right about not driving to Harrisville if she was willing to help him here in town. The question was would she be willing?

Someone knocked. "Come in," he hollered, too tired to get up.

Alex walked in carrying a couple of grocery bags. "What did Doc Newell say?"

Brandt leaned his head back against his leather sofa. "Same thing the ER doctor said. I ruptured my hamstring." He closed his eyes for the next part. "He thinks three or four weeks of physical therapy should do the trick."

When he opened his eyes, Alex was wearing the grin of satisfaction he expected. "I can go to Harrisville. That's where I went for my broken leg."

"Which is a silly waste of gas and time when Jillian is here in town." She walked into the kitchen with the bags. "I brought over the food Mom was going to bring. She's babysitting Sophia today."

"Thank you, and tell your mom thanks. I really can cook, though."

"Rita sent over her prize-winning brownies. Dad teases everyone that she caught two husbands with them, so I'd eat them sparingly."

He smiled, listening to Alex bang around in the kitchen.

A minute later she was standing next to him. "When do you start therapy?"

"I have to call and set up an appointment."

"With Jillian?"

"Yes, Alex, I'll see Jillian." *If she'll see me*. He hoped he sounded as exasperated as he felt.

"Good. While you're there, maybe you should ask her about the guy you saw her with. You might be surprised by the answer."

He raised his head. "You talked to her?"

Alex ignored his question. "You'd be crazy to let your pride ruin something special."

He couldn't deny it. The connection he felt with Jillian continued nagging at him. But so did the image of her being lifted off her feet by someone else. "I'll talk to her."

Alex patted his cheek. "I knew you were a smart man."

~

Jillian raised her fisted hands over her head in a hallelujah moment. She'd finally unscrambled the mess a well-meaning teenager made of the gym's records. Glenda and Dawson had been ecstatic to see new memberships had almost doubled in two weeks. But it was the names in the computer that had doubled, not the memberships. She still hadn't figured out how the mistake was made, but the new password she'd installed should prevent it from happening again.

Her cell phone rang and she picked it up without taking her eyes off the computer screen. "Hello?"

"Jillian? It's Brandt."

Her heart thumped hard once. Twice. So hard it took her breath away. "H-hi."

"How are you?"

How am I? she wanted to ask. *How am I after you jumped to conclusions and cancelled our date, then stopped calling completely?* Instead, she put a hand to her chest and swallowed hard. "Fine." *F* for freaked out, *I* for insecure—*thanks so much for that*—*N* for nervous, *E* for emotional. She took a fortifying breath. "I heard about your accident. Are you okay?"

"Hobbling around on crutches for the second time in a year. Doc Newell suggested I call you to schedule physical therapy."

Her chest deflated. He wasn't calling to talk or to apologize, but because he needed her help. Jillian let her head fall back against her office chair. *Thanks, Doc.* He was determined she use her degree. Just yesterday he'd paid Glenda and Dawson a visit about setting up a physical therapy space in the new addition, and they agreed.

"It would give us an opportunity to talk."

You should have looked for that opportunity six weeks ago!

"Please, Jillian."

How could she say no when she went to school for this very reason? "What day is good for you?"

He chuckled, and she imagined his dimple. "Doc said I should start next week. Any time you say, I'll be there."

She could tell him she had a completely booked schedule followed by dates every night next week. The first was true, the second a complete lie. "Are you able to drive?"

"I drove today for the first time. Luckily I hurt my left leg."

She turned to her computer and pulled up her schedule for the next day. She had solid back-to-back classes and clients, but she clocked out at five. "Can you be at the gym by five thirty tomorrow?" That would give her time to run home, feed Henry, and get back. "Let me assess the damage, then we'll set up a fixed schedule for next week."

"I'll see you then. Thank you, Jillian."

She said goodbye and disconnected the call with a pounding heart. Tomorrow she would tell him his assumptions about her with another man were wrong. She would tell him the truth, just as Alex had nagged her to do. She might even relish the surprise on his face, when she told him she'd been hugging *her brother*.

The fact he hadn't come to her about what he saw still bothered her, though she knew, deep down, she would have made the same assumptions. She still liked to think she would have talked to him rather than break everything off with no explanation.

She rolled a pencil back and forth across her desk with her fingertips. At least she would have the chance to tell him the truth tomorrow. Then she could put the entire episode behind her. The awkwardness would be gone and, she hoped, they could go forward as friends. Since baseball practice began, she'd decided she would be okay with just friends.

Alex walked in, brightening her dreary office with a sunny smile. "Hey, girlfriend."

Jillian was grateful for the interruption. "Hey, Alex. What brings you in today?"

"Flower delivery for Aunt Glenda." Alex glanced in the small mirror behind Jillian's door, touching her blond hair, which was in a businesslike knot on the back of her head. "It just started raining, and I have to attend a ribbon cutting of Harrisville's new town hall in an hour."

"You look beautiful as always." Jillian stared at the wall in front of her desk, anxious to be in her new office after the gym expansion was finished. She'd love to see the weather outside. Knowing a move was around the corner made the walls close in on her a little more every day. "I was hoping the rain would hold off until after the Smoke Eaters' practice tonight. We haven't been able to get together as often as your team."

Alex sat in the only other chair in the office. "Speaking of Brandt."

Jillian glanced at her. "We weren't speaking of Brandt."

"Technically we weren't"—Alex's eyes twinkled with merriment—"but we were talking about baseball, so we'll pretend Brandt was already mentioned."

"Okay." Jillian drew the word out, not sure she wanted to know where this conversation was headed.

"I've been to see him a couple of times. He's hobbling around on crutches."

Jillian picked up her cell phone and wiggled it back and forth. "I just talked to him."

"You did?"

"He's coming in tomorrow so we can start his physical therapy."

Alex pressed her lips together, but her grin broke through. "That is the best news I've heard in days and days. Are you going to talk to him?"

Jillian nodded. "I plan to tell him he shouldn't have jumped to conclusions."

"But in a nice way, I hope."

"Have you ever known me to be mean?"

"No, you're always nice. Too nice sometimes. You and Carolyn don't have a mean bone in your bodies."

Not true.

Alex stood. "I better get to Harrisville. I just came by to talk to you about Brandt."

Jillian narrowed her eyes. "I thought you came by to deliver flowers."

"That too." Alex was skilled enough to execute a convincingly wide-eyed, innocence. "I have faith things will work themselves out once you and Brandt spend a few minutes together."

Halfway out the door, Alex glanced over her shoulder. "Oh, we're planning a girls' night out tomorrow night at seven, but you'll probably have a hot date."

Jillian shook her head. "I'll meet you at Rowdy's."

Alex winked. "We'll see, girlfriend."

Jillian sat at her desk for a long minute after Alex left and accepted the stillness that settled over her heart. Even if she and Brandt came to an understanding and he asked her out, she wasn't going to make it easy for him. Not because she was mad, but because she was hurt and maybe a little stubborn. If he didn't ask her out, and if her heart cooperated, she would move on.

She stood and reached high overhead to stretch out her tight muscles. Time to visit Glenda and Dawson's office with the good news that she'd figured out the membership records. After that she'd walk through the gym and greet clients, offer a little encouragement. She felt too peaceful to work at her desk any longer. Now she'd figured out the problem, it would take a few more hours to straighten it out, but that could wait until tomorrow.

~

Jillian wasn't in sight when Brandt got to the gym, and he had no idea where she wanted him, so he limped over to the desk to wait. He didn't feel nervous often and wished he didn't now. In his line of work, it was far better to remain calm and in control of situations before they got out of hand. He'd botched this situation almost from the beginning.

The girl at the front desk finished what she was doing and turned to him. "Hi."

"Hey, I'm here for a physical therapy session with Jillian."

"Jillian Saunders?" The girl's mouth turned down in a frown. "She went home."

"She went home?"

"Yeah, she got off at five."

"I'm here, I'm here," Jillian said, rushing through the door. She was flushed, as if she'd been running. "Sorry. I had to go home and feed Henry."

"Wait." Brandt studied her big brown eyes a moment. "You're doing this off the clock?"

Jillian lifted a shoulder. "It's the only time I had on my schedule. This will just be a quick evaluation. We'll set up something during my gym hours after tonight."

"I can't let you do this, Jillian."

She beckoned for him to follow. "It'll take less than an hour. No big deal."

It was a big deal to him. She shouldn't have to come

back into work, but he followed rather than protest, since she'd already walked away. She opened the door to a small room with no windows. There was a massage table close to one of the walls, and a mat on the floor. "I'm glad you wore shorts. I should have told you it's easier to work with shorts on."

"Alas, this isn't my first rodeo."

She smiled for the first time. "No, I guess you know the drill. We'll start with you on the table."

He swung inside the room and she closed the door behind them. He was able to lift his weight up using his arms, only wincing slightly when his leg met the table.

She bent over his leg, and her hair, still pulled back in a ponytail, fell over one shoulder. It took a lot of willpower to resist reaching out to touch its softness as she released the compression band around his knee.

He swallowed. "Maybe we should talk first so there isn't any awkwardness between us." *If that's possible*.

When she straightened, he noticed a look of determination in her eyes and around her mouth. And something else he couldn't read. He realized in that moment he really hoped what he saw wasn't real. His desire for things to work between them was stronger than ever.

"I agree we should talk, but let me work on your leg first."

"Okay." He stared at the red strands running through her brown hair and glistening under the overhead lights. "Thank you for coming back in tonight. If I'd known you were doing it off the clock, I would have picked another time."

"I'm off the clock for the gym, but your insurance will cover some of this, and you'll pay the portion they don't." Her eyebrow arched in adorable defiance. "So you see, I'm not just here out of the goodness of my heart. When we're done, I'll have you fill out the necessary paperwork. I just wanted to see what we're dealing with first and talk to Doc Newell."

Brandt nodded, his ego deflating just a little, like the slow leak of a balloon without the squeaky sound.

"Why don't you lie facedown and let me feel around back there."

He lifted a brow and got the reaction he'd hoped for when a pretty pink spread across her cheekbones. "Sure." After some maneuvering, he was lying on his chest.

"Does your scar cause you any problems?"

He couldn't see her face but could hear the concern in her voice. "Not much. Every once in a while the skin feels tight, but I use a cream that helps."

He felt her cool hand on his calf, just below the scars on the right leg. "How bad is the PTSD?"

"Surprisingly low. Usually only a moment's hesitation. I wouldn't continue to fight fires if it was bad. As a paramedic, I'm not the first one in when we have a fire." He waited a beat. "Does my scar bother you?"

"No." Like the concern, he could now hear the smile in her voice. "I'm going to lift your shorts up just a little."

He felt his shorts moving up his leg and she tucked the excess material under the front of his left thigh. Her fingers moved along his skin, simply touching at first, then massaging only the surface of his leg.

"I bet this bruise is tender."

"I'm not sure which hurts worse."

"Doc Newell told you to wear the compression band, ice for thirty minutes every three or four hours, and elevate when you're sitting or lying down?"

She'd obviously been on the phone with Doc. "Right."

"We'll start out slowly tonight with a gentle massage followed by slight resistance work. Does this hurt?"

"No."

Using her palms, she lightly massaged up his thigh, then back down over his calf to his heel.

"If it hurts at all, tell me. Tonight is about slow and gentle. Are you taking any painkillers?"

"I took them the first four days, but I haven't had one today."

"You might want to take one before you go to bed tonight."

Her hands moved around to the side of his thigh. He felt a slight pressure along the back of his leg, but no pain.

"I'll see if I can sleep first. I don't like taking them."

"You'll need to ice again tomorrow, and continue to elevate your leg when you're at home."

They were silent while she continued to work the back of his thigh. If he wasn't so anxious to talk to her, he might have fallen asleep it felt so good. But he wanted to be wide-awake for their talk. He wanted to read her expressions, see her eyes.

"Bend your leg at the knee about forty-five degrees."

He did as she asked.

"Does that hurt?"

"No."

"I'm going to place my hands on your heel." She did. "Very slowly, I want you to try to bend it farther."

A sharp pain ratcheted up the back of his leg as soon as he tried to pull against her resistance, and his breath caught in his throat.

"Stop. You're not ready for any resistance exercises yet."

She lowered his leg and gently began to knead the muscle again. He lost track of time while she massaged him back into relaxation.

"Can I sleep here tonight? I haven't felt this relaxed since I fell." Which wasn't true. He hadn't felt this relaxed since that night on Jillian's sofa when they intended to watch a movie but ended up making out like a couple of teenagers.

She moved around the table. "Let me help you sit up."

He struggled to sit with her support, disappointed their time was up.

"How does it feel?"

"Okay. It feels…good."

"That's all for tonight. Take it easy, ice, and elevate. Try to keep your weight off it as much as possible. Can you be here at ten tomorrow morning?"

"Sure."

She thumbed over her shoulder as she backed toward the door. "I'll get those papers for you to fill out."

"I saw you."

His words stopped her. She ran her bottom lip through her teeth. "Alex told me."

His first thought was he should have known that either Alex or Patsy would try to interfere. His second was that Jillian didn't deny anything. "I know we hadn't made any promises to each other, but I thought…."

"Thought what?" She tucked a wayward strand of hair behind her ear while lifting her chin. "You saw me jump into another man's arms and kiss him. Alex said you also saw us go to Noelle's for dinner. If you'd come in instead of assuming, I could have introduced you to my brother."

He literally felt the blood drain from his face. "That man was your brother?"

"My marine-biologist brother, Sam, was passing through town on his way to his next assignment."

He wasn't ready to admit to total idiocy. "But you told me you had to work that night."

"Yes, I did, but Mason agreed to watch Sophia, so Glenda was able to teach the class after all. She gave me the night off. I was on my way to tell you when Sam surprised me."

The absurdity of what she was telling him made him throw his head back and laugh, the sound so loud it surprised him as much as her. All this time he'd assumed she was seeing someone else, and all she'd done was go to dinner with her brother.

She raised her eyebrows, her lips a tight line. "That's funny?"

The laugh died in his throat. "No, it's sad that I wasted time being angry, confused"—*and jealous*—"because you were hugging your brother. I'm a dunce."

She didn't disagree.

"I should have talked to you. I just assumed what I saw was.... I'm sorry."

She glanced at the floor. "Alex told me about your fiancée, so I can understand why you might assume. I just wish you had come and talked to me."

"I should have." He couldn't believe he'd been so stupid, and wasted so much of the time they could have been spending together. "I'm sorry I jumped to conclusions, Jillian. I hope you'll accept my apology."

She looked him in the eye for a long moment, then nodded. "I do."

"Do you forgive me enough to go out with me again?"

He watched several emotions race across her face. Wide-eyed surprise changed to a frown. Then she bit her lower lip. "I'm going to get those papers for you to fill out. I'll be back."

He was surprised when she walked out of the room without giving him an answer.

CHAPTER 16

Jillian left the gym ahead of Brandt, abandoning him to fill out his insurance paperwork.

She was confused by the clamor of emotions buffeting her. Happy because Brandt wanted to go out with her, yet hurt because he'd believed the worst and turned his back on her because of it. Elated that she had the ability to make him wait—which wasn't like her at all—and annoyed when guilt immediately overrode the elation. She'd never been in this position before.

Most of all, she couldn't believe she left the gym without giving him an answer.

He apologized. Twice. And she said she forgave him, but was it true? *Yes. People make mistakes. I've made mistakes.*

Minutes later she walked into Rowdy's and waved to Stella and Carolyn, who were already at a table. Rowdy brought over a large platter of nachos with extra jalapeños and took their drink order.

"You're awfully smiley tonight," Stella said.

"Am I?" Jillian hadn't realized she brought her smile in

with her. "Despite a mess-up with memberships, I...had a good day at work."

"Anything you want to tell us about?" Carolyn asked.

Jillian shook her head, not ready to share. "Nothing particular."

"Well, I'm in a great mood. Even though it's raining, the weather is warming up, and school will be out in five weeks," Stella said.

"You'll miss your students." Carolyn took a chip and popped it in her mouth.

"You always do," Jillian added. She turned to Carolyn. "Tell us about your wedding plans."

"I wanted something small because of the cost, but Alice wouldn't hear of it. Her baby boy is getting married, and she wants a big to-do."

"Did you tell her it's your wedding?" Stella asked.

Carolyn raised a brow at Stella. "Could you tell sweet Alice Garrett something like that?"

Stella shook her head. "No."

Carolyn shrugged. "Besides, I don't mind. My first wedding was in a judge's chambers. I was alone and nervous."

"This time around, you can be nervous in front of a whole crowd." Stella laughed until she snorted.

Jillian waved Stella's comment away. "There's nothing to be nervous about. We'll all be there for you."

Misty and Alex joined them, followed by Jolie, out for the first time since Riley Jean's birth. Alex glanced Jillian's way, sending her a questioning, raised-eyebrow, tell-me-good-news look. Jillian nodded and Alex flashed a smug grin.

The evening passed too quickly, but with plenty of laughter, as usual. Jillian enjoyed her night out with the girls, though Brandt crowded her mind with other thoughts. She had to be reminded of the conversation several times. No one but Alex seemed to notice.

He still wants to go out with me repeated like a weather broadcast before a big storm.

~

Brandt left the gym feeling a little humiliated. Her brother! He'd spent weeks being jealous because Jillian was hugging her brother.

He also feeling a little deflated. She hadn't even waited for him to fill out the insurance papers. He guessed he should be grateful she accepted his feeble apology.

Brandt hadn't expected Jillian to jump into his arms and declare her undying love. He hadn't even expected to be forgiven immediately, but he had hoped she would accept his offer of a date, hoped they could pick up where they left off. Why not? Their tiff hadn't even been a tiff, just a simple misunderstanding. He'd apologized, admitted he was a dunce, so why couldn't they just move on?

Not ready to sit alone in his quiet house the rest of the evening, he drove to Noelle's Café for dinner. Noelle greeted him with her usual cheerfulness and showed him to a booth where he could put his leg up on a nearby chair.

"You sure have a long face for a hero."

He chuckled. "I'm no hero. I did what anyone would have done, your husband included."

She whipped out her order pad and plucked a pencil from behind her ear. "Well, you're Patsy's hero, so dinner's on the house."

"You don't have to do that, Noelle."

"It's already done. What can I get you?"

Not too proud to accept a free meal, he said, "I'll have a burger and fries."

"How about a chocolate shake?"

"Sounds great."

While waiting for his dinner, he watched four Goth teenagers walk in and take a table in the back corner. He didn't recognize the kids as locals and wondered if they were part of the gang JT suspected of setting fires around town. None of them wore a trench coat tonight, and neither of the boys he saw walking in front of the hardware store a year ago were with them. He wished he'd gotten a better look at the boys behind Patsy's. He wasn't a hero, but he was glad a sense that something wasn't quite right had kicked in, otherwise Patsy's might have been reduced to ashes.

Noelle set his dinner and a milkshake in front of him. "Enjoy."

He did. Noelle's had been a town favorite ever since she opened the doors a few years earlier. She'd moved here after a distant uncle left her the boarded-up property in his will. After renovating the place into a retro café, she filled the menu with homemade comfort foods and amazing desserts.

She came back twenty minutes later, but instead of clearing his empty dishes, she slid onto the opposite bench. "Why the long face? Is it your injury that has you so down?"

"I'm mad I hurt the same leg twice in a year, but it'll heal."

"I'm a great listener." She sat back, getting comfortable. "As good as any female bartender."

He laughed and leaned back too. She obviously wasn't going anywhere until he told her what was bothering him, and he wouldn't mind the listening ear. "Okay. It's not my leg, it's Jillian."

"Aww, woman trouble. My specialty. What happened?"

He watched Noelle's expression while he told her everything. He didn't even leave out the part about him being an idiot. When he finished, he waited, but she didn't say anything. "So…?" he prompted.

She leaned forward and rested her elbows on the table. "I said I was a good listener. I didn't say anything about giving out advice."

"Well…I need some."

"Do you like her?"

He chuckled again. Her question made him feel as if he were back in middle school, passing notes with the question, *Do you like her? Check below.* Always followed by three boxes with multiple-choice answers of *Yes*, *No*, or *Maybe*. He mentally colored in the box next to *Yes*. "I like her. We have a lot in common, and I think she could be...."

"The one," Noelle said, filling in the end of his sentence. "Then you can't give up. If you think she's worth it, fight. Ask her out again and again. And again. Do whatever it takes. But also try to understand why she's feeling the way she is. You didn't trust her. And to top it off, you cancelled your date without any explanation, so you also lost her trust. That doesn't just repair itself overnight. You have to be patiently persistent."

He nodded. What she said made sense, but it would be hard to be patient. Now they'd cleared the air, he was ready to move forward, full speed ahead.

Noelle pushed to her feet with a wink and collected his empty plates. "Gosh, it's hard to be patient when you're in love."

"I never said I was in love."

She winked. "You didn't have to."

Smiling up at Noelle felt good. She was right, he was in love with Jillian. He'd do whatever was necessary to convince her he was sorry, to let her know he wanted them to try again. "Thanks, Noelle."

"Anytime. Let me know how things go." She patted his shoulder before disappearing into the kitchen.

~

Jillian felt unexpectedly exhilarated when she woke the next morning to birds singing outside her window. Her talk with Brandt had lifted a weight she didn't realize she was carrying.

An hour later she kissed Henry goodbye and walked out of her apartment to be greeted by a gorgeous day. The sun was shining, the sky was a brilliant blue, and spring flowers were in full bloom thanks to the recent rain in Eden Falls. She'd also see Brandt for his therapy appointment. Jillian wanted to skip all the way to Get Fit.

Brandt asked her to forgive him for making assumptions so they could try again. Of course she forgave him. Holding grudges only made a burden heavier. In fact, the lightness she felt this morning was proof she should have asked him why he stopped calling. Alex was right. This could have been cleared up weeks ago, which put some of the blame back on her shoulders.

Brandt hadn't intended to hurt her, only to protect his own heart. She couldn't fault him for that. They'd straightened out their misunderstanding, and her heart was singing a happy tune. Even if they never went out again, she knew they would be friends.

She felt certain, with slow, steady work, Brandt's hamstring would heal in time for him to play in the Memorial Day baseball game. Great news for the Smoke Eaters. At their last practice, everyone on the team wanted to know if he'd be back. They didn't want to lose their pitcher for the second year in a row.

After she dropped her purse in her office, she went out to meet her first appointment of the day. Still crusty but much slimmer, Marty Graw met her with a bouquet that included bright, cheerful Gerbera daisies. Tears burned the backs of her eyes as he held the flowers out. "To be clear, these aren't from me. They're from my wife. She likes the new me. And…I guess I do too." A smile twitched at the corners of his mouth. "I told her you liked those daisy things, so she got you some."

"Does this mean you don't hate me anymore?" she asked, accepting the flowers.

He hung his head in feigned shame. "I never really hated you. I just didn't like you. At all."

She laughed. "Thank you, Marty. You've worked hard, and I hope you'll keep it up. Tell your wife thank you for the beautiful flowers." She ran a fingertip over a Gerbera petal, grateful for the beauties of nature. "Have you warmed up?"

Marty's grin finally broke through. "What do you think?"

"Ten minutes on the stationary bike while I put these in water." She decided long ago that not warming up before their session was Marty's way of cutting his workout ten minutes short, so her warm-up sessions had gone from two minutes to ten. *I'm not as dumb as you think I am, Marty.*

She always felt a lift of spirits, a euphoric excitement when one of her clients met a goal, but today's was extra special. She rode the high through Marty's workout and a yoga class. She might just be able to hang on to this exhilaration for the rest of the week.

To top everything off with sprinkles, Glenda stopped her when she was headed to the front desk to meet Brandt. "I'll take your afternoon classes so you can have a few hours off after Brandt's appointment."

"You don't have to do that."

"It's done. You've picked up extra hours to cover for me

and Dawson during our many renovation meetings, so enjoy the sunshiny afternoon."

"What does one do with a Saturday afternoon off?"

Glenda nodded toward the front desk where Brandt stood. "I think you can come up with something. By the way"—she threaded her hand through Jillian's arm when they stopped in front of Brandt—"that new physical therapy room is going to come in handy if Mr. Smith keeps injuring his leg."

Jillian shook her head with an exaggerated sigh at Glenda's teasing. The new space was going to be fabulous thanks to Doc Newell's recommendations. The indoor pool would also come in handy for working with injuries.

"This will be the last time I hurt this leg." Brandt flashed his heart-stopping dimple.

Jillian smiled back.

~

Brandt took Jillian's smile as a good sign.

"How does your leg feel?"

"It actually felt a little looser this morning when I woke up. I didn't have as much trouble maneuvering around."

"Good." She tipped her head. "Come on back and we'll get started."

Brandt followed her across the gym to the same room they used the night before. She motioned to the table and he boosted himself up.

"Let's start with a massage. Lie down on your back first."

She removed his shoe and sock, and massaged him into complete relaxation.

"You have great hands," he said.

"You have great muscles."

He laughed. "No one's ever told me that before."

She glanced at him through a veil of eyelashes. “No, but I bet the thought has gone through plenty of female minds.”

Her boldness surprised him. “Has anyone ever told you that you have beautiful eyes?”

She smiled without making eye contact. “Does my dad count?”

Somehow, her admission surprised and pleased him. Was he the first? He raised up on an elbow, put a finger under her chin, and turned her face toward him. “Have you had a chance to decide if you forgive me enough to go out with me?”

A pretty pink moved across her face. “I already told you, I forgive you.”

“You didn’t answer my question.”

She lifted a shoulder in an apologetic shrug and quirked her mouth to one side. “I don’t date clients.”

“You’re joking.” He waited for the smile that didn’t come. “You’re not joking.”

“Hard-and-fast rule.” She lifted her chin away from his touch. “Time to turn over so I can work on the back of your leg.”

He wasn’t sure how to react. Laugh. Maybe punch something—namely Doc Newell for suggesting he become a client. Though without Doc’s recommendation, he might not have talked to Jillian yet.

The odds were definitely against him, but it just reinforced his determination. She was talking to him, which was a good sign. She was even joking a little, another good sign. While he was a client, he’d work on her, make her believe they belonged together. Because they did. He would be persistent and patient, just as Noelle suggested last night.

Thirty minutes later, she patted his calf. “That’s it for today.”

Brandt made a feeble attempt to turn over, but every

muscle in his body was as wobbly as Jell-O. Jillian held out her hand and slowly pulled him to a sitting position. She slid his sock into place and tied his shoe like he was a helpless child, which was almost true. "No exercises?"

"We'll start those next week. Continue doing what you're doing through the weekend. Can you come in at eleven on Monday?"

"I'll be here."

"See you then."

She disappeared before he could say anything. He limped to the door and watched her go into her office. He followed. She was bent over her desk when he stopped at the door. His gaze followed the curve of her back, all the way down to her shapely calves.

She straightened and gasped when she saw him standing so close.

"You left before I could ask you to lunch."

"I told you, I don't—"

"Date clients." He held up his hands palms out. "We won't call it a date."

She leaned against the corner of her desk, holding her purse in front of her like a shield. "What will we call it?"

He glanced at the vase of flowers sitting on her desk and wondered who they were from. "How about a thank-you for working me into your busy schedule?"

"That's very tempting since I'm hungry, but I already have plans."

He nodded toward the bouquet. "With whoever gave you those flowers?"

She laughed, the sound washing over him pleasantly. "No, with a friend."

She walked toward him, forcing him to back out of her office. He noticed she didn't tell him who gave her the flowers, or who she was having lunch with. Jealousy swung a heavy fist, hitting him square in the chest. She pulled the door closed behind her. "Rest your leg over the weekend."

He nodded and watched her walk across the gym, out into the sunshine.

~

Jillian knocked on Jolie's back door before opening it and peeking inside. "Hellooo."

"Come in. I'm in the baby's room," Jolie called out.

Jillian followed the sound of crying and stopped outside the cotton-candy pink room with flounces, ruffles, and tulle—a little girl's dream. Baby Riley was red-faced angry, and her mama, pacing in front of the bassinet, looked frazzled. She had as many tears running down her cheeks as the baby.

"Ohhh." Jillian gave Jolie a sideways hug. "Rough day?"

"She's been crying for an hour…and I can't get her to settle down. I've fed her and rocked her and ch-changed her…."

Jillian eased the baby from Jolie's arms and cradled her tense, red-faced soon-to-be-goddaughter against her chest. "What are you so mad about, sweetheart?"

"I think she's too tired to sleep." Jolie slumped against the wall, wiping tears and blowing her nose in a burp cloth she pulled from her shoulder.

Jillian sat in a nearby rocker. Already the baby was settling down. "Go make some tea or take a bath or a nap. I'll watch her for a while."

"How're you doing that?"

"I think she's sensing your anxiety. Go take care of yourself." Jillian set the rocker in motion and tucked a blanket securely around the sweet baby. "We'll be fine."

She spent the next hour rocking, singing softly, and

smelling the lavender softness surrounding them both, until Jolie trudged into the room rubbing her eyes while stifling a yawn. "Sorry. I invited you to go shopping with us, and instead took a heavenly nap."

"Don't worry about it. I completely enjoyed my time with this darling."

After looking down at her sleeping daughter's face, Jolie sat on the floor with her back against the wall. "Being a mom is harder than I thought it would be, but so worth it."

Jillian ran her knuckle over Riley's smooth cheek. "I'm sure it is. Remember how we always talked about having our kids close together so they could play with each other?"

"Yes." Jolie leaned forward, wrapping her arms around her knees. "You'll make a good mom. Look how easily you quieted my squawking daughter. By the way, a little birdie told me you're helping Brandt with his physical therapy."

"Eden Falls has too many little birdies," Jillian replied, taking care to laugh softly so she wouldn't disturb Riley.

Jolie raised her eyebrows in question.

"Yes, I'm helping him."

"You're nicer than I would be. After what he did—"

"He had a reason. Remember when Sam stopped in town? Brandt saw me hugging him and, since he's never met my brother, he thought I was seeing someone else."

"That's why he stopped calling?"

Jillian patted Riley's little bottom when she squirmed. "He assumed, but both you and I would have done the same thing."

"He could have asked you about it."

"Yes, he could have, and he agrees he should have. He apologized, and I accepted his apology. Then he asked me out and I told him I don't date clients."

"Oh, no way." Jolie sputtered out a laugh. "That is perfect. You finally clear things up, and you still can't date."

Jillian shrugged.

Riley blinked her eyes open and stared up at Jillian, who ran a hand over the baby's cap of dark hair. "Hello, sweetheart. Did you have a nice nap?"

The baby immediately turned her open mouth toward Jillian's body. "Uh-oh, someone's hungry."

Jolie stood and took the baby while Jillian relinquished the rocker. She and Jolie visited while Jolie changed and then nursed her daughter. For the first time in her life, Jillian felt her biological clock's alarm go off. More than wanting a career, she'd always dreamed of being a wife and mother, always planned to have a family.

She and Jolie had discussed it at length as teenagers. They'd plan play dates and meet at the park with the kids and a picnic basket. When the kids got older, they'd spend summer afternoons at the town's swimming pool or play on the grassy area at the foot of the waterfall. She could imagine far enough into the future to see herself sitting on a porch with grandchildren gathered around for story time.

She could even picture Grandpa Brandt beside her, a grandchild on each knee.

CHAPTER 17

The weather was so gorgeous after church that Jillian looked forward to the drive out to Saunders' Orchards. Driving with the windows down, she relished the warm breeze tangling through her hair.

Spending time with family on lazy Sunday afternoons was the best.

Maneuvering down her parents' long dirt drive, she inhaled the sweet spring air. Fruit trees laden with flowers whose fragrances were so heady, memories of childhood overwhelmed her.

When she was young, she loved when the weather warmed enough that she could open her bedroom windows and let the breeze push the curtains aside with the fragrant scent of apple blossoms, along with the lilacs lining the yard. She missed that part of living in the country. Mrs. O'Malley didn't have any blooming trees and very few flowers in her yard.

Jillian parked her car next to her dad's old pickup and waved to her mom, who'd stepped out onto the back porch.

She pointed to the orchard, and her mother nodded, understanding the magnetic pull of springtime under the trees.

Just past the barn, her father was bent over a tractor engine, and she imagined the mechanical smell of him mixed with the outdoors. Her oldest brother Joe walked out of the barn and waved. This was the brother who would continue to work the orchard after their parents couldn't. He and his wife Raelyn loved life here. Sam wasn't a farmer, and had no desire to inherit the orchards. And her sister Rachel moved around the country with her Air Force pilot husband.

Jillian ambled between the rows of trees, surrounded by sunshine. Birds flitted overhead, filling the air with happy melodies. She found a perfect spot and lay down.

Her mother found her on her back staring up at the blue sky through hundreds of apple blossoms. She looked down into Jillian's face. "I've been wandering around looking for you for fifteen minutes."

"How long have I been out here?"

"About an hour."

"I always loved to get lost out here in the spring."

"You still do." Her mom lay down next to her. "Your thinking place."

"My thinking place. I've never thought of it that way, but you're right."

"So, what are you thinking?"

Jillian felt her mom's eyes on her. "I'm not really thinking about anything particular." She took a deep breath and closed her eyes. "Just enjoying a beautiful Sunday afternoon."

"It is beautiful."

Jillian opened her eyes. "I've been working a lot of hours because Glenda and Dawson are meeting with contractors. They gave me yesterday afternoon off, and I spent it watching Riley."

"Aww, how are Jolie and baby Riley doing?"

"Jolie was exhausted, a little frustrated when I got there. Riley was crying her eyes out, her sweet little face red and sweaty. She settled down for me, though. I think she was just feeding off Jolie's frustration. I rocked her to sleep while Jolie took a nap. Both were much happier an hour later."

"I remember those days like they were yesterday. Being so tired I could barely think straight, ready to cry myself. Naptime became a favorite time of the day for me."

"Jolie shed a few tears, but was okay by the time I left."

"Is she going back to work?"

"Nate talked her into taking six months off. Owen's wife is filling in for her since her and Owen's boys are in school." Jillian watched a blossom float down from a tree and settle in her mom's hair. "I think Nate would like Jolie to be a stay-at-home mom."

"How does Jolie feel about it?"

"Now that she has Riley, I think she likes the idea too."

Her mom enclosed Jillian's hand in hers. "How was your week?"

"Fine. I've been working with fast-food-king Marty since January. He met his goal weight yesterday and was pretty excited."

"Marty, excited? Those two words don't fit in the same sentence."

Jillian laughed. "I know, but I promise he was excited. He gave me flowers to say thank you. They were really from his wife, but it beats him telling me he hates me."

Her mom's appalled expression made Jillian laugh. "He didn't actually say he hated you."

"Yes, he did. More than once."

"Unbelievable."

They lay side by side in the grass, lost in the gorgeousness of the day. A sudden breeze sent a shower of blossoms fluttering playfully through the air. Jillian's heart was peaceful, though her thoughts couldn't seem to connect to any one thing, flitting like the apple blossoms, looking for a safe place to land.

Her mother squeezed her hand. "Tell me about Jillian. I know you're working a lot, but what else is going on in your life?"

Jillian read between the lines. Her mom wanted to know if she was dating. She wanted to know if her daughter was happy.

She felt the corners of her mouth quirk up, because the answer was yes, she was happy. "Doc Newell sent Brandt to me for physical therapy, and we cleared up our misunderstanding. The whole thing started when he saw me hugging Sam. He thought I was dating someone else at the same time I was dating him. He caught his fiancée cheating before their wedding, so I understand where that fear came from. I just wish he had come to me and asked. He could have met Sam, had dinner with us. Instead, he cancelled our date with no explanation, stopped calling, and basically ignored me when we ran into each other."

Jillian studied her mom's profile, hoping she would be just as beautiful by the time she reached her late fifties. "And?" her mom prompted.

"And he asked me out again."

Her mom turned to her side and propped her head on an elbow. "And?"

"And I told him I don't date clients."

Her mom laughed just as Jolie had. "Probably a smart decision."

Jillian lied when she told Brandt it was a hard-and-fast rule. She'd never been asked out by a client before. The idea popped into her head some time between Friday night and Saturday morning. Holding off until he was finished with therapy would give Brandt time to get over his mistrust and allow her time to get over her hurt at being mistrusted.

Her mom ran a lock of Jillian's hair through her fingers. "Every mother wishes her children could be spared the hurt of heartache, but that isn't how things work. We grow from the trials and adversity we experience. How we handle those trials shapes us into the people we become. Yours have shaped you into a person full of kindness and tolerance. Very noble qualities." Her mom smiled softly, her eyes serene, like she was remembering a faraway memory. "Have I told you lately how proud I am of the woman you've become?"

"You and Dad tell us all the time, but it's still nice to hear. We can't take all the credit for how we turned out, though. We had great examples from the time we were little."

Her mother flopped onto her back, arms outstretched. "When will Brandt no longer be a client?"

"In about three or four weeks."

Her mom turned her head, eyebrows raised. "And then?"

"And then we'll see."

"So he'll be able to play in the Memorial Day baseball game?"

Jillian looked skyward as more blossoms rained down. "He should be fine by then."

She stretched her arms overhead as they lay quietly enjoying the way the sun shone through the branches above them, dappling the ground with light and shade.

On her way home from the orchard, her cell phone rang. Stella's face appeared on the screen. "Hi, Stella."

"Hey. Where are you? I just went past your apartment."

"You know I always have Sunday dinner with my family."

"Right. So, want to go shopping with me tomorrow after work?"

"For what?"

"New summer clothes. Mine shrank."

Jillian laughed. Stella had fought her curvy figure since she was a teenager. "I can't. The Smoke Eaters have practice."

"Tuesday, then."

"I can go Tuesday," Jillian said, braking at a stop sign. "I get off at five."

"I'll pick you up at your place between five thirty and six."

"See you then." Jillian turned onto her street and stopped at the curb.

"Hello, honey." Mrs. O'Malley waved from the porch when Jillian slid from her car. "Can you sit for a minute?"

These visits usually entailed a few minutes of talking and thirty minutes of moving furniture or cleaning windows. Jillian didn't mind. She tried to help her elderly landlady whenever she had time, and today she had time. "Let me feed Henry, and I'll be right back."

~

Brandt relaxed through another massage before Jillian got down to business the next morning.

"While you're still lying facedown, I want you to bend your leg. I'm going to provide light resistance while you try to bend it even farther. If you feel pain at any time, stop me."

"Okay." He followed her directions, bending his leg slightly. He pushed against her resistance, lightly at first, then a little harder when she encouraged him.

"Any pain?"

"No."

"How does that feel?"

"Okay. Kind of like role reversal."

She met his gaze. "Role reversal?"

"Yeah. I want you to go out with me and you're resisting."

Her expression was exactly what an adult might flash at a naughty child as she tugged her cell phone out of her jacket pocket. "This video will show you how to perform hamstring catches."

He watched the video and then repeated the action. Again, no pain.

"One more. For this, you'll need to stand." She helped him off the table and explained she wanted him to stand on one leg, bending the injured one using gravity as resistance. He did three sets of ten repetitions. "This exercise can be done at home tomorrow, but only if you have no pain. A little muscle soreness is okay, but if it is uncomfortable enough to keep you awake at night, stop, and we'll pick up again Wednesday."

"You don't want me to come in tomorrow?" He climbed back onto the table with her help.

"No. Take the day off and I'll see you on Wednesday." She indicated he should lie on his stomach, and she began another wonderful massage.

"I thought you had Wednesdays off."

"I do, but I'll come in for an hour. What time is good for you?"

"Jillian—"

"Don't argue. We'll only be working together for a couple of weeks. After that you can do these exercises on your own."

He hated and loved that she was coming in for him on her day off. He enjoyed spending this time with her, but looked forward to the time when he was no longer her client. He also kinda enjoyed her assertive side. The personal trainer was forefront at the moment.

"Is nine too early?"

"No."

She was all business, and he wanted personal. She gave him clipped answers and he wanted to kiss her. "Greg told me the Smoke Eaters are practicing tonight."

"We are."

I'll be there. Even if he couldn't participate, he could see how the team was doing. And watch Jillian.

~

Jillian knew from Brandt's question that he'd be at the Smoke Eaters' practice. He was already talking and joking with team members when she arrived. He glanced her way and she held up a hand in a slight wave, not wanting to call attention to herself.

Her nervousness at practices had evolved into a confidence she hadn't felt since playing softball in college. The other players looked at her as a teammate now, and she anticipated their moves as quickly as they predicted hers.

After practice, they all headed to Rowdy's for their team-building exercise. Everyone liked this part of their practices as much as they enjoyed the physical part. She found a place between Rowdy and his brother Beam. Teasing, laughing, and storytelling ensued. Even though she felt comfortable around the group, she was still the quiet one, preferring to listen rather than participate.

Brandt sat across the table from her. Their eyes met often and she always looked away first. She only felt heat flood her cheeks once when Brandt winked. Though Rowdy didn't know why she was blushing, he teased her anyway, which made Brandt chuckle.

She'd never been pursued before. The idea was a little exhilarating. She'd never take advantage of her position, but she would enjoy the excitement while it lasted.

~

"I heard you were working with Brandt after his accident. I bet there were some awkward moments involved," Stella said on their drive to Harrisville the next evening.

"The first night was a little awkward, until we talked. Now he's a client."

"Did he tell you why he stepped into the cone of silence?"

Jillian explained everything for the third time, ready to be done with it.

Stella threw back her head and laughed. "He thought you were cheating with your brother? I bet he feels like an idiot."

She laughed again when Jillian told her the no-dating-clients rule. "Was he fuming?"

Jillian remembered his look of disbelief. "No, not fuming. I think he understands." Ready to change the subject, she said, "How's Len?"

Stella's hands tightened on the steering wheel, but she never took her eyes off the road. "He broke another date."

"I'm sorry."

"I'm not sure what to do. I love the guy, and I think he loves me. At least he says he does. When we're together, he is so sweet and thoughtful. He calls and says he can't wait to see me, but something always comes up. We break more dates than we actually go on." She turned a pleading glance at Jillian. "If you were in my situation, what would you do?"

"Oh, Stella. I'm the wrong person to ask. You know I haven't dated much."

"That's why you're the perfect person to ask. What would you do?"

Jillian hated to be asked questions like this. Stella wouldn't like her answer, and, knowing headstrong Stella, she wouldn't listen to what Jillian said anyway. Well, she might listen, but she'd never follow her advice. And who was she to offer advice? What did she know about love and men? No, Stella would continue to see Len and let herself be stepped on no matter what Jillian said.

"Come on, Jillian. If it was you and Len—"

"It wouldn't be me and Len or, at least, it wouldn't still be me and Len. I would have broken up with him long before now. Like Alex, I don't trust him, Stella. I think the excuses he gives you are just that—excuses. You've been dating for two years and you've never met his family. You've never even been to his house." She pulled a tissue from her purse and leaned over the console to dab at the tears on Stella's cheeks. "I'm sorry. I didn't mean to make you cry, but you deserve better. After two years, you deserve more than Len is giving."

"You just don't trust him because you don't know him."

"Whose fault is that? You've invited him to countless events we've had, weddings, barbecues, waterskiing, and he's only shown up a couple of times." Jillian wasn't surprised when Stella defended the man she loved. Jillian—heck, any woman in love—would do the same. "Sorry," she said again. "I know you don't want to hear it, but you asked my opinion."

"I know none of you like him."

She didn't want to tell Stella she was right. They didn't like him. It was hard to like someone you didn't trust. They didn't believe his excuses were valid or truthful. He was hurting their friend and there was nothing they could do to stop the inevitable train wreck.

She put a hand on Stella's arm. "If you love Len, we'll support you." *And we'll be there to pick up the pieces when he breaks your heart.*

After all the heavy talk, Jillian tried to keep the rest of their conversation simple and fun. Stella bought way more than she probably needed, but Jillian suspected she was compensating for a bruised heart. Though she mostly wore workout clothes, Jillian also bought a summer dress, a couple of T-shirts, and a pair of sandals.

They stopped at a burger place on the river just outside of Harrisville. Stella was quiet while they ate, making Jillian feel horrible. She wished she hadn't expressed her opinion so fiercely, but Stella had asked, and then insisted, and Jillian wouldn't lie to her friend. "I'm sorry, Stella."

"I know. Me too." She picked up an onion ring and dragged it through a pile of ketchup. "Do you ever feel left out? I mean, three of our friends are married and have children. The fourth in our group is getting married in six weeks. Sometimes I think I'll be the only single one left."

"I'm single."

Stella rolled her eyes dramatically. "Yeah, but once Brandt isn't a client, you know you two will start dating again."

"Until Preacher Brenner says, 'I now pronounce you husband and wife,' I'm single. I don't see that changing any time soon."

Stella held up her soft drink in a toast. "To us single women."

Jillian bumped her cup against Stella's. "To us single women."

CHAPTER 18

Brandt's recovery was slower than he'd like, but faster than he expected. By the middle of May, he wasn't racing after the ball, but he was back to pitching. Jillian's stretching exercises and resistance training had strengthened his muscles. He was now lifting weights, and had added jogging back into his regimen just this morning. He'd also been able to resume coaching his Little League team, which JT had kindly taken over for him while he healed.

Doc Newell had released him from restricted duty today, which meant he was no longer a client of Jillian's. To top off his good day, Jillian agreed to ride to practice with him. They'd begun sitting next to each other at their team-building exercises, but she'd continued to refuse a date until their last session two days earlier.

He was going to miss his massages.

He got out of his truck at the curb and walked around to her apartment entrance. She answered after two knocks, one arm above her head, trying to hold a ponytail in place. "You're early. I was going to meet you at the curb."

He wrapped his arm around her waist, backed her inside, and closed the door with his other hand. She dropped her arms, releasing a cascade of soft hair to fall past her shoulders. He caught the flicker of desire in her soft brown eyes and knew he wouldn't meet any opposition. Still, he wanted to give her the opportunity to refuse, so he ran a finger from her cheek to her chin, lifting her face slightly to meet his. "If you'd met me at the curb, I couldn't do this."

Their slow meeting of lips turned deeper within seconds, and had his heart pounding hard enough that he was sure she could feel it against her chest. Standing here in her arms, breathing the same air, he felt as if he'd come home. *This is where I belong. In Eden Falls. With Jillian.* As suddenly as the thought ran through his mind, he wanted to fall to his knees and thank his lucky stars Kacie had a problem with scars. How had he not seen how wrong they were for each other before he proposed?

When he lifted his head to gaze into Jillian's eyes, she took a deep breath as a blush moved up her neck and across her cheeks. "You do that very well."

He was pleased that her bold statement came out a little breathless, matching his own befuddled emotions. "So do you."

"We should probably go. We'll be late."

He ran his fingers through her beautiful hair. "Or we could stay here and do more of this."

"The Smoke Eaters just got their pitcher back. I don't think they'd be very happy if you duck your first practice in favor of a make-out session."

"I beg to differ. 'I'd rather play baseball than make out with a beautiful woman,' said no man ever."

She laughed, her sweet innocence shining through. "How does your leg feel today?"

"Perfect, thanks to you."

"You did all the hard work."

"I beg to differ a second time. Your hands work magic."

Her adorable blush deepened, just as he knew it would.

"The physical therapist I worked with in Harrisville was a big, burly guy with hands the size of rump roasts. There was no cool touch or gentleness about him."

He kissed her nose, her cheeks, her lips again. She responded by leaning into him, and he knew, in that split second, as if hit over the head by a two-by-four. He was going to marry Jillian Saunders.

~

Jillian left the gym and ran home to feed Henry and grab a quick shower. She'd already wrapped Carolyn's present for the bridal shower the girls were throwing at Alex's house tonight. She spent her lunch hour stringing paper streamers of orchid, celery, chocolate, and creamy rose—Carolyn's wedding colors—and arranging bunches of balloons around the living room and kitchen. All five of her friends would act as Carolyn's bridesmaids in what would be the wedding of the summer.

JT's mountain home was the location for the reception. He had a beautiful backyard surrounded by pines. The stream running through the middle would only add to the magical, rustic setting.

When Jillian arrived, she greeted friends while she made her way into the kitchen, where the presents were stacked. Finger foods were arranged on a table in the backyard. Well-wishers surrounded Carolyn and Jillian joined in. They played games and laughed, and Jillian knew she felt lighter and had more fun because she and Brandt were dating again.

She remembered vowing with her friends, long ago, to never let a boy rule their moods, but they'd all broken that vow at one time or another. Until now, she hadn't realized just how down she'd felt because of Brandt's silence.

After games were played, presents opened, and cake served, she walked out into Alex's backyard to find some quiet. Instead, she discovered Carolyn sitting on the back step.

"What are you doing out here alone? Your party is still in full swing."

Carolyn patted a place next to her on the step. "Join me."

Jillian sat beside her friend.

"This is the exact place JT and I had our first conversation after I came back to Eden Falls. We sat right here, and he told me about the hardware store fire, and how frustrated he was that no one had been caught yet. I barely listened I was so worried he'd find out I was using my maiden name illegally."

Jillian nudged Carolyn gently with her shoulder. "Everything worked out pretty great, didn't it?"

"It did. All through school, I had such a crush on JT." Carolyn put a hand to her heart. "I used any excuse available to be at the Garretts' house, just to be near him."

"Really?" Jillian could see the truth in Carolyn's eyes. "I had no idea you liked JT when we were kids."

Carolyn smirked. "Everyone liked JT."

"True, but he was always just Alex's older brother to me."

"I idolized him. I used to be so jealous of the girls who surrounded him. Pretty high school girls. Girls with boobs."

Jillian laughed and Carolyn joined her.

"Now you're marrying your girlhood crush," Jillian said, slipping her arm around Carolyn's shoulder. "Isn't it amazing how life works out?"

"Surreal."

"Are you nervous?"

"Not at all. With Rob I was terrified. We barely knew each other, but I was so taken in by his promises of love and forever." Carolyn turned to her. "I'm terrified for Stella. I don't think he hits like Rob did, but I think he is a master manipulator."

Jillian blew out a breath. "I tried to talk to her a couple of weeks ago. She asked for my advice. I told her what I thought, but I don't think she'll listen."

"We have to do something."

"If we knew what Rob was doing to you and we came to San Francisco to get you, would you have listened?"

Carolyn hung her head, her lips pressed together. "No. After every beating, Rob said he'd change…and I believed him. He made me believe him."

Stella pushed the back door open. "There you guys are." She looked from Carolyn to Jillian. "What are you doing out here?"

"Just talking," Carolyn said after exchanging a glance with Jillian.

Stella raised a brow. "About what?"

"Old times," Jillian said.

~

Practice ran smoothly, though it took every ounce of patience Brandt possessed to keep his hands off Jillian. Why had it taken him so long to notice her? And why had he been so quick to believe she would do the same thing Kacie did?

The two women were nothing alike, and for him to make comparisons was insulting. He should have checked the facts with Jillian. She said she would have jumped to the same conclusions, but he believed she would have stepped out of her comfort zone to ask him for the truth. He'd wasted a lot of time being jealous for no reason.

Now that they were back together, he felt an urgency to

make up for lost time. They could have been skiing and skating and tubing together since January. Instead, he spent the time brooding alone.

The sun disappeared behind the mountain peaks, and the outdoor lights flickered on, throwing their shadows across the field. The air cooled, and Brandt inhaled the sweet scent of freshly mown grass. Being outdoors and active, enjoying the spring night in Eden Falls, felt fantastic.

Jillian was up to bat, her form a perfect giveaway that she'd had a good instructor. She swung hard at the first pitch. Foul ball. The second pitch was a strike. She connected with the third, a high fly straight to Jack Frazier in left field. Even so, it was a great hit. She glanced his way and he winked, not sure if she was able to see clearly enough in the fading light.

At the end of practice, the team gathered near the dugout. He slipped his arm around her, appreciating their fit. "How about a quiet night and that make-out session we talked about last week?"

Her teeth flashed white with her smile and he imagined the blush that was sure to follow. "Sounds good."

"We have two more practices before our big game next Monday," Jeff announced. "Anybody got anything before we meet at Rowdy's?"

"Jillian and I are going to skip the team-building exercise at Rowdy's tonight."

Rowdy held up a hand. "Hear that, guys? Jillian and Brandt are going to skip our team-building exercise tonight in favor of their own type of exercise."

A round of hoots and applause followed. Though Brandt couldn't make out Jillian's features clearly, he was sure her cheeks were scarlet. Selfish on his part, especially since he hadn't consulted her, but he wanted to make it clear they were together, so he bent and kissed her soundly to more hoots and hollers.

~

Jillian was a little afraid they were moving too fast, but she couldn't seem to stop herself when it came to Brandt. Besides, they were both adults and knew what they were looking for.

They settled on her sofa and, between lovely, knee-wobbling kisses, they talked about anything that came to mind. She wanted to know about Kacie. At first, Brandt wasn't eager to discuss his ex-fiancée, but finally told her the whole story, which only helped her to see more clearly why he'd assumed the worst.

"I'm sorry you had to go through that."

"Of course I didn't see it at the time, but now I think everything happened for a reason. She and I would be married and living in Tacoma. I would never have visited Eden Falls, never answered the ad for firefighter. I would never have met you."

He asked her about what happened in college and, with much cringing embarrassment, she told him about being raped and the humiliating aftermath.

"You don't blame yourself."

"Not anymore. After many sessions with a therapist."

"Please know I'd never hurt you, Jillian."

"I do."

He apologized over and over for their misunderstanding, until she finally said, "It was a mistake on both our parts, but it's over. Let's forget it happened."

They spent another thirty minutes at the door saying goodbye. When he left, Jillian touched her swollen lips and sighed. Dating Brandt, the man she'd had a two-year crush on, was worth the wait. The time wouldn't have been right any sooner. She wouldn't have been ready or trusting enough.

She still needed to heal and build up her fragile self-confidence. And he was getting over a broken heart.

Henry snaked around her ankles and she picked him up, tucking him under her chin. "Looks like you and Brandt are getting along, since you spent most of the night in his lap." She held him up higher so she could look into his eyes. "Just so you know...you'll have to share that spot."

~

After waving goodbye to Marty, Jillian dashed into the locker room and changed into jeans and a T-shirt. She was meeting her friends at Rowdy's for their last girls' night out before Carolyn West became Carolyn Garrett. And to celebrate Stella's last day of school.

She was the first to arrive and nabbed a table in the back corner. Rowdy was next to her in minutes. "Sorry I embarrassed you Monday night in front of the whole team."

"No, you're not. You did it on purpose."

"You're right." He touched the tip of her nose when her cheeks heated. "You do look cute in pink."

She shook her head at his teasing. "I might as well order Alex's nachos."

"I already put the order in. I'll be back with your drink."

After the girls arrived, Misty said she could only stay an hour because Sophia had learned to walk and was into everything. Jolie said she'd have to leave at the same time Misty did. Riley woke up from her nap with a fever. Halfway through their nacho appetizer, Alex ran to the bathroom to throw up, then came back to the table to announce she was pregnant. She left after two more trips to the bathroom. Carolyn begged off early. She'd spent the day at Patsy's, baking fifteen cakes for high school graduation parties.

That left Jillian and Stella staring across the table at each other.

Stella popped a chip in her mouth. "Sorry about the night we went shopping. I was a downer."

"You don't have to be sorry, Stella. I understand. We all have our down times."

Stella shook her head and looked down at the table. "Go home. Be with Brandt."

"He's working tonight. Even if he wasn't, tonight is girls' night. Our night. So what if it's just the two of us? Let's go to Noelle's for a piece of pie."

Stella sat for a long time, her expression shouting *no*, but she finally nodded. "Thanks. I don't feel like being home alone tonight."

Jillian hated to ask, but Stella would be hurt if she didn't act like she cared. "Where's Len? Since it's the last day of school for both of you, I thought you'd rather celebrate with him."

"He had something come up."

Jillian felt a small pinch to her heart. Her gut told her Stella was going to get hurt…a hurt more painful than the disappointments and humiliations she'd experienced so far.

She glanced toward the bar to signal for a check and spotted Rowdy staring at Stella. *Hmm*…. Just as quickly as the thought entered her mind, she pushed it aside. Rowdy had never been in a serious relationship in his life. He dated far and wide but never for keeps. Stella needed a forever guy who would treat her special.

They walked a block to the square. Rain earlier in the day left puddles on the sidewalks and the fresh scent of pine in the air. They sat at a table near the window and watched night fall over their town.

Even though Stella didn't participate much in their conversation, she wasn't home alone, feeling down because Len cancelled yet another date. Jillian wished she could offer wise advice, but didn't have a clue how to fix the situation. Other than to say, "Enough. You're gorgeous, you're funny, you're kind. You deserve someone better, someone who treats you the way you deserve to be treated. There is a man out there in this big world who is just right for you, who is probably searching for you. Stop wasting your time on Len and go find him."

Instead she kept quiet, knowing Stella wouldn't listen anyway.

~

Brandt finished jogging on the treadmill and moved over to the rowing machine. His thoughts were on Jillian, as usual. She was able to get a couple of days off next week, so he was taking her to meet his parents. He knew they'd love her as much as he did. Five weeks had passed since they cleared up his misunderstanding, and he was still mad about the two months he wasted being angry over nothing.

Jack walked into the weight room, a towel around his neck. "How's it going?"

"Good." Brandt continued to row. His leg was strong, thanks to Jillian.

"So. You and Jillian," Jack said as he lifted two twenty-pound free weights.

"Yep." Brandt chuckled. "For a while I thought it was you and Jillian."

"What?" Jack laughed. "No. Patsy said she was shy and asked me to keep an eye on her. Help her feel comfortable at the first few baseball practices."

"Your help isn't needed anymore."

Jack glanced at him. "Relax, Smith. There was never anything between me and Jillian."

"Good." Brandt remembered Patsy's confession about hoping Jack would be interested in Jillian. "Be forewarned. Patsy brought your name up recently as a matchmaking project."

Jack laughed again. "Thanks, but she's been trying for years. She thinks if she can get me to marry a local girl, I'll stay in Eden Falls."

"Do you plan on leaving?"

"Nope. I love it here. I've tried to convince her, but she's a worrier."

"Do you have a local girl in mind?"

"Nope," Jack repeated. "It'll happen when it happens. No amount of pushing from Patsy is going to make a difference."

"I wouldn't be so sure. Patsy can be pretty persuasive."

Jack flashed a knowing smile.

Brandt's crew was lucky enough to have Memorial Day off, and he planned to spend it with Jillian. They were meeting her family for the flag raising and pancake breakfast. The baseball game was next in the lineup of festivities. After the game, they'd all go to Alice and Denny Garrett's house for a barbecue. He hoped she wouldn't be sick of him by then, because the barbecue was followed by a concert on the square and fireworks.

CHAPTER 19

Brandt parked in front of Jillian's just as the sun crested the mountain peaks. Rain fell all day Friday and Saturday, but today, Memorial Day, looked promising.

As soon as Jillian answered the door, he pulled her against him. Holding on to her was the way he wanted to start every day. After a sweet, slow, good-morning kiss, he nuzzled her neck. She shivered in response. He'd found that new spot three nights ago and planned to visit it often.

She pulled back with a laugh. "Good morning."

He kissed the tip of her nose. "Good morning to you."

"Are you ready to meet part of my family?"

"As ready as I'll ever be." He'd actually never been so nervous to meet a girl's parents. Possibly because he believed he'd be asking her dad for Jillian's hand in marriage in the near future.

They arrived at Town Hall, and Jillian introduced him to her parents, her older brother, his wife, and their redheaded baby girl. They watched the flag raising, a Memorial Day tradition performed by Mayor Alexis McCreed. Then the crowd moved across the street to the square for the pancake breakfast. Jillian and her mom always helped at the griddles, but this year, when Patsy spotted Brandt with the Saunders family, she waved their help away.

"You enjoy yourselves this year. I've got plenty of help cooking and serving." She pulled Brandt aside. "Have I ever told you you're one of the smartest men I know?"

He frowned. "That's not what you said a couple of months ago."

She nodded toward Jillian. "Well, seems you've smartened up since then."

Jillian's family pulled him in as if they'd known him forever. They included him in their conversation and made him feel comfortable when he joined in. He knew he'd love being a part of this family as much as Jillian would love being a part of his.

~

While Jillian warmed up with her team, she glanced toward the bleachers, which were filling up fast. Along the fence line, people were setting up lawn chairs and spreading blankets. She'd been to every Gunslinger-Smoke Eaters' game since Dawson Garrett founded the tradition, but always as an observer.

Jack Frazier hit the ball in her direction. Even though her stomach muscles jittered in a nervous dance, she made an easy catch. After she threw the ball infield, Rowdy came toward her from first base. He stopped toe-to-toe and propped his hands on his hips.

"You nervous?"

She glanced toward the bleachers again, spotted her family. "A little."

"Why?"

The laugh she intended sounded more like a croaking frog. "Since college, I've always been on the other side of the fence."

He moved his hands to her shoulders and looked into her eyes. "Just imagine it's another practice, and everyone watching is naked."

This time she did laugh.

He grinned back. "You'll do just fine. You're a great ballplayer, Jillian. Don't even look at the crowd"—he lifted the brim of his ball cap and winked—"until you hit a homer, and then you take a bow."

"I doubt there will be any homers, but thanks for the pep talk."

"The possibility of a homer is high. We're here to cream these Gunslingers. I know Alex, JT, Stella—well, just about everyone on the other team—are friends or, in my case, relatives, but for the next couple of hours, they're the bad guys."

"I can only imagine the trouble you and JT got into as kids, but I know Alex has never been bad a day in her life."

He leaned forward until their noses almost touched. "Oh yeah, you should have heard the names she was calling you at breakfast."

Jillian laughed again. Alex had never called anyone a name—ever. But Rowdy had accomplished what he came over to do. He'd relaxed her tension and taken her mind off the crowd. She could do this. She'd participated in one sport or another since she was tiny, and there was always a crowd watching.

He ran his hands from her shoulders to her upper arms. "Good girl."

She glanced at the pitcher's mound where Brandt stood, watching her and Rowdy's exchange. His admission of jealousy over her hugging Sam had surprised her. A man had never felt jealous over her before…that she knew of, at least.

She wouldn't let it go to her head, but it did feel nice to know Brandt cared that much.

She waved to let him know there was absolutely nothing to worry about. She was his.

Jillian glanced at the blue sky. A few cottony clouds hovered over their world, leaving occasional blotchy shadows on the ground. Today was perfect in every way. Breakfast with her family was fun. She could tell her parents approved of Brandt, but she knew they would.

Rowdy scooped up a grounder and threw it to Brandt, who jumped to catch the ball. He was back to his regular routine, his leg completely healed.

He glanced at her and winked.

She bit her bottom lip with a smile.

~

The Smoke Eaters left the field as victors, with a final score of eleven to eight, which meant for the next year they would be the team crowing instead of being crowed at. Handshaking and backslapping ensued, as usual. Even though it was a rivalry, it was a friendly one.

JT approached Brandt with outstretched hand. "I see your injury didn't hold you back today. Congratulations."

Brandt glanced around until he spotted Jillian. "Thanks. The Gunslingers gave us plenty of competition."

"Little did we know you had a secret weapon," JT said, nodding toward Jillian.

She turned toward them and grinned, as if she knew they were talking about her. Brandt was proud of the way she played today. He knew she was nervous, but it didn't stop her from hitting a double, along with two singles. She also caught one ball for an out, and assisted in a double play in the fourth inning.

Jillian joined them. Brandt slipped his arm around her waist, pulling her close.

"How *is* the leg?" JT asked Brandt.

"All healed, thanks to my physical therapist."

JT adjusted his ball cap. "You should open your own place, Jillian. Maybe call it...Touches of Eden."

Jillian blushed her pretty pink. "Your aunt and uncle are making a space for me in the expansion."

"Good. The town could use a good physical therapist."

After JT moved off, Brandt leaned in for a kiss and watched Jillian's blush deepen. "Does my kissing you in public embarrass you?"

"No, I'm just not used to being kissed in public." She smiled, her brown eyes shining. "But I promise to get used to it quickly."

"Good, because I like kissing you." He tucked a strand of hair behind her ear. "You played a great game."

"Thanks. You pitched a great game."

Brandt glanced toward the bleachers, where her family waited. "Let's go over so your parents can congratulate you."

He moved his arm from her waist to her shoulder, and she reached up and laced their fingers together as they meandered toward the group waiting just outside the fence. He could see a great deal of Jillian in both her parents. She inherited her height from her father, but she had her mother's reddish-brown hair and big brown eyes. She shared a warm familiarity with her brother, who chided her good-naturedly about her strikeout in the third inning. Her sister-in-law punched her husband lightly in the chest over his teasing, and told Jillian she was impressed by the catch she made in the first inning. Mr. Saunders reminded Joe he had plenty of strikeouts in his high school baseball career.

Her family was close, as was his, which meant a lot to him, because Jillian was important. Wednesday they were driving to Spokane so she could meet his family. He already knew they'd love her as much as he did.

~

Jillian helped Brandt spread a blanket on the grass. Town Square was filling up quickly even though the concert didn't start for another hour.

Brandt sat close beside her and flashed his irresistible dimple. "I like your family."

"They like you back."

"You can't know that from the short time we were together."

"Of course I can. I know my family well enough to know whether they like someone or not."

"Well, my family is going to like you too."

"Are you sure? I'm afraid…after your fiancée…they might be a little skeptical."

He shook his head. "No. They're much smarter than I am. They saw signs in Kacie that I missed. They're going to love you." He wrapped his hand around the back of her neck and pulled her close. "They'll love you…because I love you."

Her breath caught long enough to make her chest hurt. She had never heard those words from a man. Had wondered if she ever would. "You do?"

"I do." His expression grew serious. "I love you, Jillian Saunders."

Her glance darted around at their perfect setting. The last light of the day faded, washing everything in soft watercolors. There was no better time or place to make a brave declaration of her own, words she'd never spoken to any man besides her dad. "I love you too."

He kissed her long and hard, setting her heart palpitating, something he was awfully good at doing.

"Hey, you two, get a room. This concert is G-rated."

Beam spread a blanket next to theirs.

Jillian looked up. "Where's Misty?"

Beam pointed over his shoulder. "She got waylaid by Aunt Alice. She wanted to hold Sophia."

Alex, Colton, and Charlie spread a blanket on the opposite side. JT and Carolyn soon joined them. They were hemmed in by friends, not that Jillian minded. In fact, today couldn't have been much more perfect in her eyes. The Smoke Eaters won the game. Her mom and dad approved of Brandt. And she'd spent the entire day with the man she loved.

~

Brandt left Jillian in his parents' living room. His sister was in her element, trying to humiliate him with baby pictures. He found his mom at the kitchen table, a serene smile on her face.

"What are you smiling about?"

"I'm happy you've found your other half."

Brandt pulled out a chair and sat beside her. "I knew you'd like her."

"Like her?" She shook her head. "Your dad and I love her. So do you."

Brandt looked down at the table and nodded. "I do. She's perfectly imperfect…just like me. She's so good at what she does, she makes me want to be better. A better paramedic, a better friend, even a better son and brother. I can see us together. I can see us having a family, and going through middle age side by side, growing old together. I see a future I could never quite picture when I was with Kacie."

"Things happen for a reason."

"I was saying the same thing to Jillian about a week ago. I

needed time to heal, both mentally and physically, before I found her. I had to get over what Kacie did and come to terms with my burns before I could let myself fall in love again."

He pointed at his mom. "I took your advice and showed her my scars. She said they didn't bother her."

"I'm not surprised, since she's a physical therapist, that she's not bothered by them. They aren't grotesque. They are a part of your life now, a part of you."

"I'm going to ask Jillian to marry me."

His mom blinked rapidly and offered him a wobbly smile. "And she'll say yes, because she loves you. I see it in her eyes, in the way she looks at you. I can even see it in the way you two hold hands. This will be a forever love. Grab it and hang on."

Brandt leaned over the table and gave her a smacking kiss on her cheek. "I'm going to."

"Thank you for bringing her home to meet the family."

"Thank you for being the best mom a guy could ask for." Brandt stood and offered her a hand. "Let's go out and see how much more my baby sister can humiliate me."

CHAPTER 20

Wearing a soft rose-colored dress, her hair twisted in a knot, Jillian looked beautiful. Just the sight of her walking down the aisle on Rowdy's arm constricted Brandt's chest. When she passed, their eyes met. He winked, and her blush matched her dress perfectly. She took her place in the front of the church with everyone else.

Brandt touched the breast pocket of his coat. The engagement ring was safely tucked away for the time being. When he walked past a Harrisville jewelry store, the ring—a simple, elegant emerald-cut diamond flanked by two tapered baguettes—caught his attention. Perfect. He probably should have asked Jillian what she'd like, but decided on spontaneity and what he imagined on her finger. He hoped she'd feel the same.

The music changed, and the congregation stood and turned toward the back of the church. Carolyn held on to Denny Garrett's arm, both framed in the door of the chapel. JT gazed in obvious awe, a contented smile on his face, as his father escorted Carolyn down the aisle.

Jillian wiped away a tear. Brandt liked to tease her about

being sentimental. When they watched a movie, even a thriller, he'd learned to have a couple of tissues handy, because she cried at the drop of a hat. Her crying gave him an excuse to pull her into his arms, not that he needed an excuse anymore. She liked to cuddle up close, and he liked that she did.

He turned his attention back to the wedding, taking mental notes, for soon he'd be standing in front with Preacher Brenner. Carolyn looked radiant in her white dress and veil, and JT was grinning like a kid in Patsy's Pastries when a fresh batch of brownies came out of the oven. They both deserved some happiness, and Brandt was glad he'd been invited to share in their moment.

~

Brandt led Jillian onto the dance platform built in JT's backyard and spun her into his arms. They moved around the crowded space as if they'd been dancing together forever. And Jillian decided this was the happiest moment of her life. Better than being asked on a date, and even better than their first kiss, which was pretty spectacular.

She remembered watching him dance with other partners at other wedding and always wishing she was the one in his arms. Now she was. Her dream came true.

She glanced around at the happy couples. All her friends were here. Alex and Colton, Jolie and Nate, Misty and Beam. JT and Carolyn were dancing close, moving to their own music while looking deep into each other's eyes. She hoped the photographer captured that moment, because it was perfect.

Only Stella looked miserable. Jillian wished she knew how to console her friend, make things better, or at least not hurt quite so much.

Brandt kissed the spot under her ear that always sent a delicious shiver down her spine. "I love you, Jillian," he whispered, his breath tickling across her cheek. If he hadn't been holding her up, she might have melted into a puddle at his feet.

She looked up into his smiling eyes, eyes that she wanted to look into forever. "I love you too."

He pulled her closer, if that were even possible, and they danced the night away.

~

Brandt helped Jillian into his truck after the reception, but he wasn't ready to call it a night. He drove around Town Square, turned left, and pulled into the parking lot of Riverside Park.

"What are we doing here?"

"I want to see the moonlight on your skin and shining through you hair." Sliding from behind the wheel, he went around to open Jillian's door.

She took his arm and they walked down to the river's edge. The sky was clear and full of stars, brilliantly twinkling down on them, sparkling in her eyes. This was one of his favorite places on earth, and he wanted to share it all with Jillian.

"I'm so happy for JT and Carolyn. They went through a lot before they could be together."

He tucked her against his side. "Yes, they did, but it will make their togetherness all the sweeter."

She glanced up at him. "That's an interesting way to look at it."

He turned her to face him. "I didn't know it then, but the happiest day in my life was the day I asked you out."

She beamed up at him. "Mine too."

"I think I fell in love with you on our third date...or maybe our second."

"Me too," she repeated, soft as a whisper. She sucked in a gasp when he took her hand and dropped to one knee.

"Jillian, I know this is fast, and I don't want to scare you, but you are all I think about. I want to see your face first thing when I wake up. I want to hear you tell me you love me every night as I drift off to sleep with you in my arms. I want to spend forever with you next to me. I want to have children with you, and have our grandkids over on weekends. You make me happy. You make me want to be a better man. I can't imagine going through the rest of my life without you by my side. Will you marry me? Grow old with me?"

"Yes, yes, yes." She laughed softly. "I want all those things too."

She gasped again when he pulled the ring from his pocket and slipped it on her finger. "Oh Brandt, it's beautiful."

"I never knew it was possible to feel this much happiness." When he stood, tears were pooling in her eyes. He loved that she wasn't afraid to show her emotions.

"I feel the same. I never imagined I could love anyone as much as I love you."

He picked her up and spun in a circle.

Jillian laughed through her tears. "While we were dancing, I was thinking that was the happiest moment of my life. I was wrong. This is."

He kissed her sweet mouth. "I promise you a lifetime of happiest moments, Jillian."

DEDICATION

This book is dedicated to my readers.

Thank you!

ACKNOWLEDGMENTS

As always, I wish to thank my early readers Holly Hertzke, Chris Almodovar. A special thanks to Jeanine Hopping who helped me tweak Jillian Saunders. I appreciate your kind words of encouragement and your valuable feedback. Hugs to you all!

Have you ever had a friend you've never met? That is Faith Freewoman, Demon for Details, editor extraordinaire. She helped me further develop Brandt's character—even though she wanted to "knock his block off" (yes, she actually wrote that on my manuscript). You are so careful to correct and strengthen my work without taking away my voice.

Thank you Dar Albert (another friend I've never met) of Wicked Smart Designs for the cover art. Once again, your insight and talent amazes me. Opening an email from Dar is like Christmas morning.

Thank you to proofreader JoSelle Vanderhooft. You did an excellent job of deleting all my extra commas.

Thanks to my family who quietly endure my insanity. I don't say it often enough, but I love and appreciate you all.

I’m grateful for my ever patient husband who takes care of my behind the scenes “writer-ly stuff”.

And to you, dear readers thank you for taking time out of your busy day to read my books. I appreciate your reviews, kind words, and messages. You are amazing!

ABOUT THE AUTHOR

Tina Newcomb writes clean, contemporary romance. Her heartwarming stories take place in quaint small towns, with quirky townsfolk, and friendships that last a lifetime.

She acquired her love of reading from her librarian mother, who always had a stack of books close at hand, and her father who visited the local bookstore every weekend.

Tina lives in colorful Colorado. When not lost in her writing, she can be found in the garden, traveling with her (amateur) chef husband, or spending time with family and friends.

She loves to hear from readers. You can find her at
tinanewcomb.com

ALSO BY TINA NEWCOMB

The Eden Falls Series

New Beginnings in Eden Falls - Book .5

Finding Eden - Book 1

Beyond Eden - Book 2

A Taste of Eden - Book 3

The Angel of Eden Falls - Book 4

Touches of Eden - Book 5

Stars Over Eden FallsBook 6

Fortunes for Eden - Book 7

Snow and Mistletoe in Eden Falls - Book 8

NOTE FROM AUTHOR

Thank you for reading my book, Touches of Eden. If you enjoyed it, I hope you'll leave an honest review or consider telling a friend—the two very best ways a reader can support an author.

I'd like to share an excerpt from Stars Over Eden Falls, Book 6 in the Eden Falls Series. Enjoy!

Warmest Regards,
Tina Newcomb

P.S. - For a **free ebook,** sign up to receive my newsletter at tinanewcomb.com

You can follow me on:
https://www.facebook.com/TinaNewcombAuthor
https://www.bookbub.com/authors/tina-newcomb
https://www.instagram.com/tinanewcomb
https://www.goodreads.com/tinanewcomb
https://www.pinterest.com/tinanewcomb

EXCERPT FROM: STARS OVER EDEN FALLS

Book Six of the Eden Falls Series
by Tina Newcomb

Chapter 1

Stella Adams emerged from the dressing room feeling like a princess. She threw her arms around the bride to be and one of her best friends. "Thank you, thank you for picking bridesmaid dresses that don't make my hips look two sizes bigger than they already are. I love you, Carolyn."

"You have a body I've envied since we were kids." Carolyn West held her out by the shoulders. "I love the color on you."

The burgundy lace over nude looked perfect with her skin color and her dark hair. Stella ran her hands down her hips. "I don't know about you ladies, but I look gorgeous," she said loud enough for her four friends still in their dressing rooms to hear.

Jillian Saunders stepped out. Of course, the dress looked

fabulous on her model-thin and personal-trainer toned body. She pulled at the hem. "Is mine too short?"

"Holy moly, your legs go on forever," Stella said. "Can't you share about two inches with me?"

Jillian laughed. "I wish I could."

Tiny Alex McCord stepped out next. "No you don't. You are both absolutely perfect just the way you are. Me on the other hand…"

Alex's five-foot-nothing made Stella appreciate her extra three inches. Still, Alex looked darling with her sunlight smile and messy blond ponytail. Stella wrapped her arm around Alex's shoulder. "You are absolutely perfect too."

Jolie Klein and Misty Garrett emerged at the same time. Jolie was adjusting her ample breasts and Misty was holding her midnight black hair up. "Stella, will you zip me?"

Carolyn lined them up in front of a wall of mirrors. "You all look gorgeous."

Stella raised her fist in the air. "Forever friends."

They all repeated the action. "Forever friends!"

Misty clapped her hands. "Okay lets get changed and eat. I'm starving."

The six friends didn't get the chance to come to Seattle often, so they were using a special girls' night out to make sure their bride's maids dresses fit before Carolyn's big day.

After they changed, they all climbed into Alex's SUV and headed down to the waterfront for dinner at a restaurant overlooking the bay.

Stella could hardly contain her excitement. Her boyfriend of two years was coming to the wedding as her date. He promised he wouldn't cancel, as he did so often. She didn't want to get her hopes up, but a jewelry box had fallen out of his coat pocket the last time they were together. She picked it up from her coat closet floor, so tempted to take a peek. But she hadn't. She wanted the ring to be a total surprise.

She hadn't mentioned the ring box to any of her friends. They were all a little skeptical of Len, afraid he was going to hurt her just because he cancelled dates so often.

Maybe he'd propose after Carolyn's wedding, once and for all proving her friends wrong.

She tucked the box back in his pocket and hung up his coat, smoothing a hand over the lump to make sure it was snug in its place. After Len left later that night, she worked on her look of astonishment in front of the bathroom mirror. Wide eyes, open mouth, hands to cheeks, the only thing she couldn't master were tears. Depending on the setting, tears just might come naturally.

A little niggle of uncertainty found a weak spot and wormed its way in. She loved Len, but he did disappoint her often by breaking dates. He always had a valid excuse, but still…she felt he was holding back a piece of himself.

He'll change.

But what if he doesn't? We've been dating for two years and I've never met his family.

Stella rolled her eyes and tried to brush the little haloed angel off her shoulder. *Aren't you supposed to be positive? Maybe he's embarrassed by his family. Who isn't at some time or another?*

Haloed angel was back. *If that's the case, why doesn't he talk to you about it? Especially if he's ready to propose? We can't start a marriage with secrets. After two years, don't you deserve more? Your friends don't trust him.*

Only because they don't know him.

Whose fault is that? How many times have you invited him to meet your friends and he's only shown up on a handful of those occasions?

Stella wiggled her shoulder trying to unseat the tiny angel. *My friends will support me.*

They arrived at a seafood restaurant Stella hadn't eaten at

since she was a teenager. The hostess left the desk to seat a couple ahead of them.

As they waited, Stella heard a ruckus and leaned to her right to see what was going on around the corner. Two kids were fighting at a table where a family of five sat. She started to lean back when she recognized the man at the table. Len. Her chest constricted and her throat closed. A loud buzzing silenced the restaurant noise.

The man who was supposed to propose, the same one who was supposed to be playing basketball with buddies tonight, was actually sitting in a restaurant, trying to break up an argument, between two boys, while the woman sat next to him cradling a darling little girl.

"Hey, isn't that—" Misty started.

Stella heard voices, a quick "Shush." A "Let's go somewhere else." Felt people tugging her arm, trying to turn her away, but she sidestepped them all, her feet taking her toward the family. She stopped at the table, her eyes on Len. He glanced up and his expression shifted from frustration to alarm.

"I-I think we've met…at a teachers conference." Stella was surprised the voice was hers, surprised by her comment.

"Uh…yeah, I think you're right."

"Len right?"

His alarm turned to dread. His gaze darted to the woman next to him, then to somewhere behind her where she presumed her friends stood. "No."

"No?" Stella shook a hand from her arm. "I could have sworn you said your name was Len Barlow."

The woman at the table looked up, her smile sweet. Unsuspecting. She was beautiful in a girl-next-door way. "You must have him mixed up with someone else. His name is Jerry. Jerry Winters."

"Jerry. Winters." Stella pronounced each word slowly, distinctly. "Is this your wife, Jerry?"

The woman held out her hand. "I'm Anna Winters. I can't keep track of all of Jerry's conferences. Which one did you meet at?"

"It was in Tacoma"—she said to Anna while staring at Len—"two years ago. Right, *Jerry*?"

Jerry looked down at his plate, unable to make eye contact. "Yes, I believe that's right."

"Jerry teaches in Greenwood, but we live in Seattle." Anna ran a hand over the little girls hair. "Do you teach in Seattle?"

"No, Eden Falls."

"Oh, I love Eden Falls." Anna leaned around the little girl on her lap to wipe one of boy's hands with her napkin. "We've driven through a couple of times, but Jerry never wants to stop."

"I really have my details wrong. I could have sworn you taught in Harrisville," Stella said, still staring at Len-slash-Jerry.

"Jerry's always taught in Seattle." Anna touched her husband's arm. "Maybe you have a doppelganger, honey."

"Maybe."

"Stella, we should go."

Alex. Her friends had her back. For over a year they told her something was up with Len and she'd argued. She'd given him the benefit of the doubt. Believed in him. Believed him. Her jaw felt numb.

"Come on, Stella," Carolyn said.

Her friends were afraid she would tell Jerry's wife the truth. Then there would be a scene. The buzzing in her ears grew louder. "Sorry to interrupt your dinner. I thought I recognized you and wanted to say hi."

"Yep." Jerry occupied himself with one of the boys. "Nice to see you, again."

Stella stood her ground for a long moment, staring at the cheating husband and the unknowing wife. Jerry glanced back at her and she could see the fear in his eyes.

When she turned and headed for the door, she wasn't sure if her friends followed until she reached Alex's car. Jillian opened the back door and hurried her inside. "Let's grab something to eat on our way home."

Misty slid in next to her. "I told you there was something off about that guy. Didn't I warn you?"

"Shut up, Misty," Alex said.

"I don't see why we're leaving," Misty argued. "We should sit at the vacant table next to *Len* and make the rest of his night miserable."

Stella shut out her friends, their attempts at comfort, and their words of anger. The rest of the night was a blur as she tried to focus on breathing. In and out. She stared at the distorted scenery as she fought tears. In and out. The innocent smile of Anna Winters was burned into her brain. Jerry Winters. Not Len. There was no Len. Only Jerry who had a wife and three kids. Two boys and a little girl. In and out. In and out.

They stopped for fast food to go, burgers and fries. Stella didn't dare eat for fear she'd throw up in Alex's new fancy SUV. When Alex stopped in front of her apartment two hours later, her sister was waiting. One of her friends must have sent a text full of information, because Phoebe stood at the door with a look of pity on her face. The same look all her friends, except Misty, were wearing.

Jillian and Carolyn helped her from the car like she was an invalid.

She pushed their hands away, didn't watch them climb

back in the car. They would spend the rest of the ride home talking about her, feeling sorry for her. Gloating that they'd been right all along. Feeling sorry for her behind her back.

She just wanted to go inside, shut the door on the world, and wish away the last two years of her life.